Some of My Best Friends
Are Little Green Men

Thank you to Warner Trieshman.
His creative writing class gave life
to the Little Green Men.

To Warren G, Jennifer K, and
Ron Z.
All my love.

Thank you to my mom for always loving my stories of the Little Green Men.

Previous Books

Hiding Rebecca

PROLOGUE

A crisis of unprecedented urgency unfolded in a realm reserved only for Ancient rulers of all-dimensional beings. Their lifeforce star teetered on the brink of extinction, compelling them to convene. The situation's palpable and overwhelming intensity demanded immediate action as the very existence of their realm hung in the balance, casting a shadow of urgency and impending peril.

"We haven't much time to discuss this; a great evil is being unleashed in Adam's solar system when it comes into existence," the stubborn and wise Queen Liv argued, her voice filled with urgency. "We must establish a system where all beings can settle differences without war! A being to preside over..."

The Elder thundered, his voice resonating with unwavering conviction, a testament to his steadfast determination that echoed through the chamber. His luminescence radiated from him, a beacon of steadfast resolve. "We shall maintain the peace ourselves! It is our sacred duty to govern!"

The beings turned to one another and murmured to themselves in hushed tones.

Queen Liv's ethereal skin, tinged with translucent green, rose to her full three-foot stature. A fiery anger blazed in her cheeks as she locked eyes with the Elder.

"You have failed us, Elder Hunter. Your indifference to the beings in all the parallel dimensions is a selfish testament to you. Why isn't the Ancient Elder here?"

King Laertes held Queen Liv's hand. "Love, you must calm yourself; your health is not good."

A strong, muscular, Viking-like being stood up. "The Dragons Dimension will back Queen Liv. We will not be trifled with, but some dimensions do not have the warriors or defenses we possess."

A blue fish stood up, his concern evident in his voice, his worry echoing in the chamber. "We, the Merfolk, are in alliance with the Queen. Since the Atlantians are missing, I fear they may be in danger. I know they, too, will give their alliance to the Queen."

A beautiful, regal woman with flowing white sparkling hair also stood up. "As the Queen of Anhliam, and with authority from my sisters, Queens of Alntiak and Mintaka, we will side with Queen Liv for all of the Orion Monarchy. Our defenses are in jeopardy, and we need protection. Our pleas to the Elders have so far gone unheard. Our people are suffering, especially on Mintaka, being the poorest."

Queen Liv, her frustration evident, questioned the Elder's proposal in a tone that added a layer of complexity to the discussion, even higher such power, and made the tension in the chamber more palpable.

"We agree." A dark-haired man dog featured being interjected. "Sirus, Canis Major is in peril as it is. We are being mined to extinction. We are already desperate and putting contingency plans in place if our fail-safes fail. We are in a real crisis; we need someone to protect us. Atlantis has already probably succumbed to their fate. No one knows for sure."

The Elder's hand crashed down on the table, a thunderous declaration of defiance reverberating through the chamber. "There are no guarantees in this matter. None! I will not tolerate this breach in my presence! We have listened and complied with each request. The Ancient Elder sent me to this farce of a meeting."

The Dragon King stood up once more. "As we are an Ancient Monarchy, we are all responsible. All of us are responsible for peace. We are responsible for one another."

"What about the slums? Who will represent them? They are the criminals, the worst of the worst. What about them? Do they have a say here? Do these reprobates deserve safeguarding?" A purple woman stood up. She had two eyes attached to an antenna at the top of her head. "I know that the Elders have refused to acknowledge this realm. This place is a breeding ground for danger for all of us."

"You know nothing of Elder business!" Elder Hunter argued. "Our business is above reproach and not to be questioned."

The Merfolk King announced. "The slums are everyone's business! Who are we to look down on others? Judge them? If they have evil intentions, then we punish them as such. No questions asked. We, as Ancients, will hand out the appropriate punishment until our prophecy is in place."

Queen Liv closed her eyes and spoke in a trance. "*I see a female—a young child born of Adam's solar system—planets that ring a small star. She will come from a planet born of spitting fire that will cool and foster life from water. The third from orbiting the great bright center. A father giving the last of our precious dying magic to be guarded by an intense love that ....*"

The Elder, his voice filled with defiance, declared his opposition. "I will not tolerate it. I will do everything I can to prevent this from happening." His words filled the chamber with a palpable sense of conflict, tension, and height, making the audience feel the rising tension and the impending conflict.

Queen Liv's smile was a testament to her unwavering confidence. "You will not succeed in your attempts to thwart us. My power surpasses even that of the Ancient Elders. Do not test me. You will lose."

King Leartes spoke up. "We know more than you think we do. We do not question the Elders; we question you. You are the gatekeeper, and your job and duty is to protect us."

The Dragon King stood and bowed slightly to Queen Liv. "I mean no disrespect to you, my queen. How will we ensure that this being is not abused?"

The Anhliam queen spoke softly. "I agree with the Dragon King and the others. We must send representatives to ensure power is not being abused."

Queen Liv's arm shook as she raised it to the council. "I will suffer the burden that is to occur to me. I promise from brokenness will come a bond of love sealed with magic that will be guarded eternally by all beings. I give you my word,"

"I will not have the Elder dimension trampled through with every being in the known universes." Elder Hunter argued.

The Merfolk King simply said. "Then when the magic of the stars is returned, and this prophesized being appears, then we create equally a separate realm for this being and us. We will come together and solve our differences. It will have to be a place where magic is forbidden so that everyone is on equal footing and united in the fight against this evil. This magic can not fall to evil. We must ensure that it is safe for all of us."

"No!" The Elder yelled. "I will demand the other Elders revoke this!"

Queen Liv smiled. "You can not undo what has been set into motion. The future is written by us here; no matter how much you don't like it, you can not undo it. No one can. We have chosen this path as the elite Ancient of Ancients to unite us." The queen took a much-needed breath. "The chosen one will unite these multi-dimensions into one. We will be at peace together."

The Elder seethed with anger. "Then I will be one to defy you. I will see to it that these champions of yours fall."

Queen Liv took a deep breath; her health started declining, and she needed strength. "My daughter needs me. I am disappointed in you as an Elder. As an Elder, you are our high guardians. I am grateful the Ancient Elder is unaware of your betrayal of your kind. You will fall alongside the evil in the end. Remember, I see all—past, present, and deep into the future. Mark my words, Hunter."

The Dragon King stood up once more. "I give you my word; it is to be known that this being, the Princess of Greatness, will be held in the highest of regards, and her descendants will be known to all."

Queen Liv bowed ever so slightly towards the king. "For your devotion, your lineage will be connected to one of the Princesses' descendants, and the Orion Monarchy will also be connected and will bring forth everlasting good fortune and prosperity."

Hunter growled out his frustration. "I will make sure this does not happen! I will derail this...this being and disrupt all this talk of representing one dimension! We guard! We oversee! You all just sit back and live your merry lives."

The Dragon King scowled fiercely at Hunter. "Try, and you will lose every time."

Hunter smiled. "We shall see."

A YOUNG ELDER

Time.

It is one of the most precious things people take for granted until they no longer have it. I fell in love with my wife the first moment I saw her. Her name is Grace. She is a fantastic artist. We are expecting our daughter, Nora Rose, at any time now. She is named after my grandmother, with whom I spent my summers growing up, and she practically raised me. My love for them is the anchor of my life.

I met my best friend, Roger, while I lived at my grandmother's estate. My parents were always too busy for me. Roger only had his mother to raise him; she was a housekeeper for the estate, Rose Hill. My grandmother Rose took a liking to Roger and sent him to private school with me so I wouldn't have to go alone. She was a great lady with a heart of pure gold.

"Scott, can you please go to the market for some ice cream? I forgot to buy some at the market." Grace asked sweetly, tearing my thoughts away from my thoughts of the past.

"Yes, dear." Leaning over, I kissed my wife's belly where my baby girl rested. "I'll love you always, Nora Rose." Then, on my way out, I kissed Grace goodbye. "I will be right back, love."

Roger called on my cell, and I picked up. "Hey," he said.

"What's up? How is your new son?" I asked. "I was just on my way out to get Grace another tub of ice cream."

Roger remained quiet for a long moment, sounding concerned about something. "Nothing. It can wait until I talk to you tomorrow. Love you, Bro."

I tried to interject positivity in my voice. He sounded upset about something. "Let's do lunch, my treat. Talk to you tomorrow."

I turned and looked at Grace lying on the couch, very pregnant. She practically glowed from within, which I loved most about her.

"I love you, Scott," she said as she laid back on the sofa, putting a protective hand on her swollen belly.

I smiled and blew her a kiss. "Love you too. Be back soon."

***

I could hear the rain beating against the garage door and thunder in the distance. I raised the top of my convertible as I backed out of my garage and down the driveway. As I put the car in drive, an arc of lightning stretched across the sky. Another lightning bolt came down to hit the car directly.

The only thing I saw was pure white. I felt like I was falling . . . into what I can't tell. When I regained consciousness, I was on the ground in the middle of the street. The first thing I saw was a paramedic holding a newborn baby.

"Where is Grace?" I shouted, my voice cracking with fear and desperation. But no one seemed to hear me. "Where is my wife?" I cried out again, my heart pounding in my chest. "Where is she?"

I tried to grab the baby. My arms went straight through the paramedic. Nora opened her eyes; with all my being, I laid my hand on her little head and said, "I will always be with you, Nora Rose."

Sparkles surrounded the baby. Everyone but me got into the ambulance. Doors closed. I was alone, standing in the street, watching the ambulance leave.

****

I screamed, but my voice seemed to echo in this, lost in a world I couldn't comprehend. Was I dead? Was I alive? Was I in limbo? I had no answers, only a growing dread as the air shifted and the world darkened and vanished into the void. I was alone, and the fear of the unknown was paralyzing.

I stood in what seemed to be the middle of space, with pinpricks of stars surrounding me. I was now dressed in a long, glowing white dress robe. It is hard to explain; it reminds me of a monk outfit.

Firm ground appeared under my feet. It looked like a hologram of grass with a path. In the distance, a bright pinnacle of light shot up. It felt like I was in the video game *Tron*. Authentic but not absolute.

"Where am I?" I yelled. The sounds echoed and bounced off...what?

A tiny voice said, "You are not alone. You have entered the realm of the Ancient Elders. This place is very sacred to all the known dimensions. In human terms, it would be a realm for Angels, I believe you call them."

"Who said that?" I demanded. "Come out where I can see you!" I shouted.

A little green man stepped out of the shadows. He was no more than two feet tall. Green translucent skin. A slight hint of scales. His eyes were round, and he had fuzzy dark green hair sticking up and swaying as he moved. "No need to worry. I won't hurt you. I am a guide and honored to be in your presence."

"Who are you? Please take me back to my wife and daughter. She just gave birth to my daughter. I need to be with her. I need to know they are safe...healthy." I asked desperately.

"I am Leroy, one of Queen Luna's many subjects. The Elders sent me to fetch you and guide you to them. They said something about you being exceptional." Scratching his lime-feathery hair, he shuffled his feet nervously. "I am truly sorry. I can't take you back; it is not in my power. I am a mere servant to our Queen. Come walk with me, and I will take you to them." As we walked, they were tall, ethereal beings with shimmering wings and radiant auras unlike anything I had ever seen. I caught glimpses of the Elders.

"I demand to be taken back to my wife and child!" I roared, my voice echoing in this strange space. "I have a newborn child! I have to be with my wife." The weight of my words is heavy with desperation. I fell to my knees and cried in pure agony for the first time in my life. I needed to be with Grace in her time of need. No one should have to go through this. She deserved her happy ever after. The urgency of my situation was overwhelming, and I could feel the weight of my desperation in every word I spoke.

"Yes, yes, I know. As I said before, I do not have the power to do so. I am so sorry for your loss, Young Elder. I cannot imagine your pain. Please walk with me, and you can speak to the Ancient Elder yourself," Leroy pleaded.

"I don't want to see this, Ancient Elder." After a long pause, I finally said, "I want to return to my wife and daughter." I begged.

Leroy put his tiny hand on his chest. "I promise the Princess will be well taken care of and protected. She is why you are here. Your daughter and her children will bring peace to all dimensions."

I was struck by how important this moment was. It did by no means diminish my heartache from the loss of my family. I relented as I followed Leroy down the pathway that loomed before us. The walk with Leroy seemed like miles. The blue-green grass came to an end.

Leroy stopped at the grass line. "This is as far as I can go. Follow the silver path; an Elder will guide you the rest of the way. You will be well taken care of, young Elder." Leroy bowed.

As I stepped on the silver path, I walked through a large vertical ring of moving liquid. Stepping through the ring, I followed the path up there, and a bright being awaited me.

I stood there momentarily, looking at the being standing before me as promised, trying to figure out if it was male or female.

The being read my mind. "I am not female or male, young Elder. We are beings of light—elders—guardians of all dimensions. The Ancients wanted you to know they chose you because of your devotion to others. There has never been a Human Elder. As Leroy has said, you fulfill the Ancient's prophecy. Before entering our realm, you gave some of our magic to an infant. She will have a difficult time with this; she will be different. We can't help her handle her magic. The last of ours is gone until the birth of the new star of the Ancients," the Elder said, radiating a rainbow of different colors from within as it spoke.

"I was only trying to reach for my daughter and wife. Both are very important to me; they were...are my life. I need to get back to them." I replied. My body was racked with intense love, pain, and hurt all at once. "I want to get back to them! Please send me back to my family."

The being dimmed for a moment. "I can't, young Elder... You were chosen to guide your daughter to become a leader and peacekeeper of all dimensions. She will need you to face the dangers and struggles before her. I don't understand your human emotions. They are completely foreign to us. I will allow you to guide her."

"Send me back!" I screamed. More beings of light surrounded me.

Other Elders appeared behind this leader, and they all spoke in unison. "We saved what you call a soul from death's clutches and brought you here to us. We gave you a life within our dimension. We will explain all in time."

Everything went quiet, and the one Elder remained.

The Elder held out his hand. "You need to come with us willingly. Your daughter will need your guidance as she grows into her magic. If she does not have guidance, she will die a very young death because magic will not protect her. The choice is yours: to let her die a human death and let all humanity and all dimensions be consumed by evil or to take what we offer you."

"I thought there was no more magic," I said sarcastically.

"This is the magic of a very ancient queen. She alone will protect her Princess in times of great need and will not allow her to die a mortal death. When the evil one seeks your daughter out for the first time, she will kill her instantly, ripping her to shreds without hesitation. The choice is yours," the ancient Elder said as he held one of his hands out toward me.

He continued to hold his hand out to me as he patiently waited for me to decide.

I looked at the being. "I do not have a choice, do I?" I asked.

"There is always a choice, young Elder." The Elder said.

"For my daughter, I will go with you. I will do this only for her," I said as I relented.

The being smiled in response. "The last of our magic was not wasted on you or your female child. Her magic will grow within her. She will not understand why she is different. You will be there to guide her to grow into her powers. Once the star of the Ancients is born again, so will an ancient evil be set free from its cage. There is much to learn before that time."

ORDINARY

Let me introduce myself: Nora Rose, a resident of a seemingly ordinary suburb in an equally unremarkable city. Yet, in this landscape of uniformity, my home stands as a beacon of eccentricity. While the houses in my subdivision adhere to a standard layout and modest front yards, my house does not. The stark contrast in the mailbox numbers is the only thing that sets the houses apart.

Don't get me wrong, it's built like all the others except our house, which is a very bright purple. Yes, a bright, purple house. My mother, the artist, with her unique artistic personality, just had to paint our house the brightest purple she could get her hands on. Her passion for art is so strong that she's made our home a masterpiece. Now, if that wasn't bad enough, there are sculptures in our front yard. Not one! Not two! Three! Count them. There are three giant sculptures in the front yard, and they all interconnect!

Let me describe the sculptures so you can better picture them. All three sit on a square base that curves up into a loop, then down again, and straight back up into the rectangular shape as they interconnect within the loop. Her art skills range from painting, sculpting, mixed media, and pottery to types yet imagined—more or less everything related to art.

There is supposed to be a yard with grass in front, but our yard has zero grass. A sea of rocks covers the yard, with thin but sturdy weeds peeking between the stones. Mom says she has no time to cut grass.

While I may not always understand or agree with my mother's artistic choices, I've come to appreciate the unique beauty she brings to our home. The rocks create a mesmerizing landscape with their various shapes and sizes. On the other hand, the neighbors cringe as they pass by our house. My mother is the only one who doesn't think the sculptures are eyesores.

To make matters worse, Mom always wears overalls for welding or painting. Years ago, the overalls were white; now, they are covered in a million layers of paint. It is so embarrassing when she wears them outside of the house! She claims the overalls help her create grand masterpieces. I just think it is uncomfortable to go outside like that.

I am plain and ordinary, and I am of average height. My brown hair is shoulder-length—long enough to pull up in a ponytail and forget about it. My brown eyes have streaks of gold in them. In any event, I am your ordinary teenage girl. But here's the twist: I live in a house that's anything but ordinary. Despite the eccentricity of my home, I'm just like many other teenagers.

It's a bright purple beacon of eccentricity, adorned with sculptures and a rock garden. A stark contrast to my unassuming appearance, wouldn't you say? It's like a comedy of contrasts, and I'm the lead character. But you know what? I've come to accept even the uniqueness of my home despite the reactions it elicits from our neighbors. I've learned to appreciate the beauty in the unconventional, and it's a part of who I am.

One day, as I was getting dressed, I went to my window to let some fresh air in. My window faces the front of the house. It also has a ledge that I can climb out on to sit.

The first thing I saw was our neighbor, Mr. Cranky, my nickname for him. His real name is Mr. Bernard. Here he comes, stomping across his yard, ready to fight with Mom.

"Hey, Red!" Yelled the older man, shuffling across his yard at a frantic pace. He was wearing his usual dorky clothes. "See here! You take those ugly things down! Now! Do you know what these monstrosities will do to the property values in this neighborhood?" Mr. Cranky shouted, pointing at the sculptures to prove his point. "I hear the Davidson's might be moving soon. Who will buy their house with those things staring at them!" The older man was starting to turn red and look ridiculous.

Mom was working in a crouched position. As usual, she was wearing those hideous overalls again and sporting a mass of red hair, a hue that doesn't occur in nature. She had been working on finishing the *ugly* sculpture closest to Mr. Cranky's property line.

Standing up, she wiped the sweat from her forehead with the back of her gloved hand. This left a diagonal streak from her hairline to just above her right eyebrow. In a way, it was the perfect complement to the dozen-odd hairs escaping from her messy bun.

"Hello, Mr. Bernard, and a Good Morning to you also," she said, flashing him one of her brightest smiles.

"Don't 'good morning' me, young lady! You get those horrible-looking things out of here! The property value of this neighborhood is decreasing …ah yes…decreasing by the minute with those …horrid things!" He said, pointing at the sculptures again. "I'm telling you to take them down!" Mr. Cranky said as he put his hands on his hips. "I'm an old man, you see; I'm not getting any younger!"

"I realize that not all people appreciate art," Mom said calmly, her voice unwavering. "But you do realize that this is my property. Therefore, I can put anything I want in my yard. If you do not appreciate fine art, it is not my problem, but I'm not taking my sculptures down." She said, giving him another one of her 'I'm gonna get my way no matter what you say' looks. Her response was a testament to her unwavering belief in her art and her right to express it.

"You're lucky. I'm a God-fearing man, Missy," he said, wagging his finger at her. I say lucky…yes, lucky!"

As he tucked his tail between his legs, he turned back and said, "I'm watching you. Make no mistake. I'm watching you closely!"

"Why thank you, Mr. Bernard, for your services. I am so happy that Nora and I have someone watching over us. We are so fortunate to have such a kind neighbor like you." Taking off her gloves to wave at him.

"Look, Red! I won't be so nice next time." Mr. Cranky made a nasty face at Mom and then stomped across the yard to his house, his threat lingering like a storm cloud.

"Have a nice day!" Mom called after him. She bent back down to return to her finishing touches to the sculpture. She stopped to laugh to herself as she went back to work.

`   ***

Okay, let's return to the point; I wear mostly my black hoodie. It makes me feel safe. I don't have any friends to talk to or have fun with. Bullies started making fun of me when I was little. They would call me a "loner" or an "outsider". I couldn't get away from the names. Someone would never forget and continue to bully me. So, I pretend my hoodie is my armor against the world, sometimes even against my mom's cheerfulness.

Since I was born, it has always been just me and my mom. My dad died before I was born. Over the years, I put together that his parents blamed my mom for my dad's death.

I asked why they would do something like that, but she always got a sad look on her face and walked away. Other times, she said she would tell me when I got older. Talking about my dad is the only time she doesn't smile, so I just don't ask anymore or try not to ask so often.

I miss having grandparents, especially on holidays when I see other families together. Mom's parents passed away when I was little. Mom said my Nanna died of a stroke, and my Poppa died of a broken heart a year later. I can't stand Grandparents' day at school, watching all the other kids with theirs. The class bully, Mary Jane, loves to rub it because I don't have them.

Sometimes, I daydream about what it would be like to have them, and the hurt seeps in.

INVISIBLE

I attend an art magnet school, which is a specialized school. I dislike it immensely, but who does like school? I get up in the morning before the sun does. I walk three blocks to school. I have math bright and early, promptly at eight in the morning, followed by science. The only part of these classes I like is that I sleep well through them all. The teachers fuss at me all the time about sleeping. It's not like I will ever use math or science in my lifetime.

My mission at school is clear: to blend into the background, to be invisible. Amidst the chaos of students making out in the hallways and gossiping about their romantic escapades, I remain a ghost. I don't care about their trivialities, except for one boy who catches my eye. He doesn't even know I exist.

My earbuds are my shield, my sanctuary amid my classmates' ridicule. I drown out their taunts with music, pretending not to see them. But no matter how hard I try to disappear, the popular kids always find a way to mock me. Their words, like a dork and a potential serial killer, pierce through my defenses. I pull my hoodie tighter, hoping it can shield me from the pain.

I exit the school building and return three blocks to the purple house of horrors. I have to pass Mr. Cranky's house to get to my house. So, as I see him watering his flowers again, I prepare myself for the upcoming lecture.

"Ah, Nora!" Mr. Cranky said as if he was surprised to see me. Can you talk your mom into planting some flowers? Or what about grass? Yes, grass will help improve the property values in this neighborhood. You know, with your purple house, no one will buy that house next door when it goes up for sale! You know I am not getting any younger!"

"You know my mom kills anything green, right, Mr. Benard? Besides, what does it matter?" I wonder if he ever gets tired of asking.

"It doesn't matter! You need flowers for good curb appeal!" Mr. Cranky fussed.

Faking a pleasant smile, I pretend to agree with him. "Yes, Sir, I will make sure I tell her. Have a good afternoon," I say, continuing home.

Climbing the steps to the porch, and head for the front door. Once safely inside and closed the door as quietly as possible, I tiptoed inside. I looked to the right and saw the pizza boxes still stacked on the counter. The top box has a half-eaten slice hanging out—pepperoni, my mom's favorite.

I shudder at the sight of the dishes still in the sink. Mom's cooking skills are limited to picking up a phone and ordering from a restaurant. My mother has no technical skills at all…none. She can blow up a computer at one touch of a button. I've seen it happen.

Mom has been painting all day, I assume. The smells of varnish and other art stuff assault my nose as I sneak quietly upstairs to my room before…

CREAK.

I cringe as I hit that first creaky step. I keep forgetting that creaking first step! I might as well blow a horn to announce I'm home. I hear…

"Nora! Nora Rose! Is that you?" Mom screeches from her studio at the opposite end of the house.

Curse her *Vulcan* hearing! Hurry, I think, as I run up the stairs two steps at a time.

"Come see this wonderful piece I just finished! Oh, the colors are so vibrant!" Her yelling is reaching an annoying pitch at this point.

I desperately searched for my good earbuds after entering my room and closing the door. Just then, I saw something green run underneath my bed. What was that?

"Oh, I forgot!" Mom's voice once again rang through the house.

"I wooed some more aluminum and some scraps of copper from Bennett. You remember my "friend" Bennett, right?"

How could I forget Mr. Baby Blue Eyes? He is only about ten years younger than she is. He wants to be more than a friend. So Baby Blue Eyes finds every excuse in the book to take off his shirt and show off in front of Mom. He is gross! He thinks he is a male model, which is untrue.

The only credit I can give him is that he owns his own construction company, which is pretty successful, from what I hear. I still think he has air between his ears, lacking brain cells to block the wind whistling through.

"Nora, you listening to me?" Mom yelled.

"Yes, the whole neighborhood can hear you!" I yell back, my frustration boiling over."People in China and maybe Africa can hear you, too!" I'm still looking for my earbuds to tune her out.

"Nora Rose, is it necessary to speak to me that way? I'm excited about making a new sculpture in the backyard. I think I will do it in the shape of a pyramid this time. What do you think? I am so excited, aren't you?" She yelled back.

"No," I muttered to myself.

"Yeah, sure, Mom," I yelled across the house. "I'm looking forward to it!"

I was having a hard time disguising the sarcasm. It's just incredible. Mr. Cranky constantly rants about resale value and how old he is getting now. When he finds out about the new sculpture, he will probably have complete heart failure. Isn't he ancient by now? Excellent; if he doesn't drop dead on the spot, new sculptures will give him a whole new level of complaining to do.

Suddenly, a cup I had on my dresser fell and landed on the floor. A small "oops" followed. I looked back, but nothing was there. I hope we don't have mice.

I could hear Mom coming up the steps, knocking, and letting me in the door. "Nora," I reluctantly opened the door. Mom stood in the doorway, covered in paint, as usual. "Did you have a bad day at school?"

"Don't I always? No friends, no life, and here we are another bad day." Okay, I was a little harsh. I feel awful talking to Mom that way, but my sense of drama comes from her family.

Tension, or sadness, lined Mom's eyes. Now I feel guilty. "I can't argue with you today. I only wanted you to see my new painting, but you were uninterested. Do your homework and clean up the mess you made."

I looked at the other side of the room. "I didn't do that!"

Mice?

"I don't care who did it; just clean it up." She turned around to walk back down the steps.

I cleaned up the shredded paper on the floor and picked up the cup. Feeling miserable, I sat on the floor and leaned my head against the bed frame.

It started to rain, and thunder followed by lightning sounded close to the house. My stuffed giraffe fell off my bookcase, and a flash of green appeared as my giraffe statue fell off the shelf. I rubbed my head as I tried to focus. I was starting to feel light-headed and tingly.

Another jar started to tip over but quickly straightened.

"Just my luck, vermin has invaded my room! This is Mom's fault for leaving pizza all over the place." I complained to myself.

I heard thunder in the distance. I got up and went to my window. Looking out, I could see lightning in the distance. I put my hands on the glass of the window. The thunder was closer. An arch of lightning flashed across the sky. I felt the electricity through the glass.

As I pulled my hands away from the glass, looking down at my fingers, I still felt the electricity, and then my fingers began to sparkle…

***

Two little green men watch Nora intently in the shadows of her room. She was so magically vibrant. The pair had wandered beyond their borders to be caught within the dimension bending and thinning around them.

This female human fascinated them due to her intensity of familiar magic. She may be the key to breaking their people's ancient curse…

THE ONE

I felt dizzy, looking around and wincing at the strange scene before me. The room, now a kaleidoscope of iridescent colors, began to sway. I saw these colors reflecting and swaying with every small motion I made. I don't know how much time has passed, but things have settled as they were before.

I sat down for fear of falling. The sparkles that had mysteriously appeared on my fingers were now gone. They were like tiny, shimmering particles, each emitting a soft glow. *'What in the world is going on?'* I desperately thought.

I heard tiny voices talking.

"Who are you?" I asked, "Where are you? I hear you." This was more of an accusation.

An argument was happening close by, in tiny voices. "Come out!" I demanded, looking around my room.

Everything fell silent. Then, a diminutive green figure emerged from behind my bean bag in the corner of my room. He stood about two feet tall, with round eyes, translucent green skin, fuzzy lime hair, and large ears, and his appearance only added to the enigma of this bizarre situation in the button-nose encounter.

"Hello, my name is Link; this is my brother, Lonnie." Link gestured to the bean bag, a large, plushy seat in the corner of the room. Nothing appeared.

With an eye roll, he strode to the bean, another little green figure from its hiding place. Lonnie was plumper than Link, with slightly more rounded ears that flopped when he moved his head. At first, he avoided my gaze, but then, he slowly raised his eyes to meet and extracted a mine.

Link shook his head. "We have been watching you for a little while."

Link folded his arms, waiting for me to say something.

I rubbed my head in disbelief. "Who are you?" I said, trying to grasp the reality of the situation without freaking out.

"I just told you, I'm Link; this is Lonnie. What part of this didn't you get?" Link reached out his hand in greeting.

Link, growing impatient with me, placed his hands on his hips. "Look, we're not a threat," he said, pointing to himself and his brother. "What's with the sparkles?"

I looked at my fingers. "I don't know?" Was this little green man getting an attitude with me? I relented. I lowered my finger down for Link to shake.

"Nice to finally meet you. Please let me try to explain where we come from. All dimensions are parallel, like layers that sit on one another. There are thousands of them. Every once in a while, dimensions connect, touch, or cross over."

My curiosity piqued, I asked, "Are there other humans like me?"

"Some look like humans but aren't. Like the Dragons and the Orion Monarchy, they look human but are not. I do know this one human...he was one at one time.

Our father was given the honor of escorting a new human Elder across. It was said the Elders used the last of their magic on this human. It is also rumored that the magic was shared with a human child." Link stopped to look at Nora.

"You look a lot like him. Doesn't she, Lonnie?" Lonnie looked up at me, nodded in agreement, and smiled.

"How many others are like you?" I asked. To be honest, I didn't know what to say. "Shouldn't you be gray?"

"Why do humans always ask that stupid question?" Link huffed and threw his arms up in the air in frustration as he walked closer to my foot, looking at me with a sour expression. "And NO! I will not take you to my leaders! We are all different." His foot is tapping rapidly. "Can't you think of anything original? No, we are not aliens! Those gray dudes are wack! Out there! My cousin Lennie, the crazy one in the family, used to hang out with one of those gray guys. Major trouble they are with their wiggly fingers and nasty black eyes. Yuck!"

"What? I just wanted to know if there are others like you. It's a simple question!" I shot back at Link, feeling a mix of frustration and confusion.

Link decided he wanted to get closer to me. He struggled a bit but was able to climb onto my leg. Lonnie scurried behind Link and tried to climb up, but he needed help. I put my hand down to lift Lonnie.

Lonnie smiled. He looked bashful as he sat beside Link, close to my knee. "I like to sneak an extra helping of seeds on occasion." Redness tinged under his translucent green skin.

That statement caused Link to shoot Lonnie a nasty look.

Lonnie blushed again. "Okay, I like to sneak a lot." He confessed, "I'm Lonnie. I am very sorry about the things we broke."

Lonnie looked down and then back up at me, looking remorseful. It was a moment, a step towards understanding the consequences of his actions.

"It's okay," I said, relieved it wasn't mice. I've got to be imagining this, I thought. "How did you get here?" I am genuinely questioning my sanity right now.

"I don't know. We were out collecting dandelion herbs for our Queen's potion. We wondered outside our borders; we must have gone through a portal. From there, we traveled over the great white stone path and encountered mountains of stones, where we spied the great shining Metal Tower! The air around us began to bend, then ripple and . . . change. We started to feel different. Everything began to stretch, and it all started to shimmer into other colors. We began to glow green but brighter. We were frightened and started to feel different."

Lonnie jumped up, saying. "Electric!" His lime-fuzzy hair began glowing slightly as tiny puffs flew into the air. "This could be the way to break the curse!"

Link yanked on Lonnie's ear. "Why don't you tell her all our secrets!"

"Ouch!" Lonnie squealed. "But Link, just think about it! We both saw the magic in her hands! She could be the one! The one to…" Link put his hand over Lonnie's mouth.

"Wait!" Curiosity gripped me. "What is this curse? Come on, you have to tell me I don't have any friends, so who can I tell? Your secret is safe with me." I said, crossing my heart.

"Naw, you're going to rat us out. Humans always talk too much!" Link gave another sour look.

I held my finger out to him. "I'll shake on it." Link looked at me warily. He put his hand out to grab my finger. Something unique began to happen. The sparkles started to form as his hand and the tip of my finger connected.

Lonnie's eyes widened. "Magic Link!" Tapping Link on his shoulder. "It's our magic! What if it is her magic Link?"

Lonnie continued to watch as the sparkles encircled both Link and Lonnie. "Queen Luna needs to know! We need to go back and tell the Queen and Lana!"

The sparkles stopped as I pulled my finger away to break the connection. Link was left speechless, with his mouth hanging open in awe. "Ah…wow, this will cost us hours of interrogation. I can see it now." He sounded very annoyed.

Link took a step back and looked up at me in reverence. "You are the one we have been waiting for. She is the one, Lonnie."

"Will you please tell me what's going on now?" I said, sighing. Or do I have to guess? Sharades, maybe?"

Sitting back down, Link paused momentarily. "You are the first human we saw in person. Your magic…" trying to find the words, "Your feelings are so colorful. You see, we can't see colors or feel. Our people were cursed millions of years ago until you or… The metal tower has something to do with thinning the barriers between the dimensions to allow us through...like a portal.

"I am not colorful. I hate the color. You are confusing me with my Mom. She likes colors." Self-consciously, I ran my fingers through my tangled hair. Besides, I am bored. I get up, go to school, come home, come to my bedroom, and I am miserable for the rest of the night. Ta-da, that's all there is."

"Wow, you have the Elder's magic! Link, think about it." Lonnie smiled.

I looked at my hands. 'Elders?' 'Magic?' "I want not to believe you. I want to wake up from this dream. I need someone to pinch me to make sure I'm not dreaming. I don't want to be the hero; that's not who I am. I am a nobody. Plus, I want to stay that way." Despite my denials, deep down in my heart, I knew my life would never be the same again.

Link said, giving me a dirty look. "It doesn't look like she will help us, Lonnie. Let's go." Link got up and started to hop down."She isn't the one."

"You don't understand. I can't feel it! I spent most of my life hiding! To feel anything hurts too much!" I said, starting to cry. "It hurts too much to feel. You don't understand what it's like to grow up alone. Never knowing who you are or where you came from. I only have my mom."

Link turned to face me. "Never feeling or seeing color is just as painful. You have the choice. An evil being took that choice away from us all." Link's voice had taken on a note of resigned sadness. Turning to Lonnie, he snapped, "Let's go!"

Lonnie looked up at me with sad puppy dog eyes."I wanted it to be you, Nora. It is worse never knowing sadness or hurt. You have the choice to make a difference for us. For millennia of nothingness, generations lost not knowing the simple things humans take for granted." He got up and turned away.

I've longed not to feel. Something compelled me to want to help them, whispering and urging me to choose to do something for these little beings. I felt responsibility for them, for their people.

I squeezed my eyes shut and said, "Okay! Just come back." I was so going to regret this.

THE LEGEND

Lonnie turned around with a determined smile on his face. "I't let us down, Nora. We're in this together," he said with unwavering confidence. Knew you would Nora."

Both Link and Lonnie returned to their seats. Link took a breath. "Until now, we all lived in a world of black and white. Our Queen could rule fairly only through a potion made from dandelions. The potion allows her to offset the curse and rule fairly, but only briefly."

"Did you get cursed too? Is that why you don't like colors?" Lonnie asked with a childlike innocence that was both endearing and amusing.

"Humans aren't cursed, dummy," Link replied, his patience with Lonnie's questions evident as he yanked Lonnie's ear again.

"Ow, that hurt!" Lonnie said, rubbing his ear. His eyes looked sideways at Link, and his lips pouted.

"Okay, you keep talking about some curse. I'm not cursed…well, maybe," I said, throwing my hands up. Why is the Queen the only one to drink the potion? Why can't everyone drink it? See, problem solved." I asked all the questions in rapid succession. I took a breath and rubbed my head. A significant headache was beginning; I could feel it. I am so starting to regret this. "Continue. Please."

Link sighed, "The Ancient Seer has forbidden it. No one but royalty can drink the potion. We eat seeds of the earth." Link pointed at Lonnie. "Some eat more than others."

Lonnie raised his hand, his excitement palpable. "That would be me!" He said, smiling from ear to ear and jumping up and down. "Me!"

Link gave Lonnie a dirty look as he continued. "Anyway, Lonnie and I come from a nonroyal family. Our Queen favors our parents and sister. Our sister Lana guides and advises and can see things in the future. Our older brothers Lann and Leo are the Crown's record keepers. They keep all the ancient records and future ones. Lonnie and I have not earned our place in the court yet. Sounds boring, if you ask me."

"I would love to have a family." The words just flew out of my mouth. Link looked at me peevishly. "What?" I realized I interrupted him.

Link took an extra second to make sure I was done. "Our brothers recite the ancient story on the 'The Day of the Curse' every eve. "

"Oh, It's scary, Nora, but it's a good story. Do you have any seeds to eat?" Lonnie asked.

I chuckled. "No, I don't. Let Link tell the story before he gets mad again." I said, rubbing his fuzzy head. Lonnie rolled over, his belly jiggling as he laughed.

"Stop interrupting! I am telling a story here!" Link shouted. Lonnie instantly stopped laughing and sat up. I covered my smile with the back of my hand.

"Okay, if everyone is finished." Link said.

I could tell he was getting irritated. "Link, please proceed."

Link began to tell the story:

`

Our Ancestors saw colors and felt emotions millions of years ago. In the beginning, Great Ancient Queen Liv and Great Ancient King Laertes held potent magic—ancient Magic that had to be balanced by true love. They were heads of the counsel of dimensions. All royalty looked up to them and their wisdom.

It has been secretly whispered that an evil force attacked Queen Liv, and the star of Adam exploded into a galaxy—your galaxy. Queen Liv suspected that her child held the evil that attacked her. They both decided to try to counteract and balance their magic with the true love of two sisters…

Queen Liv confided to her most trusted confidant, Seer, "Promise me you will not bestow this child with our sacred letter. Under no circumstances or anyone's pleading keep this promise. This child is evil. I fear for the future of our people and all dimensions. "

The Seerer took the Queen's hand. "I give you my sole word, Your Majesty."

Queen Liv smiled. "Thank you. Place me where no one will find me after the birth of this child. Conceal me where no one will ever find me, then send word of my death to everyone."

"My Queen?" The Seerer questioned.

"I must hibernate to maintain and accumulate my powers so my Princess can survive this evil I carry. She will be the salvation for us all. Her survival and her children's survival depend on me. I will need all of my powers to help them." Queen Liv drifted off into sleep.

Ancient Queen Liv became ill within a year of the Younger's birth. Ancient King Laertes had been away trying to negotiate a peace treaty. He rushed back when he heard the Queen was ill, wanting to be at her side before she passed away.

After her death, the Ancient King continued to rule, but she was overwhelmed by grief over his wife's passing; he separated himself from everyone he loved and his colony. He ruled until both his daughters came of age. With time, he joined his wife with the Ancients...

As I began to visualize the story, lights projected from my hand and played out the scene that Link Between Us was narrating. It played out like a spectral movie—almost like a hologram. I gasped in surprise. It was awe-inspiring to witness.

…In the beginning, the Queen sisters ruled side by side in the colony of their Ancestors. Slowly, the colonies split into two territories, and magic became vulnerable and weak.

The oldest Queen, Liana, ruled her tribe with fairness and, most of all, compassion. Her colony prospered under her rule because she was devoted to her people, and the colony, in return, cherished her.

The Younger sister—we are not allowed to speak her name—was lazy, envious, and angry at her older sister. She retreated to the forest, where the trees circled a piece of land where nothing grows, and everything that enters it suffers and dies.

She made her home within a hollow tree. Its branches bent in agony towards the ground, probably because she practiced her wicked magic there. As the years passed, her clan started to starve and weaken from neglect.

Those who could leave and escape to live under Queen Liana's rule did. This angered the Younger and deepened the wounds of her resentment between her and her older sister. The Younger punished her people, who could not escape severely.

When word of the abuse reached Queen Liana, she vowed to end their fear once and for all. She journeyed to what became known as the Forbidden Forest Grove, which was dark and dangerous to see the Younger.

As Liana arrived at the edge of the Forbidden Forest, the Younger walked out to meet her older sister and her entourage with resentment. "Go away, Liana. How dare you intrude on my home. Go back to your perfect paradise."

"My beloved sister, why are you punishing your clan? What have they done to cause your displeasure? Can we settle this feud between us once and for all time?" Queen Liana asked her sister as she walked closer.

"You are not welcome here!" The Younger spat. A breeze picked up some leaves and swirled them around, hitting Liana in the face.

Panic and fear snaked down Liana's spine, and her translucent green skin prickled with warning bells that she should turn back and flee. *"I will not back down. I will continue to try and do the right thing by my sister."* she thought.

With a deep breath, "I come in peace. I want to put all this anger between us to rest. It is what our parents would have wanted for us. It has been going on far too long," Queen Liana said, pleading with her Younger.

Jealousy flared in the Younger's face. "You were always the smartest, the fairest, and most loved by all, especially by Father! There can only be one beautiful sister, and it is you, he always said to me." The Younger threw a rock in the direction of her older sister.

The rock missed the Queen and struck her guard on his chest. He put his hands on his sword, waiting for the order to attack, scowling severely at the threat before him.

Queen Liana gently looked at her Guard and shook her head. He replaced his sword with the safety of his belt and resumed his stance. Queen Liana nodded in approval and turned back to her sister, trying to smile and stay calm.

"Please, let us make peace." Queen Liana said quietly. *"I want my sister back,"* she thought.

"It's all your fault that I am the only one whose name does not hold our people's sacred L!" The Younger shouted!

A strong breeze picked up once again, and the leaves on the trees swayed in warning. Leaves flying and swirling viscously around.

"It was Mother's illness. Her mind was not well when it was time for your rite of passage through the name blessing. When you were born, our mother fell ill so fast that she was barely clinging to life. You know this! I pleaded and begged Mother, plus the Seerer, to stop the name blessing." Queen Liana pleaded, a tear starting to fall from her eye. "Father wasn't here then, but he was trying to get back to us as soon as possible."

"Where was Father while we were growing up? Has he locked himself away in his chambers? Shutting himself away from everyone and, most of all, ME! He couldn't even look at me, Liana!" Raw pain was in the Younger sister's voice.

A small animal scampered through the trees, and a low, unnerving rumble echoed throughout the Forbidden Forest as the ground began to vibrate.

Liana tried to stay calm. "I tried to fill the role of mother for you. I did the best I could to raise you. I told you many times before that father was devastated at mother's passing. He loved her so very much." Tears began to fall from Liana's eyes.

"That is not an excuse!" the younger screamed. A louder, intimidating rumble once again rippled through the forest. The ground began to lift and drop as if taking a breath.

"My Queen, pardon the interruption; I fear we must leave for your safety." Queen Liana's Chief Guard interjected.

"She is my sister, and she will not harm me." Queen Liana nodded at her Guard and turned back to her younger sister, but her hands trembled in fear.

"Now, together, we can have a future. I have come all this way to make peace with you so we may live in peace, harmony, and happiness. It does not matter what your name starts with. I love you, sister. I always have. Our parents loved us both so much that they entrusted our bond to balance the ancient magic." Queen Liana pleaded.

"Father did not love me! I was nothing to him! I was blamed for Mother passing." The Younger said, taking a deep breath as she struggled with the intense pain.   "You were his prized daughter—the sparkle in his eye.

The ground shook, trees swaying violently, and leaves swirling everywhere.

The Younger screamed in a fury, clenching her fists. "I curse you, Liana…and all of your people for all eternity!"

The Younger let out another scream of pure fury. *"YOU WILL NEVE AGAIN…FEEL EMOTIONS…YOU WILL NEVER AGAIN ENJOY COLORS OF OUR WORLD…NEVER AGAIN! I CURSE YOU!"*

The younger sister's blood-curdling screams rang through the air and echoed throughout the trees. The younger sister took out a silver wand and waved it wildly in the air. Purple streaks of light began flashing out of the wand's point, and the ground started to shake. The time they stood still at that moment.

"My Queen, please let us go!" The head Guard reaches out, protecting his Queen. As the rest of Queen Liana's guards advance toward the Younger sister to capture her, the ground begins to shake violently, slowing their advances. They struggled to keep their balance. Looking at her Younger sister, Liana sees no color and feels no emotions toward her.

An eerie green fog seeped up through the leaves, encircling Queen Liana and the guards and spreading from the grove throughout the lands.

Queen Liana stopped the guards from getting her to safety to watch the younger and let out another high-pitched scream. The younger accidentally stepped into the dead ring. Snake-like branches that oozed black liquid sprouted out of the ground, trapping the younger's legs and pulling her inside the earth.

The more, the younger struggled to free herself, the tighter the branches held onto her until she disappeared beneath the Earth. The ground rumbled as if the younger struggled to get out, fighting the branch-like arms with all her strength. The ground sealed, holding her steadfast, her imprisonment a fit punishment for all her wickedness.

Everything went silent. Not one bug or animal dared to make a sound. Minutes she was passed as the environment settled around Queen Liana. Only then did her Majesty allow her guards to escort her back home, taking with her the rest of the residents of the Younger, as nothing else could be done.

The Queen and her guards traveled back silently and solemnly. The two colonies will now be reunited—now and forever, never to be split again.

Evil had stolen the Ancient Magic as a punishment to all beings across the dimensions. It will only be restored when true love balances it once more.

Once Queen Liana returned to her village, she begged her Seer to help remove the curse. The Seer tried, but she failed to find the magic.

The Seer said in a prophecy, "After searching through her herbal records for an herb called dandelions could ease the symptoms of the curse. The dandelion potion will allow you, my Queen, and all Rulers who follow to lead fairly towards the people." The Seer stopped and took a deep breath...

... "I see the curse ending when the last Elder's magic is given. He will pass some of this magic onto an infant. She cannot feel love, and the two stars, once prophetized, become one when she is united with her other half. When the unfeeling feel, then and only then will the curse be broken. We will have colors and feelings returned once more, learn and trust another with her heart, and in true love, we will balance magic." Taking a deep breath, "Be warned. Mark this Day of the Curse so that future generations will remember and look for the foretold day."

The spectral hologram disappeared as the story finished...

"From then on, no one of our kind has been able to feel or see colors… until us." Link finished the story, wiping tears from his eyes, and sniffled. "I never realized how sad that story was." I handed him a piece of tissue. He blew a little button nose. "Queen Liana fought so hard for us." Tears continued to fall as he wiped his eyes.

"When you see only black and white with shades of gray and can't feel it's so…" Lonnie began to shudder.

"Horrible! It's just horrible!" Link finished. He said, sniffling again.

"Oh yes, it is!" Lonnie said, starting to cry also.

"Every Queen and King since has sought a way to release their people from the curse." The link was quiet for a moment. "Lonnie and I were fortunate enough to stumble into a possible way to break it."

Asking Link, Lonnie's eyes began to sparkle. "Do you think if we were the founders of breaking the curse, we would be admitted to the Royal Court? Oh, oh! Do you think we will be honored and awarded the highest and most powerful position? Do you know the ones who wear the Hats of Honor? Do you? Do you? Huh?"

Link gave Lonnie a glaring look, took a deep breath, and continued. "As I told you before, most of my family is in the Royal Court. I do not wish to be a part of it." Link looked at Lonnie. "And now all he can think about is Royal Hats!" Rolling his eyes.

Lonnie looked at me in confusion. "What's wrong, Nora? What do you think about us getting a Royal hat? "

Looking at my hands, "How did I do that? Play…those images…?" I asked

Lonnie jumped up. "I know! Magic! You have Magic of the Elders! We are getting Royal hats!"

SLEEP TIGHT

Link and Lonnie's story was awful. It is so easy to look past the everyday things in life. How many times have I ignored Mr. Cranky's flowers? I don't even look at my mom's paintings half the time. I should. I wonder if it makes her sad that I don't enjoy her creations…I guess it does.

I've taken for granted something these little men can't have. I choose to close my world off to anyone or anything. It was like I decided to live in a black-and-white world, not seeing the world for what it is or could be. I closed my eyes to imagine a life in authentic blackness. I tried to see how hard it was for Link and Lonnie's people. A pang of guilt hit me squarely in the stomach.

"So, I have a question," Link said matter-of-factly. What made you so mad you hate colors so much? I mean, look at you. You are dressed in all black."

Exasperated, I said, "They are just colors! Colors don't hold feelings." Looking down at my hands and frowning. I felt like I was getting upset over something trivial, so I said, "At least I don't think so."

I felt like an idiot for saying that. I thought back to every time Mom finished a painting. The colors brought her so much joy and happiness. Besides, Mom wears many colors and is among my happiest people even though she won't talk about my dad…besides the point.

"Are you sure you don't have any seeds? I'm starving." Lonnie asked.

I looked over at the clock. It was late, and I had missed dinner.

"Stay here, don't leave. Let me go downstairs and see what I can find." I scooped both Link and Lonnie and set them down on the floor.

I ran downstairs and rummaged through the pantry. I found some sunflower seeds and poured a bunch into a cup.

As I stuck my head in the refrigerator, I overheard Mom on the phone. Tiptoeing into the hall to keep an eye on what she was saying, I only caught Mom's side of the conversation.

"Thank you for the metal, but I am not ready yet… You know why…" Mom said softly.

I didn't want to hear any more of the conversation. I returned to the kitchen, grabbed the cup of sunflower seeds and a yogurt container, and headed back up the stairs to my room. As promised, Link and Lonnie didn't move. They looked up as I entered my room. I laid the sunflower seeds on a paper napkin in front of them.

"What are these?" Link asked. "They look funny."

I had just put a spoonful of yogurt in my mouth. "Seeds. Sunflower seeds. They are good. Those are the only seeds I could find." I explained.

Lonnie tried to put one of the seeds in his mouth. His face twisted in disgust. "These aren't good," he said, handing the sunflower seed back to me.

Sighing, I took one of the sunflower seeds, opened the shell, and presented the inner seed to Lonnie. He looked at me skeptically.

"Go ahead; it's the inner seed. I thought you knew," I told him. Lonnie looked at it again, picked it up, and took a bite.

"Oh, now this is good!" Lonnie's eyes brightened. "Can I have another?"

I smiled and showed him how to open up the outer shell.

Link cracked open a sunflower seed and proceeded to eat the inner seed. Both little green men went through the whole cup full of sunflower seeds. I gathered all the discarded shells and put them in the garbage.

Lonnie yarned, "Nora, I'm sleepy." I went into my closet, looked around, and found an old doll bed in the back. Thankfully, the bedding was still attached. As I set the bed down, Lonnie crawled into it and fell fast asleep.

"It's pink!" Link complained. "and besides, Lonnie will take up the whole bed!"
"And what do you want me to do?" I asked.

"A bed for me?" The look on Link's face told me he would not back down.

I went into the bathroom cabinet and took out a towel and washcloth. When I returned, I laid the towel down like a makeshift bed. Link climbed on the towel, and I placed the washcloth beside him.

"Sweet dreams, Link." I kissed my finger, placing it on his head. Link smiled and snuggled into his makeshift bed. I turned off the light on the ceiling, flipped a night light on, and crawled into my bed.

I lay on my back, staring at the ceiling. How did all of this happen? When did I go from being invisible to having magic? I know I have always been different. Mom always says being different is better than boring, but I never really agreed.

A ball of light glided over the ceiling, followed by another until they were circling…above me. I sat up in bed and backed up against my headboard. My heart was pounding, trying to jump out of my chest.

A human formed out of all the lights. A translucent male figure sat on my bed. At any other time, I should have flipped out.

He looked at the little green men sleeping. "I mean no harm. I see you have met Link and Lonnie. They are good boys, and their parents are very proud of them." He chuckled.

"Forgive me. I'm an Elder, a guardian if you will. Your magic has caused quite a stir among the Ancients, young lady." The Elder smiled.

"Magic? I...don't know..." Will this day end already? I thought irritably.

The walls fell away, and we stood in open space. In the distance, two stars were close to colliding. I panicked.

"Do not worry; we are safe. Once these stars collide, it will usher in a new era. Ancient magic will once again revitalize, and the prophecies of old will come to pass." The Elder held my hand.

"I don't understand. What do I have to do with it?" I asked.

"Once the stars are one, you will receive the total amount of your magic. You will need a partner who will give up his soul for you. To become one and balance such a colossal burden that Ancient magic bears. The small amount of magic you hold was given to you the night you were born. It was the very last of the original ancient magic. This is why we could not counsel or train you properly." The Elder held out his hand with his palm up. "Place your hand in mine."

I placed my hand on top of his. A flurry of sparkles, every color of the rainbow encircled our hands. A tingle started at my hand, ran up my arm, and traveled down my spine. Smiling, he broke the connection. He closed his eyes for a moment.

Opening his eyes, he resumed looking at me. "You are very vulnerable. Evil will influence you, sway you. I will always be close by to guide you. Listen with your heart. You hold the last of the Elder's magic."

We had returned to my bedroom. Things were as they were before. It seemed like he wanted to say something more but thought better of it.

"Why me? I don't know if I can do this. I can't even pass a math test." I complained.

"You can't pass a math test if you sleep through class. Be well, Nora Rose. Stay Safe." The Elder faded away into the night.

"How exactly am I supposed to sleep now? How did you know I slept in math class?" I whispered. There was no answer.

"Hello?" I whispered again.

Again, there was no answer.

It took me the longest time to get to sleep. I watched the ceiling for the better part of two hours, trying to go to sleep. I thought of various things, but one thing kept crawling back. Who would give up their soul for me?

Eventually, I had dreams of sparkles, Queens, and little green men.

* * *

 Sitting on the other side of the room, the Elder watched Nora toss and turn. He gently waved his hand over her head in the air; Nora finally settled down and fell fast asleep. He placed both Link and Lonnie next to her.

He stood beside her as he looked down. "Good night, Nora Rose. I love you, my daughter."

CROSS OVER

A monster truck engine roared next to my window. I jumped at least three feet off my bed. Then I realized it was Baby Blue's stud mobile.

I looked in the mirror across the room; drool hung out my mouth, and my hair looked like a rat's nest. I turned around to find Link and Lonnie sleeping on my pillow.

The doorbell rang throughout the house. "You have got to be kidding me," I groaned as I lifted my head up and then dropped it back down on my pillow.

Hey, wait, how did they end up in my bed? Link was the first to wake up. He looked at Lonnie, still asleep, bent down, and yanked on his ear.

Lonnie jumped. "I'm awake!" he said, looking up at me. "Good morning, Nora! Can we eat now?"

Link rolled his eyes, and I giggled. "Yes, Lonnie, I will go downstairs and get more sunflower seeds for you and Link."

Lonnie's eyes widened. "Oh, yummy!"

I could hear Baby Blue Eyes and Mom talking downstairs. I walked over to the window and looked outside. As promised, Baby Blue Eyes had a truck full of metal scraps. Another guy got out of the car; at least this guy had on a shirt. Maybe Baby Blue Eyes should take fashion lessons from his best friend on how to cover himself.

They both began taking the scraps from the truck and dumping them in the backyard.

"Let me put my hair in a ponytail, and I'll go down to get you some breakfast, okay, guys?

Lonnie nodded his head in agreement, smiling. I brushed my hair and went downstairs. I grabbed a cup and poured more sunflower seeds into it.

As I bounced down the stairs

"Nora, please don't forget you have chores today." Mom said. As I turned around to look at her, Baby Blue Eyes was behind her, shirtless again. Gross!

"Whatever," I said as I ran back upstairs with the cup of Link and Lonnie's seeds.

While Link and Lonnie ate, I wandered over to my window to watch the two guys unload the scrap metal. 'You are vulnerable' kept replaying in my mind. How do I protect myself? I thought as I looked aimlessly out the window.

"Nora!" Lonnie said as loud as he could, "Nora!". I turned to look at him. "I couldn't get your attention." He smiled. "Thank you for the delicious seeds and a good night's sleep."

"You are most welcome, Lonnie. How did you sleep, Link?" I asked.

"It was…fine." Link paused. He started blushing. "It was very nice. Thank you."

I helped both Link and Lonnie down from the bed. Lonnie whispered into Link's ear, and whatever he said, Link agreed.

"Nora," Lonnie paused. "We need to get home. We need your help getting there. The magic you hold can send us back. We both agree we want to stay with you, but…" a small tear escaped Lonnie's eyes.

"We knew who you were as soon as we saw your magic… feelings." Link shook his head, trying to find the right words. "We didn't want you to live in blackness for the rest of your life; we want color and happiness. Our people know it all too well, but Lonnie and I know better now. We know what it is to feel again. It hurts us to ask you to return us, not knowing if we will see you again." Link sat and wiped a tear from his eye.

Lonnie took my finger in his hands. "It feels so good to care and love you. We want you to feel it, too."

Looking at Link and Lonnie, I asked, "How do I get you guys back? I don't know the spell, or whatever…" throwing my hands up.

A whispered thought passed through my mind. "Take them back from where they came." It took me a second, then I looked at their little faces. I could feel the love they had for me. Link smiled in return. The feelings were so overwhelming. I felt a tear run down my cheek. These little green men helped me feel….

Lonnie spoke up. "We love you, Nora. You are our very best friend."

I could only answer him with a smile.

Lonnie looked down as if he was debating something. He pretended to kick around something on the floor. He looked at Link. Link nodded his head in agreement. Lonnie smiled in response. Looking up at me, he said. "Your dad resides amongst the Elders. He is always close by. So, you can talk to him whenever you get sad, and he will hear you."

Tears welled in my eyes and ran down my face when I heard those words. Link pulled the washcloth off the makeshift bed and over to me so I could wipe my nose.

"Thank you, both of you." I didn't know what else to say. These little men who don't owe me anything and care enough to want to help me. I had never had friends before, and I'm not used to this feeling. Is this how it feels to have friends? I never thought that I would have friends, ever.

I laid my hand down next to Link and Lonnie. I brought them up parallel to my shoulder as they crawled into my hand.

Lonnie reached over to catch my tears, but it only got him wet. Link started chuckling at Lonnie and soon began rolling on his back in a full belly laugh. He almost fell out of my hand. I just had to join in. They were both shocked to see my laughter. We all fell into fits of laughter. For safety's sake, I gently put Link and Lonnie on the floor.

They started glowing bright green like glow sticks, an impressive sight. Lonnie and Link looked up at me; I returned their look and smiled at the two little men who showed me what friendship could be.

I had an idea, so I stopped momentarily and said, "I have an idea."

DON'T SAY GOODBYE

Link and Lonnie started to shimmer again.

"What's happening, Link?" Lonnie whimpered.

"It's time to go," Link said sadly as his glow faded. Link and Lonnie looked up at me.

" I don't want to go Link. Please, I beg you, make us stay." Lonnie's voice quivered, tears threatening to spill. "Nora, I want to stay with you."

"We can't stay, Lonnie. It is time for Nora to make a heart-wrenching choice." Link's shoulders drooped slightly, mirroring the weight of the decision.

Without a word, I gently cradled Link and Lonnie in my hands and placed them in the cup that held the sunflower seeds from last night. I carried them, feeling their weight, downstairs, through the house, and out the back door. Metal scraps were scattered across the backyard, a stark reminder of the change.

Mom was sorting out the scrap metal that was left in a pile. She had markers put down where she intended to start building the new sculpture.

"Are you here to help?" Mom asked.

"I…I can't right now. Maybe…" I looked down at Link and Lonnie for a moment.

"What do you need me to do?" Can I be any more obvious?

Mom handed me a handheld shovel. "Dig a little trench around the markings, please." "Sure," I answered.

I took the tool and reviewed the lines drawn out for the base. I set the cup down sideways so Link and Lonnie could get out. They walked out onto the soil, staying within the lines. They shimmered once more.

I laid my hands on the ground and, closing my eyes, whispered these words:

"I desire to align myself and my magic with the Ancient Queen Liana for good, for peace for all. I claim this ground and the sculpture to be put upon as a doorway for Link and Lonnie's people to reside if they choose to do so."

I opened my eyes again and looked at Link and Lonnie. "I will help in building the sculpture. I will try to infuse magic to create a portal for you and your people to come through...well I'll do my best. I can't thank you enough for all you have done for me. I love… the both of you."

A tear ran down my face and landed in the soil. Sparkles ran along the markers' outlines and slowly filled the rectangle. The sparkles went into the ground and spread out to look almost like roots. Link and Lonnie started glowing once more.

Link and Lonnie looked up at me in amazement. They put their hands across their hearts. Link spoke first: "I feel the curse will be broken, and our people will be free from it."

Lonnie said quietly, "We…our family…our people, and the Ancient Ones will be forever grateful to you. Your name will forever be remembered throughout our kingdom's lands and passed down for generations." He looked down and paused. "I know for sure we will get our Royal Hats! I just know it!" His smile lit up his face.

Link looked at Lonnie and shook his head. "You will look silly, just like Lann with a big yellow thing on your head." Link gestured erratically around Lonnie's head. "That hat is just ridiculous!"

Link turned back to me and put his hand on my finger. You will always be close to my heart." As they started to glimmer again, Link said, "Lonnie, it is time we return. Queen Luna is trying to bring us home." Taking Lonnie's hand, they began to fade away.

"We will always be watching over you…and close by," Lonnie said.

I leaned down as Link reached up to me. He was fighting to leave. As he kissed my cheek, a tear fell and soaked Link. Lonnie laughed this time but quickly stopped when Link threw him a look.

Wiping the moisture from his face, he said. "You are my life friend. You gave me, my brother, my family, and our people an extraordinary gift." A tear slipped down his little cheek. Wiping his tears with his hand, he smiled.

They were both waving goodbye as they gently faded away. I felt sad that Link and Lonnie had to go, but I was secure that they would be nearby whenever I needed them.

I didn't have enough time to sulk. However, Mom came over to see what I was doing. She sat down beside me.

"Nora, what is the matter? You seem troubled. Sad," She asked gently.

I jammed the shovel into the ground. "You wouldn't understand."

"Try me. You never know." Mom coaxed.

"No, trust me, you won't. Just…" I didn't understand what she was trying to do.

"Is it about Bennett? You know…" Mom said cautiously.

I stood up and brushed the mud off my knees. "I don't like him! I never will!"

I stomped back into the house and yelled back at her, "I wanted my dad back!"

ORDINARY LIFE

I lay in bed, unable to muster the strength to face the day. Emotionally drained, I finally gave in and trudged downstairs for sustenance. As always, Mom was lost in her painting. I stood at the doorway of her studio. I hesitated.

She looked up as I walked in. "Finally decided to talk to me?"

"I don't know, maybe." I pouted. "Why won't you ever talk about Dad? I just want to know. It feels like a big part of me is missing, and you won't tell me anything." My voice trembled with the weight of my unspoken questions.

Mom looked at me for a moment, debating what to say next. "Nora, you know how hard it is for me. Please, don't push. When it is time, we will talk. I promise."

Some things never change, I thought. "Ok, whatever, I guess." I looked down at my feet, deciding I wasn't hungry. "I'm not hungry. Night."

I walked back upstairs into my room, feeling so confused. I stopped in front of my closet; the door was still open from last night. I smiled, remembering when I used to play with dolls. I reached for the handle to open the door wider.

For the first time, I looked at my wardrobe; most of the clothes in my closet were black, brown, or grey. I never really stopped to think how dark all my clothes had become.

"No color," I thought. Link and Lonnie were correct, "I need color." I said out loud.

"You sure do," a voice behind me said.

Startled, I turned around, thinking it was Mom, only to see that the same Elder had spoken with me last night.

"Can't you even knock? It would be polite to do," I said, my heart still racing.

"It doesn't work that way," the Elder said, smiling. I am worried about you. You seem upset. Would you like to talk?" He stood up from the bed he was sitting on. I am proud of you…what you did for Link and Lonnie. You have transformed their lives in such a positive way."

"Are you like my Yoda? You know, like in…." I was so annoyed that he was translucent and couldn't recognize his facial features.

"Yes, and I know very well who Yoda is," he said with amusement. "Nora Rose, it is not enough to love someone else; you must choose to love yourself first. Only then can you love others. This is the hardest part; you must do it. No one, not even I, can do that for you." I looked at him for a while, trying to understand his meaning.

As he stood up, a heart appeared on my mirror. "Wait! What is that for?" I said, pointing at the mirror.

"Learn to love who you are, Nora Rose. Be well." With that, He vanished.

I plopped down on my bed, looked at my closet, and returned to the mirror. The heart was still glowing in my mirror. I sighed. I wonder if there is a book on 'How to love yourself?' That would be easier than having to figure it out for myself. I wonder if I can *Google* it.

***

The alarm clock blared. Groan, it's Monday. Dragging myself out of bed, I went to find something to wear. I stood in my closet, fingers itching to grab a grey shirt, continuing my no-color policy.

Then I looked up at the copy box where I stuffed all the colorful clothes Mom bought me, and I never wore. Taking the box off the shelf and setting it on the bed, I opened it up.

Taking a deep breath, I chose a green T-shirt. Next, I rummaged through my dresser for a green headband for my new hairstyle. I am not giving up my black hoodie yet.

I looked at my reflection, checking that the headband would stay in place. I smiled, thinking the green headband would remind me of Link and Lonnie during the day.

***

As I walked into school wearing my hoodie unzipped, hood down—something that had never happened before—curious looks followed me as I walked past. I became self-conscious of the changes I made. I had an overwhelming urge to hide once again. Looking down, not wanting to look anyone in the eye, I ran into something solid…

I looked up into a pair of hazel eyes. "Uh, sorry," I said, almost stuttering. "I wasn't watching where I was going." Looking down, I tried not to turn pink.

"It's ok. Aren't you in my class?" Mr. Hazel's eyes said, holding my shoulders to keep me from falling. "I'm Dane, by the way…math, right?"

I was looking for the nearest escape. "I…I've got to go, sorry. I'm late for class." I rushed around him and started down the hall.

"See you in class…Nora." Dane said, looking after me as I disappeared down the hallway.

Trying to look for my books in my locker, I overheard everyone talking about the new girl in school as they walked down the hall. I heard them say her name was Allison. She transferred here from another state, and I heard them say, Good, the focus is temporarily off me.

Walking into class, I saw a pretty girl with blonde hair sitting at the desk behind mine. Sitting down quietly, I opened my notebook.

Allison tapped me on the shoulder. "Hi, I'm Allison. I'm new."

I was turning around to face her. "Oh, hi. I'm Nora."

"I was wondering if you have notes so I can catch up," Allison asked quietly.

"I can let you see the notes at lunch if you want," I said hesitantly. I wasn't sure if she would want to even eat lunch with me. No one else had in years.

A smile crossed her face. "Thanks. We are going to be the best of friends. Oh, by the way, I think someone is looking at you, "Allison said with a sheepish grin, pointing toward a familiar set of hazel eyes.

Oh no. Knowing who she was pointing to, I said, 'Please don't turn red.'
It didn't help.

DANE:

I keep watching her. It's like she is magnetic. Nora is such a pretty name. She thinks that no one can see her; I do. I have been watching her for a long time. I have always been drawn to her.

I have dated other girls, and they always seemed shallow. They were debutants my mother wanted me to date, girls who had a list of what they wanted you to be or how you should be. I expected gifts, flowers, and the best places in town. I think they only see one thing: my parents' money.

It is the worst-kept secret in the town since my Mother flaunts our supposed wealth all over town.

We live very much above our means. The sad part is that we are broke, but no one will ever find out if my mom has anything to do with it. Looks are everything my mother always says.

"Hey dude, who are you staring at?" Greg asked. "Dude, check out the new girl. She is hot."

He likes the nickname JoJo because he is a big gamer. He looks the part, too, with messy hair, rumpled clothes, headphones, a constant accessory around his neck, and saggy clothes. We have been friends since we were old enough to walk. His parents are way cool, and they love each other. His parents do have money, but they are not frauds like us.

I can't keep my eyes off of Nora. It is the first time I've seen Nora smile, and she is so pretty when she does. She seems to have made friends with the new girl. Oh, God, the new girl caught me staring at Nora. Shit! I looked away as fast as I could. Peeking back at Nora, she turned a bright shade of pink. Maybe she likes me too. That is interesting. Perhaps I will ask her out.

"Dude! You have no game, Dane. Were you staring at the black hoodie chick?" JoJo asked.

"Yeah, she is cute. Her name is Nora, by the way." I said, trying not to look in her direction again. I was trying to hide my hard-on.

"You owe me! You get the hoodie chick, and then you get me the blonde." JoJo said. "Hanging with me today?"

"Got swim practice," I muttered under my breath.

"Still lying to your parents about that? Dude, eventually, you will get caught. Mommy is going to put a tracking device on you and will rip you to shreds when she finds out." JoJo said.

"They are only interested in themselves. They will never find out." I said sullenly

A GLITTERY NEW FRIEND

Allison has blonde hair and brown eyes. She is about my height. Allison is the embodiment of "girly." She wears pastels and lots of pink. Her hair is always perfect. I also noticed that all her accessories are fuzzy, glittery, and fruity, with a never-ending supply of lip gloss.

Ever since that first conversation, we have become inseparable. We had so much fun the first time we had lunch together. I haven't laughed that hard in a very long time. Having someone to eat with is excellent. Allison thinks I'm super cool. We now have sleepovers at my house quite often since we have met.

At our first sleepover, Allison pulled out her zebra pajamas lined with pink faux fur. Me? I wore my old ratty T-shirts and sweatpants. Occasionally, Mom insisted that Allison model for a project she was working on. Allison gets a look of pure horror and tries to back out of the room to find the nearest escape. Once or twice, I had to rescue her from Mom's clutches.

I will have a massive bowl of popcorn and any type of candy, and I will eat pizza with Allison. We lip-sync to music, dance, binge-watch movies, or surf social media. One night, in my bedroom, Allison pulled out her makeup bag from inside her overnight bag.

"You know, Nora, you have gorgeous eyes. I love the gold lines in them. I have some eyeshadow that will bring your eyes out," Allison said as she put a handful of popcorn in her mouth. Highlights of gold eyeshadow will make those eyes pop ."

"Why? Nobody sees me. I just want to fade into the woodwork again. Plus, Dane doesn't even like me." I grumbled as I picked up a handful of popcorn.

"You are most definitely not invisible, Nor." Allison said as she threw a kernel of popcorn at me. "Dane watches your every move. Besides, he and his nerdy friend JoJo talk about you constantly in study hall."

I picked up a handful of popcorn and threw it her way for that remark.

"Hey!" Allison giggled. "What is the story with you and him anyway?"

"There is no story. I just literally ran into Dane that morning I met you." I said, shrugging my shoulders. I could feel the heat rising in my face just at the thought of him. "Not a big deal."

Allison looked at me suspiciously. "C'mon, Nor, let me show you how to accent your eyeshadow to bring out your gorgeous golden eyes. And if you want, I can fix your hair, too," she said as she grabbed the hair brush.

Ultimately, I gave in. Allison taught me how to apply my eye makeup. She looked at me in the mirror and showed me how to fix my hair. "I need to talk to you about an issue bothering me." I made a face to let here."The hoodie has to go. It does. I know it is your safety thing, and I know to continue, but you have me now.

"Allison, I don't think I can." A pang of fear went through me.

"You can trust me. Okay, just try for it for one day. Please, for me." I looked up into her pleading eyes. As if on command, the heart appeared in the mirror. I don't think Allison saw it, and even if she did, she didn't say anything.

"Love yourself before you can love others." I never forgot the words.

Smiling, I promised I would try for one day. Allison squealed with happiness. She gave me a big, squishy hug.

As she finished my hair, I looked in the mirror and smiled. Allison was right. The makeup did bring out the gold lines in my eyes. Allison started talking about how she knew someone to put highlights in my hair.

I lost track of what she was saying. The shimmering mirror caught my attention. I turned around and asked if she had seen it to see where Allison was.

She was walking towards the door. She picked up her cell phone and stepped out into the hallway. "I'll be right back." She said.

Looking back at the mirror, Lonnie was staring back at me.

"Hey Nora, I've missed you," Lonnie said. "I wanted to let you know everyone can see colors now!" He said, smiling.

"How are you doing this?" I whispered.

"Oh, my sister Lana is doing this for me. I wouldn't stop asking to talk to you. I haven't gotten my hat yet, but Queen Luna promised. Aren't you excited?" Lonnie looked so innocent.

"Yes, I'm very excited; I can't wait to see your new hat. Tell Lana to thank you. I have a friend over, Lonnie, so I can't talk long. Where is Link?"

"Link is with our older brothers. I'm so happy for you, Nora! I just wanted to let you know the good news. I love you, Nora." He blew me a kiss, and I returned it to him. The mirror shimmered, and he was gone.

I chuckled. What a 'Magic' phone call. I miss them so much. It feels like they were here with me yesterday, filling my life with love and laughter. The nostalgia of their absence lingers in my heart.

NORA:

Allison, my energetic and unpredictable best friend, burst into my room ten minutes later. "Guess what! I got some news! I'm so excited!" She was practically bouncing with anticipation, her excitement infectious as always.

"What? Tell me!" I said, trying to act excited. She had something up her sleeve, I thought.

Allison was way too happy for my peace of mind. "Okay, Greg. Well, Dane calls him JoJo because of the game thing. Eek, he just texted me and told me that Dane wants to go out with you." Pitched squeal.

"No way! He won't, not in a million years! Stop it right now!" I exclaimed, my disbelief palpable, my heart racing, and my mind struggling to process the news. Terrified.

Allison had a massive grin on her face. "Ok, we'll see who is right Monday at school."

Allison grabbed one of her stuffed unicorns from her bag and threw it at me. We both burst out laughing so hard I had tears in my eyes. It felt perfect to laugh like this.

Of course, I didn't believe Allison. Why would he ask me out? But a thought, a tiny seed of hope, crept into my mind. Could he like me? For me? The possibility was both terrifying and exhilarating, filling me with a sense of hopeful anticipation.

After talking, laughing, and more candy, Allison fell asleep right before dawn. I was lying down, just about to fall asleep, when I felt the familiar tingling of magic in my fingers.

As I pulled my hand from under the covers, sparkles encircled my fingers. Sitting up, I closed my eyes and knew what to do.

I stepped lightly to avoid walking through the back door—the grass from the morning dew. I approached the half-finished sculpture, a project I had been working on for months, its rough edges and its unfinished form as a testament to its potential. Placing my hands on it, I could still feel the lingering traces of magic.

I bent down to pick up a thin piece of metal and wrapped it around one of the support pieces. "I accept that I am beautiful on the outside and the inside." The piece that I wrapped glowed and bonded to the attached piece.

I smiled, returned to the house, crawled into bed, and fell asleep, feeling self-assured and confident, ready to face whatever the future held. I felt a piece of my click into place...completed.

THE ARTIST HOUSE

A few weeks later, Baby Blue Eyes delivered some more scrap metal. I was at school. Thank God that I missed that one. I can imagine the neighbors, a collective sigh of disapproval, gathered alongside Mr. Cranky, grumbling with dismay over the arrival of more scrap metal. Mrs. Erma, the old lady who lives across the street, one of the braver neighbors with a no-nonsense attitude, knocked on our door to ask Mom if she was adding to the house.

"We, the neighbors, and I are wondering if you are adding to your house," Mrs. Erma said with a sour face. Mom said she wore her light blue housecoat with a neon pink flamingo print, knee-high stockings, and purple slippers.

"No, I'm not expanding the house. I'm adding a sculpture to my backyard," my mom replied, leaning casually on the door frame. Her voice was filled with quiet determination.

"Oh, how wonderful! Adding to the eyesores I see." Mrs. Erma said, adjusting the black-rimmed cat eyeglasses. Erma looked at Mom disapprovingly through the thick lens with her hand on her hip.

"How many more elaborate things are you planning on all day? I feel sorry for Mr.Bernard; sweet thing loves his flowers. NOW he has to live next to this metal jungle you have here. And what is going to happen when the Davidsons move? Who is going to buy a house with a view like that?" The air was palpable, each word a sharp jab in the ongoing battle of wills. Making us see the tension in the

"Mrs. Erma, can I do anything else for you?" Mom asked, smiling sweetly.

"Young lady, do you know how many rats and such you attract with that so-called art? However, that young man is mighty cute." She briefly mused before returning to the point—and property values. I'm warning you. You will run off any decent potential buyers. The next thing you know, the whole neighborhood will be vacant," she said with an icy undertone.

"Mrs. Erma, I appreciate your concern, but I have an excellent pest control company. You do not need to worry about vermin getting into your yard. Why don't you come in for some herbal tea, and we can talk about your concerns? I can show you some of my new canvases, or maybe you can pose for one of my figure drawings." Mom said sweetly. "Or maybe you can…"

"I don't think so. I'm too old for all that nonsense," Mrs. Erma said in a huff as she turned back to her head. "Young inconsiderate," she mumbled under her breath. "Yes, but he is a good-looking fellow. Yes, sir, he sure is," Mrs. Erma mutters.

Mom just smiled and watched her walk back across the street."Have a nice afternoon, Mrs.Erma." She closed the door and went back to her painting.

So, that encounter with Mrs. Erma was the last straw. But we didn't give up. While running errands with Mom, we forgot the plants in the car too long; they were wilting when we got them home. We bought some plants and continued our journey.

Mom and I planted somewhat droopy purple flowers and other plants around the sculptures the next day. I don't think they will survive due to Mom's black thumbs. They look sick even now.

The sculpture is a two-in-one pyramid shape with little ramps connecting the bar leading to the top of the base. One pyramid points up and intertwines with another pyramid pointing down.

There is a piece of metal that was bonded by magic. Mom knew she hadn't welded it, and I never told her how I did it. How could I? How can I explain magic to her?

We have officially earned our reputation in the neighborhood as the "Crazy Artist House." Mr. Cranky still complains about property values daily, but now he just looks funny, muttering to himself as he cuts his grass.

I just have to describe him. He loves to wear his black socks up to his knobby knees, sandals, a floral fanny pack around his waist, and noise-canceling headphones with flower stickers on them. I have no words for his ensemble. But then again, who am I to judge? The rest of the neighbors have given up hope of us being 'normal.' What is the definition of normal anyway? If they did come up with a definition, would anyone have to follow it? Can you imagine Mom being traditional and boring? Ha, when pigs fly.

The flowers and plants we planted died within two weeks of being planted around the sculptures. The only flowers to survive were the ones planted closest to Mr. Cranky's yard. I wonder if he is secretly watering them for us.

Whenever I walk past Mr. Cranky's house, I try to be cheerful, give him my biggest and friendliest smile, and wave every time in his traditional ensemble. Did I mention his floppy straw hat with plastic flowers when I see him now? And he calls us weird? I try not to laugh as I tell him hello. It's our little way of acknowledging each other.

And this is what I get in return: "Tell your mother to water those flowers, they're dead. Get rid of the weeds. Clean your yard. Tell that young man who keeps coming here to wear a shirt and cut his hair. Grow some grass in your front yard! I'm old and getting older every day. Your house is lowering my property value, young lady! Plant more flowers and take care of them this time!"

Yep, he is warming up to us and growing to love us all right.

I nod in a happy response accompanied by a "Yes sir, and I will make sure I tell Mom first thing. Have a good evening! This weekend, I promise we will plant flowers," and I get a nasty look and a humph for my efforts.

PYRAMIDS

Mom always inquires about the enigmatic ramps, but I choose to keep their allure intact. Her question, "What sparked this idea?" "Who are the ramps for?" or "Where did you find this inspiration?" remain unanswered as I maintain the enigma, asserting my independence and mystery, much like any typical teenager.

Pyramids are structures that can be metaphysical and move energy, vibrations, and magic to their point and concentrate their apex. Combining the two concentrates the momentum into the center, creating a portal or a connection between the two dimensions. The ramps are for Link and Lonnie... It's my secret.

Another detail is the one in the front serves as a conduit, drawing Link and Lonnie into the portal for them and their people. Unbeknownst to many, these sculptures hold a special place in my heart. They not only enhance my life but also a growing fondness back, also bringing me closer to Link and Lonnie as my emotions deepen and evolve, strengthening our bond.

DOODLES

Since the Elder's comment about my tendency to doze off in class, I've been waging a relentless battle to stay awake. It's a constant struggle, and I find myself doodling in my notebook to cope. I sketch intricate patterns around the edges and draw images of Link and Lonnie. Doodling is my lifeline, but it also means I miss out on most of what's being taught in math class.

After math class, I was putting away my stuff when Allison gave me the daily 'Dane update.'

"He stared at you all during class again today. Nor, just talk to him," she said, flipping her blonde hair off her shoulder. "By the way, I am so proud of you for ditching your hoodie. It's been a…week?"

She stuck the end of her glitter purple pencil between her teeth as she momentarily contemplated. Allison, my classmate and newfound friend, was always full of advice, whether I wanted it or not.

It's been a challenging week without my hoodie. It was more than just a piece of clothing; it was my shield, my refuge from the harsh realities. Without it, I felt exposed, like a turtle without its shell. I had a friend now, even if she was a bit too glittery for my taste, but at least I did.

"Hey, Nor, meet me by your locker after lunch, okay?" Allison's smile was as secretive as ever, a sight that filled me with a potent mix of anticipation and dread, like waiting for a surprise that could be delightful or daunting.

She picked up her sequined purse and left the classroom, leaving me to wonder what she had in store for me. I dread cleaning this locker at the end of the year, looking at my mess. I threw another crumbled sheet of paper in my locker. I'll clean it later.

***

"Where is my Poetry book?" I muttered to myself as I was digging through my locker after lunch.

"Guess what I got?" Allison announced, coming up behind me and dancing happily in place. "Guess, I'm not telling. You have to guess." A squeal and more jumping in place followed this.

I pretend to think, "Um…answers to the test today? No, don't tell me." I said, still pretending to think. "Oh, I know, a one-way ticket to Mars. No, no, wait. I bet anything it is a bucket of glitter!" I plastered a huge smile on my face, laced with ample sarcasm.

Dane walked by and briefly stopped. He looked at me and opened his mouth like he wanted to say something but closed it again. He lost his nerve. Dane shoved his hands in his pockets and continued down the hall.

We both giggled as he disappeared down the hall. What was that all about, I wondered? I couldn't deny my stomach whenever he was around, but I tried to push those feelings aside. After all, he was just a guy in my class, right? The flutter in

As Allison watched the scene unfold, she looked at me. "Really, Nor, he likes you! Greg, JoJo, I keep forgetting that he is trying to advise him on how to ask you out. I offered advice, but no, HIS best friend said this is 'man' talk, and I should stay out of their conversations." She huffed. "You're my best friend, and I should know better, right?"

"Ah…" was the only word I could say. Not being able to say a word is common when Allison starts talking.

"Anyway, back to me. Close your eyes." Allison opened her bag and took something out of it. "OK, now open your eyes." She said as she handed me a sketch pad full of unicorn stickers with glitter.

"It's a sketch pad for your doodles. I've been watching you during class, and I think you are an awesome drawer," she said as she handed me the sketch pad. "I put the glitter stickers on it so you don't forget that me, Allison, your best friend, gave it to you." She said in a happy squeal, clapping her hands together. Fruity hugs followed.

"Thank you, Allison. You didn't have to." Holding the sketch pad, I ran my hand over the book. "Thank you."

Giving her a big hug in thanks. This is my first official 'friend gift.' Wow, she is so sweet to think of me like that. With this gift, I belonged, like I was a part of something special. I felt like I t

As I gave Allison another 'Thank you hug,' I looked up as Dane passed in the hall again. He turned around, walking backward, and smiled at me with his crooked smile. I waved, and I smiled back, feeling my face turn pink. Then he turned back around and continued to class.

"Oh, girl, you have a stalker," Allison said with a smile. "He is so charming and sketchy at the same time."

***

It took me two days to open the sketchpad. I think I have drawing anxiety, if that is a thing. It was another couple of days until I got the nerve to ask Mom for a graphite pencil. The cost of that question was an hour-long lecture on different pencils with coordinating erasers. I just needed one pencil. Geez!

Once I had my pencil, eraser, and sketch pad, I sat by the newly finished sculpture and started drawing. I had a bit of anxiety in the beginning, but now I found my safe spot to draw. With each stroke, I could feel my confidence growing. I was becoming a better artist, and it felt good.

After a few weeks of sitting outside in a kitchen chair, Mom made me a bench out of recycled wood, which I placed by the sculpture. Sometimes, I lose track of time when I draw out here. It's peaceful. When the sun hits the pyramid at the right angle, a green glow surrounds it like an aura. This routine, this place, it's becoming my sanctuary.

This was one of those days. I was absorbing the sight of it when… "So, what do you have there?" The Elder said nonchalantly.

I jumped at the sound of his voice. "Are you crazy? Someone will see you? You need a bell to wear around your neck."

"No one can see me but you. What are you doing?" The Elder gestured to my sketch pad.

"Allison gave me a sketch pad. It's… my first friend gift." Shrugging my shoulders. "It is just special here. Quiet."

"It's your magic. I'm glad you found something you like. I was sent a message from Link and Lonnie. They said they miss you and will see you soon. The Elders are busy preparing the portal for them." He smiled.

"Good, now the Elders won't need me anymore." I looked at the Elder. His facial features were never prominent. You could tell he had eyes and a nose, but they were almost blurred.

The Elder stood up and sighed. "You have just started your journey, Nora Rose." He walked to the sculpture. "She has such talent, don't you think?" He looked at me for confirmation.

"Mom is good at whatever she does," I asked curiously. "Do you know her?"

"I know everyone." The Elder smiled. "Be well, Nora Rose." And he was gone.

I just shook my head in disbelief. "He is getting weirder by the minute," I muttered.

Later on that night, Mom got ahold of my sketch pad. She went on and on about how good she thought my drawings were.

At dinner, Chinese takeout, she said that I had a natural talent and how I get it from her side of the family, of course. I thanked her for the compliment, and she was happy as a clam.

She keeps bugging me to go to her Art Gallery Openings to show me off as her new protege. To get out of going to the openings, I formulate a plan to get out of it by telling Mom that Allison has a terrible family issue. So, of course, I have to be with Allison. Poor

Allison, but a best friend must do what she needs to comfort a friend. Or so I'm told. I'm still learning the rules on that one.

FIRST DATE GONE WRONG

Allison was correct in her assumptions about Dane asking me out. He finally got the courage to ask me to get ice cream after school on Friday. It was the longest week ever.

Allison irritated me about getting my hair done, a new outfit, a manicure, and a pedicure. I gave in. So, Mom, Allison, and I went shopping; we got manicures and pedicures. It was enjoyable hanging out with both of them. As for the new outfit, I put my foot down. It didn't do any good.

I seem to be the talk of the school again, and this time, it's good. Everyone seems to like my new change. Of course, I give Allison all the credit.

Friday arrived, and Mom made sure everything was perfect. I wore a white blouse with tiny yellow polka dots and a yellow skirt. Mom and Allison wanted me to wear these new sandals out of the house, so I did.

When I got down the street, I changed into my tennis shoes. Other students complimented my new outfit so much that I blushed. Mary Jane stuck her nose in the air as usual. She was such a snob.

Standing at my locker, Allison came up behind me. "Where are your sandals?"

"They hurt my feet, Al, and we are walking to Scoops," I explained.

"Scoops? They named the ice cream shop Scoops. I'm assuming the owner has no imagination." Allison said. It was more of a statement than a question.

"I guess so." I was at a total loss as to what Allison was carrying on.

"Anyway, back to you. You get to destroy my creation this time, but only this time. I'm so excited for you. Everyone is talking about it." Allison's smile was huge.

"Really? Don't they have anything else to talk about?" I said, wanting to hide under a rock.

"Nope," Dane said as he walked up to my locker. "Still on for this afternoon?" He asked.

Allison very quickly said. "Yes, she is."

I just had to look at her in amazement.

"So Allison, how about you going out with JoJo? Like a double date." There was a glimmer of hope in his eyes. "He likes you and thinks you are pretty."

"Um, No. I am waiting for Prince Charming to ride up on a white horse and take me away." Allison frowned.

Dane's eyes widened. "Okay… what about the meantime…while you wait for Mr. Prince Charming?" Dane asked.

Allison looked at Dane like he had just lost his mind. "I'll let you know. Now, go away; we have girl stuff to talk about."

I just looked at him helplessly.

He smiled as he turned to walk away. "Later, Nora." He turned to continue to walk down the hall.

Allison and I both started laughing hysterically.

When the first bell rang at the end of the day, Allison was by my side in minutes, giving me last-minute advice. She claims to be an expert about romance from reading about it in magazines.

After the third bell, Dane showed up at my locker, and Mary Jane did too.

"Well, well. Going out to scoops, I hear." Mary Jane said sarcastically.

Allison stepped in front of me. "Yes, go away."

Mary Jane shrugged and turned to face Dane. "When you get tired of boring, let me know. I will give you everything you want." She smiled at him seductively and walked away.

Dane frowned at Mary Jane. "No, Thank you." He stepped around her and offered his hand to me. "Ready?" He smiled. God, I love his smile; those eyes are enough to melt any girl's heart.

"Yep," I said nervously.

Allison yelled after us. "Have fun!" She said, waving goodbye.

I waved back at Allison, and papers flew out of her locker. *Did I do that?* I looked at my hand and quickly tucked it behind my back. *Damn magic!*

Dane gently took my hand and turned me around. He stared into my eyes. Was he going to kiss me? My lips parted in anticipation. He smiled, and then the spell was broken.

SCOOPS:

We smiled at each other as we walked out of the school building. Scoops Ice Cream is located nearby.

I could tell Dane was nervous; he didn't know what to do with his hands, so I put my hand in, and he smiled. It was cute seeing him nervous.

Walking into Scoops was like stepping back in time. An original jukebox, a long pink and silver fifties bar, graced one end of the shop, with teal leather stools sitting under them. Booths lined the windows of the shop.

As we entered, a middle-aged lady in a pink dress, red lipstick, and black-rim cat-eye framed glasses greeted us warmly. Her eyes followed us as we found our seats, adding to the nostalgic charm of the place.

"Sit wherever you want." The lady said as her eyes followed us as we sat down.

I looked over to the right side of the ice cream shop; an older guy was leaning on the bar that rounded the kitchen by the window, looking at me. He had intense blue eyes and long, white, weird-looking hair. He was dressed in a weird-looking blue metallic jumpsuit. He smiled at me. The same tingly feeling skidded down my spine. I looked over at Dane for reassurance, and when I looked back, he was gone.

Dane guided us to a booth. As we sat down, menus were placed in front of us.

"So, what can I get you two?" The lady's teal name tag, on top of a white handkerchief, read "Georgia."

We ordered ice water and ice cream and handed our menus to Georgia. She smiled knowingly and went to get our drinks and ice creams. Nerves hit me in my stomach.

"You look pretty today. I like your…outfit." I could see he was inwardly cringing.

Smiling, I replied. "Thank you. Allison put it together for me. She is my self-appointed personal fashion designer."

Dane smiled. He wore a tight blue T-shirt with a denim button-down on top, jeans, and tennis shoes. I could not stop looking at his eyes. I felt a little overdressed but didn't worry much about it.

I was saved when our waters were set in front of us. I was about to speak when Georgia came back with our orders. I got a hot fudge Sundae with whipped cream, nuts, and a cherry. Dane ordered a Banana split, and it was huge.

"Are you going to eat all that?" I asked.

"Of course, I am a growing boy." Dane smiled. "Want a bite?" My stomach did a flip-flop, and I shook my head no.

We talked nonstop about school, assignments, and other things; we both forgot to be nervous.

After we finished our ice creams, Georgia happily brought us the check. Dane dug in his pockets, his school bag, and then back through his pockets. A look of pure horror crossed his face. "I left my wallet in the gym locker."

A sense of panic went through me. Georgia frowned and cast a disapproving look at Dane.

"I'm assuming y'all need a minute." And walked off.

I dug my wallet out of my school bag. "It's okay; Mom gave me a card for emergencies. I think this qualifies."

Dane looked utterly horrified.

"It's okay. It happens." I told him.

Georgia reappeared and took the bill and the credit card, giving Dane a look as she left.

I tried hard to keep from laughing. "Dane, please don't worry so much about it. Really"

"So you'll go out with me again? This time, I won't forget my wallet, I promise." Reaching over the table, he took my hand. Tingles raced up my hand.

"Yes, I will," I said, struggling to keep myself from blushing.

Georgia reappeared, returning my card. She looked at our hands and smiled. Turning to Dane, she said, "Don't let this one go. I don't know many girls who would pay the bill and not give her man hell." With that, she left.

We both looked at each other and burst out laughing. The walk home was made in silence.

Dane walked me up to the porch. He said he wanted to meet my mom. I explained that she was out running errands.

I promised him that he could meet my mom on our next date. He didn't want to leave until I was safely in the house. But instead of going in, I stood within the front door frame and waved goodbye until he was halfway down the street.

DANE:

I wonder if it is possible to die from embarrassment. I left my fucking wallet in my locker! Could I be any more stupid?

I thought as I cringed at the thought.

"Where have you been?" My Father asked as he stood in the doorway of his office.

"Out," I said.

Dad swirled the amber liquid in his glass. "I'm not playing twenty questions with you. Where have you been? Your mother is worried." Dad said, still waiting for an answer.

"I'm sure she isn't. Probably off with some other guy." The cutting remark didn't go over well. He grabbed my shirt and slammed me against the wall. The mirror next to my head wobbled with the force.

"You are pissing me off!" Dad said through clenched teeth. His face was inches from mine.

"I'm not the one who has to drink himself to oblivion to survive being in this farce of a family," I said. I hated both my parents. They were conceited and narcissistic; they didn't they a shit about me.

"You are to be home after school. Do you understand?" He said, losing none of the anger.

"I have practice. You want me to the star, don't you?" No, I wasn't helping much.

"Who is she?" Dad asked as he let me go with a slight shove.

"I have homework. I'll talk to you when you're sober," I said, walking past him.

"Dane! Stop!" Dad called out from behind me. I stopped in my tracks.

Turning around, I looked closer at him. I would say that he has been drinking for a while. "What?" I asked. I just want to get away from him.

My dad stood there waiting for me to say something.

"I have homework to do. I'll eat later." I went up two steps and turned back to face my father. You don't know her." Then I went up to my room.

I texted Nora, Me: Hey.

Nora: Hey

Me: I had a great time with you.

Nora: Yeah, me too.

Me: See you in school tomorrow.

Nora: See you.

NORA:

Two weeks later, Dane came by to meet Mom. His thoughtful gesture of bringing her flowers was met with a warm smile from Mom. She was instantly charmed by his appreciation for her paintings, which earned him double brownie points with her.

One in particular captivated him. It was of a gazebo in a rose garden, with vines of roses growing around it. A small white iron table and chair sat close by with a pink teapot sitting on top of it. A straw hat with a pink bow was sitting on the chair seat.

"This is my favorite, too," I said. Dane looked over at me and smiled.

All the compliments did not save him from Mom interrogating him thoroughly. I was waiting for Mom to bring out a spotlight, pull out the polygraph machine, and tie him up to it. I wondered if she would take his DNA and fingerprints, too. I feel so sorry for him right now, watching Mom questioning him.

Mom gave her approval, warning him not to hurt me. It's a good thing she was kidding…I think. I don't want to be around her when she gets mad.

Once we escaped Mom's interrogation, we stepped outside and onto the porch. The sun's rays bounced off the sculpture in the front yard, casting a warm glow over my home's familiar surroundings.

I was leaning on the railing when Dane came up beside me.

"I like your mom. She is cool, and her art is awesome." He hesitated. "You're pretty impressive yourself, you know."

"Allison?" I said, knowing exactly who the culprit was. "She is such a traitor," I said with a smile.

"Nah, it's my fault. I asked her to take pictures of some of your drawings. I was curious. Besides, Allison talks about how awesome your drawings are. She is already planning our wedding in the study hall. Did you know that?"

"I wouldn't doubt it, knowing Allison." I looked at him. "Thank you for the compliment."

"No worries," Dane said. She talks a lot, always gets in trouble for talking, and wants to be the Maid of Honor."

By the look on my face, he knew he said the wrong thing.

"Well, that's Allison for you," I said, smiling.

Looking relieved, he just smiled. "Allison has big plans for everyone."

"I want to show you a place that is special to me; it's my special place. It's a secluded spot in the backyard, surrounded by trees and flowers, where I often come to think and draw. I said a little nervously.

"Sure, I would love to." Dane hopped down the porch steps. I followed him and led him to the backyard.

Walking around the house, he held his arms out. "Point the way."

As we approached the backyard, I felt the familiar magic tingles in my hand, a sensation that always accompanied my powers. 'Not now,' I whispered. It wouldn't stop.

"Oh, WOW! The sculpture is breathtaking!" Dane exclaimed as he approached it. I looked over my shoulder to my left and spied Mr. Cranky watering his flowers. I waved to him but couldn't tell if he smiled back at me.

I led Dane to my bench.

"It's not much, but I like it." Nervousness crept into my voice as I said. "Mom made my bench out of recycled wood." I sat down, but Dane kept standing. I held out my hand, and when our hands connected, sparkles erupted from my hands.

"*Oh no,*" I cringed.

He didn't seem to notice and sat down. We were both looking at the sculpture.

He stiffened for a moment. "Did you see that, Nora?"

I did.

"Wh…What?" A lime-green glow surrounded the sculpture, and I smiled.

Dane looked at me, astonished. "The sculpture glowed...green." He looked at me wide-eyed. "You saw it, right?"

My knees went weak, and I instantly became mush. Just for a single moment, the sculpture glowed brighter, as if Link and Lonnie approved.

"It's magic," I said to Dane. I couldn't help but smile at him and squeeze his hand tighter.

He smiled in return. For just a moment, I could hear what he was thinking. "*I could love you, Nora.*"

I choked at his thoughts.

"Are you all right?" Dane asked, concerned.

I looked at him and saw it in his eyes when he thought, "*Yes, you are the one.*"

"The one?" I asked out loud.

Dane frowned and thought, "*Did I say that out loud?*"

I realized I could hear his thoughts. I blushed fiercely.

"Uh…um, nothing," I said, trying not to die of embarrassment. "The one…um… the song?"

I was trying to think, but my brain was failing me. Dane looked skeptical but chose not to say anything. *Damn magic!* I thought.

"*Is she reading my mind?*" He thought. "*No*"

Oh God, it must be magic! I thought frantically.

"*I wonder what she would think if I kissed her.*" Dane thought.

I could feel the heat in my cheeks deepen.

"Are you okay, Nora?" He asked out loud. "You are red."

I tried to control my blushing. He looked at me with those gorgeous eyes. I did want him to kiss me.

Gently, he pulled me close and into his arms. I wanted to stay here forever.

***

I waved goodbye to Dane a while later as he left to go home. As I turned around, the Elder appeared, suddenly adding to the moment's mystery.

"Why do you keep popping in like that!" I demanded.

He just smiled. "You like him?" The Elder asked as he sat on the bench, patting the seat beside him. I didn't sit.

"As if you didn't already know that. And why could I hear his thoughts? Is that why you are here?" I was freaked entirely out by this point.

He chuckled softly. "Nope, that's not why I am here." I looked at him skeptically. "Then why? I heard what he was thinking—actual thoughts!"

Smiling, "It's your magic, Nora Rose; it's getting stronger. The stars are getting closer together as we speak. You must be bonded with your Guardian before it happens."

I looked at him, not trusting him. I had no idea what he was talking about. It didn't feel like magic. It felt like something else. What did magic feel like anyway? I looked over at the bench, and he was gone. *I wish he would frickin' stop doing that!*

My cell buzzed with a text from Dane.

Dane: Hey, I'm home.

Me: I'm glad. Miss you already.

Dane: What did you mean when you said the one?

Me: It was off the top of my head.

Dane: I like you.

Me: I do, too.

ALONE

When flyers at school started going up for the school dance, Dane, a close friend, asked me to be his date. Of course, I said yes. My best friend, Allison, reluctantly agreed to go to the dance with JoJo at my urging. He wasn't a bad-looking guy if you asked me.

It has been a whirlwind of a school year so far. I went from feeling unloved and unwanted due to my unique abilities, which allowed me to control elements and set me apart from others to the completes, which are still going very well.

Allison and I, with our struggles, found solace in each other and are still inseparable. Dane, a new friend who understands my situation, is the opposite. Thing and I are taking things one step at a time.

I'm sitting on my window ledge when it drizzles, my heart heavy with the absence of Link, Lonnie, or even… The void their absence leaves is a constant ache, a reminder of our shared bond.

"You called?" The Elder appeared standing on the roof of the porch.

I jumped. "Can you knock or something?" I felt scared again! I wondered why Link or Lonnie haven't …" I didn't want to say they'd abandoned me because that would hurt.

The Elder smiled sympathetically. "They haven't abandoned you. They have been busy. Queen Luna is keeping the boys very busy. Lonnie is defiantly earning his hat. I give you my word of honor, and you will see them again soon." His words were cryptic, leaving me with more questions than answers.

I looked away for a moment, then looked back at the Elder. "They are my friends. I miss them."

"I know you miss them. They miss you also," the Elder replied. "They miss you also. There is much preparation to be done before magic is reborn again."

I was quiet for just a moment. This feeling bothers me every time I see the Elder. I asked him, "I feel like I know you. Who are you?"

"Be well, Nora Rose." The Elder smiled, then dissolved into thin air. As he vanished, I felt I knew him from somewhere but couldn't place where. I couldn't shake it.

SOMETHING LOST, SOMETHING FOUND

It's the last day of school, and I am waiting for the big hand on the clock to strike twelve. Even though it is a half day of school, it feels like an eternity with each tick of the second hand. They make us come to school just to clean desks and lockers.

I would be excited not to be in class for a whole summer. On the positive side, I spend my entire day with Allison, my new BFF, at the neighborhood pool watching Dane lifeguard. Speaking of Dane, we are officially 'going out.' Although, he hasn't kissed me yet. Allison thinks there is something wrong with him. I think taking his time with the kissing department is kind of sweet.

The sudden ringing of the school bell announcing that we are free for the summer echoes within the halls. Everyone in the class jumps up and runs out of the class.

"We are FREE!" Allison exclaims as she jumps out of her desk. "Free Nora! Free of this place! For three whole months! Free!"

Our teacher clapped her hands loudly to catch our attention. "Make sure your lockers are cleaned before you leave!" she announced over the chaos of the students leaving the classroom.

I looked around, thinking I was unsure who she was talking to, for everyone in the class had left the room or was not listening by the time she said it. Oh well, it's time to see what icky things are in my locker.

As I got up, I looked at Allison, who patiently awaited me to be as excited as she was. "You know we will return here in two and a half months," I said, yawning.

"Nor, you are always such a ray of sunshine," Allison said in a sarcastic tone,

Allison folded her arms. "What's up with you?"

"I don't want to clean out my locker." I lied. I sighed and gave in, telling Allison the truth. "The thing is, I dread meeting Dane's parents tonight." Just the thought of it sent a wave of panic racing through me.

Walking to my locker, I realized I didn't have anything to put the trash in. "Hey Al, do you have anything I could use for the trash?"

Completely ignoring me, she proclaimed. "Dane won't let anything happen to you. He is gaga over you." As she followed me to my locker. "They will love you. I," Dramatic pause. "love you, and I have exquisite taste in friends." Allison tossed her blonde hair back without taking a breath between sentences. "I insist on helping you dress for tonight. Besides, you aren't dating his parents."

That earned Allison a glaring look from me, but before I could utter a word, a pair of hands closed my eyes.

"Guess who," Dane whispered in my ear.

Allison frowned at Dane. "Excuse me. We are discussing important issues here. Nora has no time to play Dane." Shooing him away. "Please go away. We are discussing important issues here. Fashion, hello. "

Ignoring Allison, I looked at Dane. "A lifeguard?" I said, smiling at the thought of my boyfriend's lifeguarding. I asked Dane, "Want to help clean out my locker?" as I ducked out of Dane's hands.

"I…" Dane tried to get a word between Allison's chattering but couldn't. He sent a desperate look my way.

"Hello, discussing clothes here. I'm going to wear my yellow dress and cute sandals." She is mentally making notes on her outfit for tonight.

"Sorry, Allison. My mom and dad are only expecting Nora. My Grandmother came into town, and the reservations are for five." Dane said, waiting for Allison's wrath.

"Oh, okay, I didn't know Nora was meeting your Grandma. This requires more thought into accessories." she pouted to Dane. "Are you sure Nora will be okay without me?" Allison looked Dane in the eye. "You better not let anything happen to her, or you will deal with me and feel my wrath. You hear that, mister?" Allison said, standing on her tiptoes, pointing her finger in his chest. "Not a hair on her pretty head. Get it?" Allison gave her best mean look.

With that, Dane said. "Got to go." As he hurried out of the school building. "See ya later, Nor!"

I watched as he ran out of the school building. I found it funny that Dane is or was scared of…Allison. Or was it me meeting his family? Allison pulled me out of my thoughts with…

"Has he kissed you yet?" Allison said in a loud whisper.

"Stop asking, Al," I said, getting irritated. "For the billionth time, when he is ready. I'm not going to force him." I found an offending ball of goo covered in fuzzies amongst the discarded looseleaf. "I knew it!"

"What? Can we focus on Dane, please?" Allison asked. "There is something seriously wrong with him. I have to talk to him about that."

Stuffing all the discarded balls of looseleaf in my backpack, I picked up a pair of earbuds I thought I lost after Christmas break. I examined them, ensuring the woolly goo didn't ruin a good set of earbuds. Oh, good, they appeared to be uncontaminated. I shoved them in my bag, back to the icky thing.

As I picked through the locker, I wondered how to eliminate the slime. I picked up the sticky substance, looking around to see if anyone was watching. Oh, good. No one was looking but Allison. So, back in the locker it went.

Horrified, Allison exclaimed, "Nora Rose! I saw that! Here, let me." She picked up the problematic glop with two fingers and walked it to the class' garbage.

Allison dug into her glittered, bubblegum pink backpack, pulled out a bottle of pink sanitizer that smelled fruity, and rubbed some on her hands.

With a satisfied smile, Allison declared, "There, the crisis of the syrupy ickiness is over," and put the bottle back in her bag.

As I finished cleaning out my locker, Allison smiled at me. "This is going to be the best summer ever! Think about it, Nor. We get to hang out at the pool. There is no homework or tests, and we get to sleep late! Oh, I am so looking forward to my summer vacation!"

Allison was leaning against the lockers, digging in her backpack, searching for her glittered lipgloss. I stared at hers. She was amazed; she didn't need a mirror to apply her lipgloss and talk simultaneously.

Okay, let me finish cleaning out this mess. Getting frustrated, I chastised myself to refocus on the task at hand.

Once I was finished, I closed the locker door and sighed in relief. "The job is done," I announced to Allison. She jumped up and down with excitement, clapping her hands.

"Come on, smile. It's summertime, Nor!" Allison said, smiling widely and bubbling with happiness.

"Okay, let's start our first summer together," I said. Allison and I walked out of the school together.

I am glad I have Allison to talk me into being positive. It will be a good change for me. It will. I found myself smiling at the thought. However, I wonder if Allison will talk more than ever now that we are out of school with no teachers to tell her always to be quiet. Oh no, what did Allison just say…

I looked back and saw the white-haired blonde man standing in the middle of the hallway, smiling at me; who was he? He waved, and he was gone.

"Come on, Nor," Allison whined. "It's summer." I stumbled as she pulled me further from the school.

DANE:

       My father sat on his side of the bed and set down his glasses of wine. "Who are the girl's parents? Do we know them?" he asked me, pretending that was his space.

       I was sitting opposite; they thought I didn't know about their secret arrangement. This family is all an illusion of perfection. Mom and Dad believe I will never figure it out if they continue to play this farce. I knew better. I know of her affairs; my dad remained loyal for some reason. I wonder what she has on him.

       Mom sat at her vanity, brushing her hair and watching me in the mirror. "Have we socialized with them? Then where did you dig her up from?" Her voice was laced with venom.

       "No, you don't know her, Mom," I said, not wanting to talk to either of my parents. This is going to be wrong. Mom is starting to gear up to have a fit as we speak.

       "I don't see why we have to meet this girl. Besides, she is not in society. What is the point? Can't you just spend time with your grandmother? Can't you date that gorgeous girl, Mary Jane? I wholeheartedly approve of her. I heard she is having her coming out this coming spring. God knows she shouldn't wear white when she marries. I also heard the whole football team had her and then some, but she does come from money." My mom huffed as she applied another layer of hairspray.

       "Stop it, Cordelia. Give her a chance." Dad said as he put on a tie.

       Mom flipped her blonde hair with red highlights as she looked at Dad in the mirror. The daggers in her eyes gave away her displeasure at the situation.

       "I will pick out his wife, thank you very much. I know best. Look at the tramp you wanted to marry. It's a good thing I intervened and asked you to marry me," Mom said, forgetting I was in the room.

       "You didn't give me a choice, did you? She married my best friend. And she wasn't a tramp, unlike a gold fucking digger like you!" Dad retorted.

       "You are the asshole, Roger! I didn't know I was digging in an empty mine! Too bad the tramp got the one I wanted most." Mom replied, glancing at him in the mirror and shooting him the same 'I am going to kill you look.'

       "You were the asshole who thought I had money…" Dad looked at me and decided to stop.

       I shook my head; *I hate my parents. I wish they would just divorce.* This is not the first time I thought this. It has become a mantra.

       "Never marry, son." Dad patted me on the back, and I sighed. "All you get is hell." Roger walked out of the room, heading for the steps.

I followed him, stopping halfway down the flight of steps. I turned and checked that we were out of earshot of Mom.

"Dad, please keep Mom from attacking Nora. Please. She is 'the' girl. She is the one," I said, really like this, not meaning to give out so much information.

Dad looked at me, muscles in his jaw flexing. "You're a kid; you don't know what you want yet. You're especially not ready to settle down. You have your life ahead of you. Bang several girls...whores if you have to and, for God's sake, use protection...then settle down."

I stared him down. "She is the one. I am certain of this."

Roger rubbed his forehead in frustration. "Shit, I've seen that look before. I'll see what I can do." Roger rolled his eyes.

ROGER:

I stood at the doorway, watching Dane go into his room. My temple throbbed with the weight of my thoughts, a silent storm raging within me as I grappled with the fear of history repeating itself.

He had seen that look before on his best friend, and he contemplated it. When Scott first saw Grace, his best friend, at a frat party, he fell hard for her; the rest was history, even if it ended badly.

He often found himself lost in thoughts of Grace, his mind a maze of questions. How was she doing? How had his best friend's daughter coped without a father? He had seen advertisements for her art gallery shows, but the fear of the unknown always held him back. Was she truly happy? Or...

Cordelia yelled from inside the room."How long are you going to stand there looking like an asshole? We need to get ready!"

RAINING TROUBLE

I decided to be positive and not worry about meeting Dane's parents. I wish there were some way I could talk to Link and Lonnie. To ease my mind. They would help cheer me up, and I miss them so much. I crawled out the bedroom window, sat on the ledge, and put my feet on the porch's roof.

Looking down, I noticed the 'For Sale' sign had disappeared from next door. Wow, they sold the house that fast? Someone bought the house next to us? Would the new owners think we are crazy? So much for property values going down.

"Nora? Where are you?" Mom's cheery voice filtered through the room. Mom stuck her head out of the window."What are you doing? I want to help you dress for tonight. Get down from the ledge, please,"

"Oh, Mom," I sighed. I climbed down and crawled back into my room.

"Why were you on the ledge?" Mom said with a tinge of concern.

I shrugged my shoulders. "I don't know. Just…nervous, I guess." I couldn't decide whether to cry or not.

"You'll be fine. Just be your sweet self." Mom said in a weird tone and quickly turned to my closet.

"Are you crying, Mom?" I said anxiously. Mom is always cheerful no matter the situation. I thought,

Okay, that is strange. "Hey, Mom, what's up?" Mom turned around, wiping her eyes. She was never good at hiding her feelings. "You are crying?" Ok, now I'm concerned, I thought.

"No, I'm not!" She said, trying to swallow the tears away. She paused. "Okay, you caught me." She said with a halfhearted smile. "Nothing for you to worry about. You're just growing up so fast, Nora Rose." She said, trying to wave her feelings away. "Are you wearing a dress…the one I got you for the dance?" She is still trying to choke down her tears.

"No way, it's just a dinner Mom. What about a skirt?" I said, still caught off guard by Mom's reaction. Before another thought, she scooped me up in a big bear hug and whispered that she loved me.

I could have sworn I felt a tear fall. I replied, "I love you too, Mom." I savored this moment in her comforting embrace. I pulled away, feeling self-conscience, from my Mom's embrace. With that, she turned back to the closet, looking through the lights of the outfits at increasing speed. Mom yanked out a navy blue polka-dotted sundress and turned around with a massive smile.

Mom declared, "This is one! You look so cute in it, and you can wear your red sandals that will match perfectly, Nora." A forced smile crossed her face. I cringed.

I thought I was going to be an American Flag. I didn't have the heart to tell Mom no, so I put the sundress on… my phone on the bed started ringing.

It was Allison calling on video chat. I reached for my phone on the bed and answered it. I remembered I had forgotten to call her. Darn!

"You didn't call!" Allison's tone was not exactly happy. "Let me see, let me see what you're wearing! You know I'm a fashion expert!" I handed the phone to my mom so she could hold it up for me to model for Allison.

Allison said as she was trying to get a better view of me. "Pan down the phone so I can see your shoes?" Allison frowned. "I don't think the red shoes will go. What are your accessories? How are you going to do your hair? You must wear some makeup. A first impression is the most important."

Before I could answer, Mom said. "She is wearing the red sandals, Allison."

Allison pouted. "But she will look like a flag." I rolled my eyes as Allison continued, "And besides, don't you want her to look glamorous?" fashion critics voiced.

Mom took my phone and said, "Nora will talk to you later."

"But wait! Ahh…" Allison exclaimed.

"Goodbye, Allison, she looks fine." Mom said. Allison tried to get a word in...and Mom wouldn't let her finish.

"I'll call you later, Allison!" I called out hopefully before Mom hung up. I hope she heard me, I thought.

"Goodbye, Allison; Nora will call you later." Mom disconnected the call and gave me 'A look.' I just smiled and twirled around to model for Mom.

"Perfect," Mom said with a smile as she clapped her hands.

"Thanks, Mom." I tried to sound enthusiastic as I got up to hug her. Mom braided my hair. She added a simple ribbon and applied a little makeup that looked natural.

After Mom finished putting on my lipgloss, she sat back with a look of satisfaction, and then the doorbell rang.

I bounced down the steps and opened the front door, expecting to find Dane to be there. I was wrong. Oh, so very wrong. Instead, Baby Blue Eyes stood in the doorway, wearing a shirt! Oh, geez, it's a miracle! I thought, that's a first, and holding a dog by the leash?

"Is your mom in?" The dog woofed in agreement. Baby Blue Eyes shifted nervously under my glaring response as he stepped inside and closed the door behind him and the dog.

"Bennett! Oh, what do you have here?" Mom said as she came down the steps with her usual cheerful smile. She turned her attention to the dog. "You are so cute. Aren't you a darling?" Mom said, bending down to pet the chubby face.

"It's a she, I looked. Hey, here's her tags; I checked her out with the doggie Doc." With another perfect smile of the pearly white teeth. It's like he did something clever. I rolled my eyes.

My eyes widened. Did he just say, ' Doggie Doc?'I thought with horror ."Oh, good, he can think." I felt out loud. They both looked in my direction— muttered way to even the dog!

"Nora, you are close to losing all your privileges this summer! Apologize…now." Even though my Mom has changed her hair color to teal, she still has a redheaded temper.

Bennett shifted again, saying, "She is a Puggle, half Pug and half Beagle. Isn't that cool? Her name is Gigi. A buddy of mine gave me the dog. I thought you may like company when you paint." He flashed another display of gleaming white teeth.

I cringed. Tonight, of all nights, does this have to happen? I thought. Really? "This is gross. Eww," I mumbled.

Mom's head popped up in shock. "Apologize now, or you're grounded." Mom was still petting the dog, who was licking her face.

I folded my arms, stating, "I'm not feeding that dog or cleaning up after it." I said defiantly. The dog walked over to me and smelled my toes while flopping on her side, begging me to rub her belly. The dog is just as dimwitted as the man who brought it here.

The doorbell rang, and I jumped. I saw Dane through the glass door. Bennett turned around and opened the door for Dane.

"Hey…is Nora…." He looked over Bennett's shoulder and saw me. A look of relief crossed his face. Bennett let Dane in the house. Dane looked from the dog to me. Why was he wearing a tie? He looked nervous. He shook Bennett's hand and told Mom hello. He bent down to pet the dog. *Traitor,* I thought.

I blurted out, "Should I change? You have a tie, and I feel underdressed." Dane looked at both Bennett and Mom. Then his gaze fell back on me, and he smiled. "No, you look great."

You know when people say you can cut the tension with a knife? This would be one of those times. So, I had the good fortune to break the tension.

"Bye, Mom. I love you. See you later. Are you ready, Dane?" Everyone seemed to relax as we walked out the door.

Mom said after us. "Have a good dinner!" She watched us walk down the sidewalk, where

***

We walked a few blocks to his house as we were walking up his driveway. Dane said, "Nitzie and my parents are going to love you. Don't worry." He stopped walking to face me. "You know how much I like you, Nor... I...I have a gift for you."

Dane pulled out a box, opened it, and pulled out a gold bracelet with a bit of heart. He took my hand in his hand; he fumbled with the bracelet. He finally got it hooked on my wrist. "I hope you like it." He said.

I put my hand over the bracelet. I was overwhelmed. "I love it," I said, taking a deep breath to keep from crying. I didn't want a puffy face when I met his family. A sneaking suspicion crossed my mind. Dane knew the look well and answered before I could get the words out.

"No, Allison had nothing to do with it. It was me." Dane said. "It was my idea." He smiled as he gently held my wrist and brushed his thumb across the heart attached to the bracelet.

At that moment, I looked into his gorgeous hazel eyes. His blonde hair reflected the setting sun. I could smell the gel he used. My heart started beating widely. This is it, I thought. I began to lean into him, wanting desperately to kiss him, wanting his lips on mine. He leaned down to kiss me....

"Dane, is that you?" A female voice called out from the front door.

Dane stopped instantly and straightened up. "Hi, Mom. This is Nora."

His Mom looked down at me like I was a bug to be squashed, then shifted to daggers.

Dane took my hand as if he could sense my panic and pulled me closer to him. Could he know what I was feeling?

Before I could say anything she said. "Let's get going, or we will be late for our reservations. You know I don't like being late, Dane." His mom glared at me again, and I wanted to melt through the ground.

I was introduced to his Dad and Grandmother as we got into his Dad's brand-new silver SUV. It still had that new car smell. No one spoke as we drove to the restaurant. I honestly just want to go home. I have a bad feeling about tonight.

A NEW MAGICAL FRIEND

Dane and I walked back to my house in silence after we returned from dinner while holding hands. Dinner had been a disaster.

When we got to my house, Dane walked me to the door. I thanked him for the bracelet again and for dinner and hugged him goodnight, promising to text him in the morning.

I dread that conversation. I don't think this relationship is going anywhere; his mom hates me.

When I opened the door, I saw Mom asleep on the sofa, snuggled with Gigi. The dog lifted her head and looked at me as if she accused me of disturbing her rest. Dumb dog! She didn't even bark when I came in. Gigi put her head down, but her ears perked up as if I was going to say something important to her.

I didn't go upstairs; instead, I walked through the house to the backyard to sit on my bench. I looked at the full moon and decided not to turn on the back porch light. Maybe Link and Lonnie would return, and they could improve things and my current mood. Instead, a voice came out of the dark, and I jumped.

A girl about my age emerged from the shadows. She was a little taller than Allison. "Hey, my name is Jewels, like the gems. My little brother calls me Lala, only he is allowed, so don't do it. He is a fourth in an ever-so-long line of Reginald's, so we call him Finch." Her presence was enigmatic, adding to my intrigue.

Feeling a mix of confusion and intrigue, I introduced myself. "Hi, my name is Nora. It's just me and my mom," I said quietly. What are you doing out here? Your mom let you out this late?" I felt a bit awkward asking that. Ugh!

Jewels sat on the rock garden across from me by the sculptures. "Sorry. No, Mom, just a Dad…it sucks, but that's the way it is. I saw you sitting on the roof earlier. I didn't get to say hi before a parade of guys started knocking on your door. Both are yummy, I must say. I'm a Wiccan. I love being outside during a full moon." Jewels said, drawing circles in the dirt.

Jewels looked up at me, "You have some wicked vibes here. They're solid right…here…why?" she said, drawing a line pointing to the sculpture's corner. "Wow, really…bizarre vibes." Jewels closed her eyes for a moment and took a deep breath in. "So much energy, and you," she said softly as she smiled at me. I looked at her, intrigued. "Yes, you seem to fuel it," Jewels smiled.

I felt a momentary sense of panic. What does that mean? I thought. Her eyes were an intense green, with black hair framing her petite heart-shaped face. Her complexion was on the border of deathly white, but since there was no direct light source, I hoped the moon's glow made her look so white. Under her intense stare, I started to get extremely nervous, so I said the first thing that popped into my brain.

"How do you like the neighborhood so far?" Geez, that sounded dumb. Could I be any more of a freak?

Deciding to change the subject, Jewel shrugged her shoulders. "What's with the old guy?" she asked, gesturing towards Mr. Cranky's yard. Mr. Cranky was a neighbor who had a reputation for being, well, cranky. He was known for his strict rules and love for flowers, which he tended to in his yard daily.

Jewels asked, picking weeds from between the stones, throwing them to the side, and continuing to pick other weeds.

"I call him Mr. Cranky. His real name is Mr. Bernard. He has an unnatural obsession with flowers and runs the neighborhood safety patrol. He is extremely concerned about property values, curb appeal, and ensuring everyone cuts grass every weekend. He has no fashion sense, which is very scary. And, Oh! I heard rumors that he has flowered wallpaper in every room of his house." I need to stop calling him, I thought. I do.

"Your boyfriend is cute. I saw him earlier this afternoon," Jewels said, still swirling her fingers in the dirt. Your mom seems cool. There are not many Moms with teal hair around here. It looks sort of boring around here if you ask me."

As Jewels looked up at me, she exclaimed, "The bodybuilder? You got it made, girl. Or is that your mom's man?"

"NO! Can't stand him."I replied, "That's Baby Blue Eyes; he has air between his ears. He is dumb as dirt. He owns a construction company, can you believe that? He just occasionally brings Mom scraps for her sculptures, and today, he got us a dog! He is such a dumb ass."

Pausing for a moment, I continued. "These are her sculptures," I said, pointing at the sculpture next to Jewels. "We're known as the Crazy Artist House." With that mouthful, I took a deep breath. "I don't have a Dad."

Jewels reached for my hand and turned my palm up. Surprised, I could only get out, "What…?" she held my hand firmly when I tried to pull it back. She picked up some dirt with her other hand, placed the dirt in my palm, and drew some sort of shape. A wave of nervousness went through me.

Jewels put a finger to her lips, "Shh…can you feel that?"

"What? What did you do?" I asked nervously.

"Be quiet. Your magic is so...wicked!" Jewels said.

"I...no...I don't have magic." I almost choked.

Jewels looked at me with a knowing smile. "Okay, you can deny it if you want to. I know magic when I feel it, Nora." She said, smiling.

I closed my eyes. A calm started to wash over me. I recognized the feeling from when I sketched in my book, but there was something… I felt tiny, cold prickles on my hand…

"Nora," the words whispered past my ear… Or was it in my mind? My eyes flew open, and Jewels was sitting across from me with her hands in her lap, looking at me, smiling.

"You did well for the first time," she said, taking a deep breath. The little ones have been busy. But that was something else. Old." Jewels smiled, got up, stood, and smiled. "See you around. Bye, Nora," she turned.

Walking away, Jewels stopped mid-step and turned back to face Nora.

"They'll be back soon." With that, she smiled and went back to her house. Jewels called a farewell greeting, "Peace," giving me a peace sign as she walked into the darkness.

I was stunned. What did she mean by that? What vibes? She couldn't possibly know about Link and Lonnie…. Could she?

"Nora Rose?" Mom called out from the back door. "Come in, it's late."

I jumped and got up from the bench, walked inside past Mom, and stopped at the steps when I heard Mom again. "Do you want to talk about it?" Her voice was full of concern. "I'm here if you need to talk. I'm here to listen."

I walked past Mom, not wanting to talk right now. I paused at the first step, desperately trying to hide my feelings. I went up several steps and looked back at Mom.

"I don't want to talk about it now." And continued to upstairs to my room

As I walked into my room, I kicked my sandals off. I crawled into bed, still dressed, not caring, and burrowed into the covers. The tears started and didn't stop.

I wanted to hide in my room all day and never come out. Mom walked into my room, sat on my bed next to me, and started gently combing her fingers through my hair as I opened my eyes and looked at her with tired eyes.

"What happened during dinner?" The dog followed Mom into the room, jiggling her tags. She looked up, whined, lay on the floor, and put her head down.

"It went all right. His Dad and Grandma were nice, but his Mom didn't like me. She treated me like a bug that she wanted to kill. Glaring at me and making a face every time I used the wrong fork. There were like forty of them and cloth napkins! Who does that any more? Didn't they do that in the last century? His mom looked like she had just walked off the magazine cover, and I was in a plain, dumb sundress. We went to a fancy restaurant. Some very high-end place." I said with my voice hitting a high pitch.

Pulling the covers over my head, I said, "I wanted to die!" Peaking over the covers, looking up at Mom, and taking a deep breath, I continued. "At least Dane was nice enough to whisper in my ear, *'Start with the fork on the in.'*"

I got out of the covers and sat up next to Mom. I looked and asked, "Is that a thing? We use one fork and outside and work on a paper napkin; that's it! Right? Why do you need so many forks and spoons to eat one meal?"

"It's high society showing off." Mom muttered as she reached over to take my hand in hers. "Maybe Dane's mom is the problem? She isn't worth it, Nora."

It eased some pain, but this was the most challenging part of the confession. I had to keep going. "His Mom said that I am not the debutant she wants for her son. I heard her say that to his Dad when she thought I couldn't listen to her.

His Dad talked about his job and how successful he is. Grandmother Nitzie couldn't hear anything, even if a bomb had dropped. She spoke only about her cats. She told all of us the same stories fifty million times!"

"Well, when you get old, it tends to happen. I like your bracelet. Did Dane give it to you?" Mom asked, looking at my wrist.

I blushed. "Last night before dinner. He almost kissed me, but his mom butted in before he could."

Mom took a deep breath and sighed as she leaned over to hug me. "Nora, I know how hard it is sometimes. Remember to stay true to yourself and don't change for anyone." She sighed and held me tight. "I'm happy Dane watched out for you."

I leaned back out of Mom's hug and looked at her curiously. "It's so easy for you. Everyone you meet loves you. You know who you are; you make it look so easy." I said.

A bark interrupted the moment. We both looked at Gigi, who insisted on being in the conversation. Mom reached down to pet Gigi, changed her mind, and placed her on my bed. Gigi, feeling comfortable, turned around several times and plopped down on my bed.

Without thinking about I started petting the dog.

"Mom, did you have to put her on my bed?" And with that, the dog licked me on my hand in affection. Ugh, now she is attached to me, I thought.

Mom smiled and continued petting Gigi as she said, "It took a long time for me. There was a lot of heartache and pain in between. It wasn't easy, Nora. Sometimes, it would've been easier to fall in with the crowd. Your Nanna gave me the same advice… to be who I am and not what everyone wants me to be." She lifted her hand and cupped my face. "Your dad would also be so proud of you."

I blinked. Did I hear that? "What did you say?" I hoped I heard right. Mom was just as shocked as I was by what she said.

Mom blinked a couple of times, not knowing whether to repeat it. Then, I took a deep breath and then another. "Your dad would be very proud of you," she started again. "We'll talk more about that later."

VICTIM OF NEWTON'S FIRST LAW

`The sun barely peeked through the curtains when the cell phone rang incessantly. Then, the dog started barking loudly. I barely got the phone to my ear when the ever-energetic Allison began to talk.

"WHY did you NOT call ME? What happened? How did it go? Was it horrible? How was the food? What did you eat? Was his Grandma freaky? Did they question you? Did Dane kiss you yet? Do they like you? And when on God's green earth did you get a dog? I'm coming over, no, I can't…wait…Mom! Hello?… Are you there?" Allison said, trying to catch her breath, her questions pouring out rapidly.

I smiled, amused by Allison's rapid-fire questions. Leave it to her to ask so many in one breath. "Are you okay? Can you breathe?" I asked, trying to keep up with her energy.

Allison was momentarily stunned. "Hello? Is that all you have to say? Am I ok? NO! I'm dying here! You didn't call. It's morning, and you didn't call! Oh, It must have been dreadful. Stay right there! Don't move. I'm coming over. Don't Move! Mom!" Allison hung up with an abrupt click.

I looked at the phone in stunned disbelief. How could one person ask so many questions in one breath? Ok, I know I asked that question already, but really? I was exhausted just listening to her. Allison never ceases to amaze me. After this morning's emotional escapade with Mom, I just want to crawl back under the covers.

I rolled over, and a wet nose was in my face. This is so not cool. I sat up and looked at Gigi.

"No one asked you or permitted you to sleep in my bed. Don't get comfortable." Gigi looked at me and tilted her head, her floppy ears lifted like I was going to tell her a secret. "No begging, you hear." A woof said otherwise, and she laid her head back down.   My cellphone rang again. Dane

He sounded worried. "Hey," his voice sounded like he was trying to be upbeat, " I was worried and wanted to see you today, but I have to be at the pool." He said, pausing for a moment. "Are you okay?"

I took a deep breath. "I'm fine. Allison is on her way over…I think. She was in a question frenzy, so I will probably be busy. Don't worry about me. You can come by later if you want…for an ice cream?"

Dane sounded panicky. "I'm sorry, Nora. Nitzie is only here for a few more days, and … I won't be able to come over later. Can we make plans after she leaves?"

With the silence on the other end of the phone, I cringed. "No, that's okay. I'll hang out with Al. Tell your Grandma I said hello to me." *If she can hear you,* the nasty thought crossed my mind.

Defeated, Dane replied, "I know things didn't go well. My mom is… well…you know."

Uncomfortable, I said, "I have to go. I think Allison is here…" Looking out my window, I saw Jewels drawing weird circles with sticks around the sculpture in my backyard. "What are Jewels doing?" I muttered.

"Who is Jewels, Nor?" Dane was surprised by my sudden change in subject. "I gotta go. Have fun with Nitzie. I'll call you later. Talk to you later, Dane." I hung up on Dane, and I was sure he was left asking himself, 'Who is Jewels?'

I hurried down the stairs. As I was passing the doorway, Allison rang the doorbell. I opened the door and let Allison in the house. Dane texted me again.

"Did you hang up on me?" I ignored the question from Allison.

Allison opened her mouth, and I told her, "Wait." As I put my hand up to silence whatever rant Allison would start with. "I'll answer you in a minute. Come with me."

Running down the hall in flip-flops with Allison behind me, I flung open the back door. The flip-flop got caught under the backdoor mat. I sailed forward as I braced myself for the fall.

You know how I said I would never use anything I learned in school? Ha! Newton's First Law states that an object stays in motion until something stops it, like my head moving towards Mom's new mammoth pottery planter, and said obsession stops my head moving in said direction. I'm living proof that the law still applies. Go figure. I used what I learned in school in real life.

***

. I cracked my eyes open. "I hit my head," I said, cringing. I tried to stand up.

"Relax," a man said, steadying me as I swayed from dizziness. "Shh," a voice said gently as he sat beside me.

I looked at the translucent man sitting next to me on my bench, and he smiled at me and said, "I got you. Are you okay?"

"You look familiar now that I can see you." I asked."Why can I see you clearly when before I..."

"We are in a sub-realm. Think of it like a small room beside a large arena. The rules of magic are different here. I am an Elder. Something like an Arch Angel." The Elder tilted his head to listen to something off in the distance.

I wasn't sure who he was talking to, but he said. "No, I'm not taking her! Give her another chance! She is the chosen one. Hunter, I'm warning you."

He looked back at me and smiled. His short, brown hair with streaks of blonde highlights. He has brown eyes. Kind eyes.

"Thank you for your kindness." He muttered again. He gently put his hand on my head. "You will be okay soon. As soon as you feel better, you can sit up."

I could hear my Mom in the background saying:

"Nora! Oh no, no!" my mother whimpering. Then she yelled, "Get Ice, Allison!" I could feel her place me in her lap.

LINK

"Hi, Nora! I'm so excited to see you again!" Lonnie's voice was echoing in the distance.

"Mom…Nora? Are you all right?" a male voice asked. "Hit your head? Huh?" Link commented in a sarcastic tone. Did you knock something loose?…" the words echoed.

"No! It was an accident. See, I'm fine, or not." I looked around.

***

Everything shimmered around me. "I hear my mom. I need to tell her I'm okay." I started to panic a lot. " I have to go. Please." I said, panicking.

"They won't be able to hear you right now. Your physical body is hurt." He took my hand into his. "I'm here to watch over you while you heal."

I am in big, big trouble, I thought. "Who are you? Your eyes. They're the same as mine. I'm confused. I feel like I should know you, but now that I can see your features, you look so different. Tell me who you are." I should be in full panic mode, but the funny thing is, I'm not.

He chuckled. "You have your mom's streak of distrust, I see." His smile faded. "I knew your mom."

I thought for a moment. "Did you know my dad also? I wish I had the chance to know him." I frowned. He took my hand and squeezed it. It felt weird but right.

He smiled. "He was a great guy. He fell in love with your mom the second he saw her at a party." He stopped for a second. And then he continued, "They met in college, but he lost touch with her for a while. The next time he saw her, he wouldn't let her escape him…"

He trailed off in thought and smiled again. "Determined, she tried to escape, but he finally wore her down. After their first date, they were inseparable." He chuckled at the thought.

"Yeah, Mom is pretty stubborn. But that is so romantic, I never knew that." I paused.

"Mom never talks to me about my dad. Ever!" It was so awesome to know some minor details about my dad.

I blurted out, "Dane gave me this bracelet." I held out my arm, and the little heart glistened. "I can't wait for him to kiss the man. I blushed as I realized what I said. "He is shy, but," I said, blushing more. I looked down and thought. Why am I telling him this?

The Elder smiled again. "Take your time. I like him. I think he is a great guy. You were meant to be with him." He stopped to listen to something I couldn't hear again.

I hesitated to ask, "Tell me another story about my dad, please. I want to know so much more about him."

"What do you want to know?" He said simply.

I was stunned. I replied, "Anything? Everything! Please!"

He laughed."We don't have much time left. I will tell you about their wedding day. It was a perfect day at his grandmother's Estate. Rose Hill. His grandmother Rose loved your mom and was happy to provide her with a rose garden for their wedding ceremony. It was the happiest day of our lives. We promised to name you after her when we found you were a girl. She died not too long after I did." His voice trailed off as if he was reliving it.

I gasped at the words 'our' and 'we.' I couldn't think for a minute, too many thoughts racing through my head. Was this my dad sitting here? It can't be; he died. Am I dead? I thought, looking at his face.

"Am I dying?" I didn't want to know the answer, but I had to ask.

As if he knew what I was thinking, my dad took my hand, kissed my fingers, and put my hand back down.

"No, you are not dying. You were supposed to, but you have so much more to do. You will live a long, happy life... Extraordinary beings chose you." Pausing, he was deep in thought. "I can't wait to see your mom with our grandchildren," he said, smiling, but then he realized exactly what he had said.

"Wait! You're my dad? Children?!" I choked. My eyes filled with tears. "How?" My frown deepened. "How are you here now...?" Realization hit me. "You...before? Why didn't you say something?"

A tear fell from his eye. "It's forbidden. The Ancients are not pleased you now know the truth." He took my hand once more. "I have been by your side your whole life, since the minute you were born, guiding you."

"I always hoped you would be. Link and Lonnie said you were. Do you hear when I talk to you?" I hoped he didn't hear some of the things I said to him.

A big grin crossed his face."Yes." Then his smile faded. "Your mom feels responsible for my death, you know. She shouldn't; it was my time. I was chosen to be an Elder. To help guide you through the transitions you will be going through. The Ancients brought me into their dimension." Dad took a deep breath, reached up, and touched my cheek.

"You are the best thing that ever happened in my life, along with your mother." He pulled me close into a hug. "I am so proud of the young lady you have become. You're so special to have two little green brothers for friends. I wish I had more time, but I don't. It's time for you to go back. Trust Dane, Nora Rose. Don't repeat history."

A flare of anger ran through me. "No! I want more time. It isn't fair! I want you to stay!" As I reached for him, he started turning transparent.

Before disappearing, he kissed my forehead. "I will see you again soon. I love you, Nora Rose. I will always be close by. Be well, Nora Rose." With a smile, he waved goodbye and faded away.

***

Wow, pain! I could hear someone beeping in the background and crying. It hurt to open my eyes, but the beeping hurt my head. I tried asking someone to stop the noise, but my mouth felt like it had cotton in it.

Once more, I tried to open my eyes. I groaned with the effort. *I just needed to rest,* and the crying suddenly stopped. Those were my last thoughts.

Several hours later, I could finally open my eyes and look at my Mom. "You look horrible, Mom." I croaked.

Mom looked at me and laughed. Her eyes were puffy, her nose red, and her hair was messy. I wasn't exactly sure what she was happy about; she still looked horrible."Oh, Nora, you're awake!"

"Why am I in the hospital? What happened?" I looked around at all the monitors and down to the IV in my arm. Oh Boy, I thought—big trouble.

ELDER DIMENSION:

"She was meant to perish!" Hunter's voice thundered a direct challenge to the youthful Elder Scott, the tension between them palpable. "I deliberately caused her fall!"

"How dare you!" Scott retorted, his voice echoing with the gravity of the prophecy. "She has been chosen by Queen Liv herself to fulfill the prophecy of peace to all dimensions."

"I told her I would not stand for it at that shame of a convention. I will not allow a human...to take over what we, the Elders, are assigned to do. Govern, "Hunter declared, his voice filled with determination.

"I advise you never to touch my daughter again, or you will have the Ancients to deal with. They do not take kindly to being disobeyed, even an Elder," Scott warned, his voice carrying the weight of the impending danger.

Hunter sneered as he walked off. "We will see, young Elder. I would worry more about you breaking the rules. Dealing with an Ancient Elder is sometimes worse." The words hung in the air, thick with the anticipation of what was to come, leaving the readers on the edge of their seats, eager for the next part of the story.

I spent a day and a half in the hospital, 'just to make sure,' the doctors said. One good thing was that Allison, Jewels, and Dane came to see me in the hospital and stood in the doorway. I looked over towards the wall.

The same man with the white blonde funky hair stood looking at me, smiling…then he disappeared.

"Nor?" Dane drew my attention to himself. He looked at me with concern. "Who were you looking at?"

I felt my cheeks turn pink. "No one, I just spaced out."

Dane sat on the edge of the bed and held my hand. There was something in his touch, the way he looked at me. My heart began to pound. What was he thinking? He brought me pink roses, which were sitting next to me. The smell of the flowers was sweet, and the pull of his eyes was heartbreaking.

"Please forgive me." He looks with sincerity as he picks up my hand. My hand was still an IV as he brought it to his lips. They were so soft. Electric sparks raced throughout my body. I didn't know what to say to this.

Dane bent down closer, "I won't give up on you, no matter what you say. My parents are jerks. You didn't deserve to be treated like that."

A tear fell down my cheek, and he caught it with his finger. "Don't cry."

I struggled to sit upright. Our mouths are so close together. Please kiss me, I begged in my mind. My heart was beating so hard that the monitor started to beep…loudly. The nurse appeared in the doorway and frowned. "Young man, you are wearing out your welcome. Let her rest."

I smiled and cupped Dane's face. "It will be all right." His forehead connected with mine, and he smiled.

"Nora!" Allison squealed as she stood in the doorway.

***

Allison came by to see me next, but she was reticent. That was weird. When Jewels came, she smiled like the cat that swallowed a parakeet. Everyone told me countless times never to scare me like that again. Jeez! Mom was overly protective and wouldn't let anyone stay too long. To be honest, I was worn out after each visit.

When I got home from the hospital, Allison was by my side constantly, telling me all the latest gossip.

Jewels and Allison got to know each other while I was "away." Allison also said that Dane constantly texted her to see how I was doing.

"I'm not talking to him right now," Allison said as she flipped her straight hair back.

"He said I was hogging all your time, and I'm being selfish and not letting anyone see you." Allison turned around to pick up her ringing phone. With a click of a button, it stopped.

"There, you need to rest." Allison kept putting my stuffed animals next to me. It was getting annoying.

"Who texted?" I asked. "I'm fine. I can talk to Dane or… anyone for that matter."

Allison raised an eyebrow. "You need rest, and you don't need to be disturbed."

"Al, I'm fine." Getting irritated with Allison, I took a deep breath and blurted. "Really I'm fine. You are acting weird. What's wrong with you?"

Allison looked away. "Nothing," she stated, putting her hands before her face. Oh boy, what now? "Al, talk to me, please. What is going on with you?"

Allison turned away from me. Through the sobs, she whaled, "Nor it's my fault! I am so very sorry. I tried to catch you. I'm a horrible friend. I couldn't stop you from falling. I was right behind you. It happened so fast. I couldn't stop you from…. I should be fired as your best friend!"

Mom entered the room at that particular moment. I swear she was born with Vulcan hearing. "Okay, Allison, your mom is here; it's time for you to go." Mom looked at Allison, crying. "What's wrong, Allison?" Mom pulled Allison to her feet with her arm wrapped around her back, talking to her calmly while walking her to her waiting mother.

***

After Mom left the room, I closed my eyes. Why am I so tired all the time? I heard the car door close and Mom saying goodbye. A few minutes later, she appeared in my doorway.

"You okay?"

With that, I hurried up to sit against my headboard, trying not to hit my sore head. I gestured for Mom to sit with me. "Can we talk for a minute?"

Mom started pulling her hair up in a messy bun as she walked into the room and sat on my bed. It looked like cotton candy on her head. "Sure, what's up?" she said.

I was nervous about what I had found out about my Dad, but I had to. "This is important, and I need you to listen to and believe me."

Mom looked at me and didn't say a word for a minute. "What is it?"

I took a deep breath. "I met Dad." There it was out. I know you may not believe me, but I can prove it. I was named after his grandmother, and you married him in her rose garden. He said you were stubborn." I dared look at her. Her mouth was open. Mom was speechless.

"How?" Mom stuttered. Mom didn't move a muscle. "How Nora?"

"I don't know. He said I was hurt, and he…said that he needed to watch over me." My throat felt like it was closing up from the nervousness. I gulped and swallowed several times to keep going before I lost my nerve.

"I'm stubborn? He said that about me, huh?" Mom looked into space for a minute or two like she was struggling with a decision. "Okay, I believe you. You win. You want to know about Scott; I'll tell you about your dad."

She took two deep breaths."Your dad went to an Ivy League School. A friend took me to a frat party on his campus. That's where I first met your dad. He asked me out on a date, and I simply told him, 'I don't date rich frat boys.' If I left, I'd never see him again and go on with my life."

A smile crossed her lips."Several years later, I was modeling for an art class, and one of his friends recognized me from that night. This guy contacted your Dad, who tracked me down and kept asking me out. I tried to avoid him, but he showed up everywhere I went."

I gasped."Did he stalk you? Why didn't you just go out with him?"

Mom frowned."I didn't like his friends. They were troublemakers. I needed to concentrate on school. Nanna and Poppa didn't come from money. I had to work my way through college."

A smile crossed her face again."Your dad promised he would go away if I went to dinner with him. At that point, I would do anything to get rid of him. When he picked me up that night, he brought me a simple yellow rose…I always wondered if it was from his Grandmother's rose garden but never asked."

Mom looked over to the roses that Dane had brought me and looked back at me. "I couldn't help it; I fell in love with him that night." Mom took my hand and kissed my forehead. "That's all for right now. Sleep tight. Call if you need me."

"He told me he fell in love with you the second he saw you," I said, hoping she would tell me more.

Mom walked to my doorway and turned around."Goodnight, Nora." As I left my room, I heard her walking down the steps.

KISS ME

I had to spend a day and a half in the hospital 'Just to make sure,' the doctors said. One good thing was Allison, Jewels, and Dane came to see me in the hospital and stood in the doorway.

I looked towards the wall, and the same man with the white blonde funky hair and the blue metallic suit stood smiling at me. "You're going to be okay, Mom," he said, put his fingers to his head, and saluted me.

"Nor?" Dane drew my attention to him. He looked at me with concern in his eyes. "Who were you looking at?"

I felt my cheeks turn pink. "No one, I just spaced out."

He sat on the edge of the bed and held my hand. There was something in his touch, the way he looked at me. My heart began to pound. What was he thinking? He brought me pink roses, and they were sitting next to me. The smell of the flowers was sweet, and the pull of his eyes. "Please forgive me." He looks with sincerity as he picks up my hand. My hand was still an IV as he brought it to his lips. They were so soft. Electric sparks raced throughout my body.

I didn't know what to say to this.

Dane bent down closer, "I won't give up on you, no matter what you say. My parents are jerks. You didn't deserve to be treated like that." A tear fell down my cheek, and he caught it with his finger. "Don't cry."

I struggled to sit upright. Our mouths are so close together. *Please kiss me*, I begged in my mind. My heart was beating so hard that the monitor started to beep…loudly. The nurse appeared in the doorway and frowned. "Young man, you are wearing out your welcome. Let her rest."

I smiled and cupped Dane's face. "It will be all right." His forehead connected with mine, and he smiled.

***

Allison came by to see me next, but she was reticent. That was weird. When Jewels came, she smiled like the cat that swallowed a parakeet. Everyone told me countless times never to scare me like that again. Jeez!

Mom was overly protective and wouldn't let anyone stay too long. To be honest, I was worn out after each visit.

When I got home from my stay in the hospital, Allison was by my side constantly, telling me all the latest gossip. Jewels and Allison got to know each other while I was 'away.'

Allison also said that Dane constantly texted her to see how I was doing.

Allison said as she flipped her straight hair back. "He said I was hogging all your time, and I'm being selfish and not letting anyone see you." Allison turned around to pick up her ringing phone.

With a click of a button, the text ringer stopped. "There, you need to rest." Allison kept putting my stuffed animals next to me. It was getting annoying.

"Who texted?" I asked. "I'm fine. I can talk to Dane or… anyone for that matter."

Allison raised an eyebrow. "You need rest, and you don't need to be disturbed."

"Allison, I'm fine." Getting irritated with her, I took a deep breath and blurted."Really I'm fine. You are acting weird. What's wrong with you?"

Allison looked away. "Nothing," she stated, putting her hands before her face.

Oh boy, what now? I thought. "Al, talk to me, please. What is going on with you?"

Allison turned away from me. Through the sobs, she whispered, "Nor it's my fault! I am so very sorry. I tried to catch you. I'm a horrible friend. I couldn't stop you from falling. I was right behind you. It happened so fast. I couldn't stop you from…. I should be fired as your best friend!"

Mom entered the room at that particular moment. I swear she was born with Vulcan hearing. "Okay, Allison, your Mom is here; it's time for you to go."

Mom looked at Allison, crying. "What's wrong, Allison?"

Mom pulled Allison to her feet with her arm wrapped around her back, talking to her calmly while walking her to her waiting mother in the car.

After Mom left the room, I closed my eyes. Why am I so tired all the time? I heard the car door close and Mom saying goodbye. A few minutes later, she appeared in my doorway."You okay?"

With that, I hurried up to sit against my headboard, trying not to hit my sore head. I gestured for Mom to sit with me. "Can we talk for a minute?"

Mom started pulling her hair up in a messy bun as she walked into the room and sat on my bed. It looked like cotton candy on her head."Sure, what's up?" she said.

I was nervous about what I had found out about my Dad, but I had to."This is important, and I need you to listen to and believe me."

Mom looked at me and didn't say a word for a minute. "What is it?"

I took a deep breath. "I met Dad." There it was out. "You may not believe me, but I can prove it. I was named after his grandmother, and you married him in her rose garden. He said you were stubborn." I dared look at her. Her mouth was open. Mom was speechless.

"How?" Mom stuttered. Mom didn't move a muscle. "How Nora?"

"I don't know. He said I was hurt, and he…said that he needed to watch over me." My throat felt like it was closing up from the nervousness. I gulped and swallowed several times to keep going before I lost my nerve.

"I'm stubborn? He said that about me, huh?" Mom looked into space for a minute or two like she was struggling with a decision. "Okay, I believe you. You win. You want to know about Scott; I'll tell you about your dad."

She took two deep breaths."Your dad went to an Ivy League School. He was brilliant. A friend took me to a frat party on his campus. That's where I first met your dad. He asked me out on a date, and I simply told him, 'I don't date rich frat boys.' I left; I'd never see him again and continue with my life."

 A smile crossed her lips."Several years later, I was modeling for an art class, and one of his friends recognized me from that night. This guy contacted your dad. Where he tracked me down and kept asking me out. I tried to avoid him, but he showed up everywhere I went."

I gasped."Did he stalk you? Why didn't you just go out with him?"

Mom frowned."I didn't like his friends. They were troublemakers. I needed to concentrate on school. Nanna and Poppa didn't come from money. I had to work my way through college." A smile crossed her face again."Your dad promised he would go away if I went to dinner with him. At that point, I would do anything to get rid of him. When he picked me up that night, he brought me a simple yellow rose…I always wondered if it was from his Grandmother's rose garden but never asked."

Mom looked over to the roses that Dane had brought me and looked back at me. "I couldn't help it; I fell in love with him that night." Mom took my hand and kissed my forehead. "That's all for right now. Sleep tight. Call if you need me."

"He told me he fell in love with you the second he saw you," I said, hoping she would tell me more.

Mom walked to my doorway and turned around. "Goodnight, Nora." As I left my room, I heard her walking down the steps.

***

The following day, I woke up to Mom yelling in the stairway. "Nora, wake up it's noon,

Dane is here to see you!"

That got my attention. I jumped up out of bed and threw some clothes on. I was going down the steps, putting my hair in a ponytail all at the same time. I stuck my head around the fence to see Dane looking at one of my Mom's current paintings.

"I'll be right back," I said breathlessly.

Dane smiled in response. I raced back up the stairs to brush my teeth. One last check, my shoulders dropped.

"You're a mess, Nora Rose," I told the reflection in the mirror. I bounced down the steps. I couldn't help smiling when I saw Dane.

Putting on my brightest smile, I walked towards Dane. "Hey, I've missed you." I looked over; Mom was across the hall in her art studio.

Dane looked up, putting this phone away. "Hey, I missed you too. Allison is still mad at me." He said, running his hand through his hair. "She blames me for everything. That's why I haven't called. I…"

I placed my finger over his lips, "shh."

Mom must have decided we needed some time to talk. "Nora, why don't you and Dane go outside and get some fresh air."

I can only imagine Mom smiling to herself.

Dane jumped from the sofa, took my hand, and led me outside. I looked back at Mom; she was smiling! I was right, I thought.

So we walked hand in hand until we got to my bench. We both sat down in silence. I was uncomfortable with the silence, remembering being here with my dad.

Dane straddled the bench. "I didn't mean for the dinner to get so messed up," he said regretfully; "Mom shouldn't have been mean like that. I don't care what anyone thinks, Nora. I…I…" Dane looked at me with his intense, beautiful hazel eyes.

My heart started to pound out of my chest. I straddled the bench to face him. He leaned into me. My heart felt like it was going to burst out of my chest. Catching my breath waiting...

He pulled me closer, a few inches apart. The look on his face told me what was coming next. Being so close to the pyramid, I could hear his thoughts again.

I can't wait anymore. I have to do this now. I took a deep breath—a huge, deep breath—to try to steady my heart from beating out of my chest.

Dane moved closer until I was practically in his lap. Then I did something I had no intention of doing…I wrapped my legs around his waist; Dane groaned as our bodies touched. My fingers threaded his dirty blonde hair, and his fingers slid through mine. His hands tilted my head, bringing my mouth to his as his head dipped closer. A sigh escaped my lips, and things slowed to the point where minutes felt like hours.

His hands held my head firm yet gentle. His other hand slides across my back as if I was a cherished heirloom. My skin tingled everywhere. As his lips met mine, my eyes fluttered close, wanting to cherish this moment forever. His lips were soft as they pressed against mine.

My hand slid under his shirt, feeling the smoothness of his skin, which encouraged him to kiss me deeper. His body went rigid and stopped.

OLD FRIENDS

Out of nowhere, Link leaped and playfully struck Dane's nose, turning the situation into a humorous spectacle. He then hopped onto Dane's shoulder, adding to the scene's absurdity. Now, with a hand on his nose, Dane tried to flick Link off his shoulder with the back of his hand. But Link, the mischievous acrobat, was too quick, stepping in all attempts to get caught and keeping the audience entertained with his antics.

Watching the ridiculous scene, I screamed, "Dane, stop!" Dane froze, his hand in the air, ready to squash. Link ran from under Dane's hand and looked up at Dane, sticking his tongue out Link to the gro.

Shocked, Dane insisted, "Nora, what is that?" Pointing his finger towards Link.

Getting up from the bench, I leaned over. "What are you doing, Link? How did you get here?" I asked while helping Dane up from the ground.

Dane looked stunned, holding his nose. I laid my hand on the ground so Link could climb onto it.

"Where is Lonnie?" I said to Link. I looked over my shoulder at Dane; his mouth was still open.

"Nora, what is that thing you are holding!" Dane said

"He isn't going to hurt you, Dane. Link is a friend." I said calmly,

"No, that thing is not a friend!" Dane said, intense fear in his voice.

I turned towards Dane, my hand holding Link in it. "Dane, I'd like to introduce Link. Link and his brother Lonnie are from another dimension. Mom's sculpture connects the two dimensions." Dane still looks at me like I have three heads on my shoulder.

"It does NOT explain what he is! An Alien?" Dane said nervously.

Link threw up his hands."Here we go again. Humans!" Link turned to Nora, "This human was attacking you! My only choice was to protect you! That must be how I got through again." Link scratched his fuzzy lime hair.

Dane shouted, "Hey, I wasn't attacking her!"

"Nora Please! I am freaking out?" Dane countered.

Link scoffed. "Okay, genius! I'll say this only once!…" Interrupting Link, Lonnie excitedly said, "Nora! Look at me! Nora, look, I got my Royal Hat!!" Lonnie jumped up and down on the bench, trying to get Nora's attention. "See, isn't glorious."

I bent down to Lonnie, and Link groaned. "Not the hat again!" Link frowned.

Dane moved closer to look at Lonnie. "There are two of them? Nora, please tell me I'm dreaming." I couldn't resist the pleading look on his face. I took his hand and interlocked my fingers in his.

Lonnie jumped once more. "Nora!! Look! I got my hat! From the Queen herself! Nora!" He said with a beaming smile on his face.

I placed Link next to Lonnie on the bench. Link shot Dane a nasty look.

"You aren't gonna kill them?" Dane asked.

I started to explain."Remember when you saw the green glow the first time I showed you my spot? It was Link and Lonnie's people. I don't know how the dimension was broken this time…." Maybe it was Jewels. It had to be Jewels, I thought. I closed my eyes and rubbed my forehead. I could feel a headache coming on again, but I didn't want to stop trying to explain.

"It's a long story. I…I …" I lost my explanation.

"Nora is trying to tell you that she has powers, Elder powers from her Dad." Link said.

"Like a magician? I thought your Dad...died." Dane was so confused.

"He did the night I was born. There is magic in the world…different dimensions. Here, let me show you." I took his hand, and with the other sparkles, they flew and brought up the images of us sitting on the bench in hologram form.

"Nora…" Dane pulled his hand away from me. "This is not right. They are not right!" Dane said, breaking away and stepping back from me.

Tears welled in my eyes. "I thought you were falling for me. You said I was the one for you!" I let out a sob.

His confusion was apparent. "I heard your thoughts last time we were here. The sculpture is like a magical power source. I am the same…Dane, please."

He ran his fingers through his hair. Dane kept looking between me, Link, and Lonnie.

Link looked at me and said, "You're a real genius, Nora. You figured it out faster than he did," Link said, pointing a finger at Dane.

Frowning, I said, "Stop it, Link. Be nice! Dane is my boyfriend." I turned to Lonnie, who looked neglected. "Lonnie, I love your hat. I'm so proud of you." I rubbed the fuzz peeking out of his hat.

I laughed, and Dane chuckled, too. "Link, I want you to be nice and apologize to Dane for hurting his nose. Please, for me."

"How did they get here? How did you get…get ma…magic?" Dane asked.

Link put his hands on his hips. "I never apologize! But since you asked me to, I will. I apologize to your boyfriend, Dane." Looking at Nora, "Don't make me do it again."

"It is sort of new. It happened when Mom finished her sculptures in the front. It bent the barriers between dimensions. It was a while ago, the night of the hard rain. I was just as freaked out as you were. My…father, whom I…just met, was chosen to be uh…"

"An Elder! Her father is an Elder!" Lonnie shouted. "She holds the last of Ancient magic! Are you scared of us?"

"Why can Dane see you and Link?" I asked Link

"Becwas," Lonnie piped up with a mouthful of seeds. "He is your Gawdian," Lonnie said as he shoved more seeds into his mouth.

Link rolled his eyes. "What Mr. Gluttony means is that Mr. Genius over there is your

Guardian."

"I'm her what?" Dane asked.

"Nope, no, you cannot do genius. It is something you have to choose for yourself," Link said. "You either take our Nora, or you don't. If you don't do well, you will be dealt with. There is much more here than meets the eye. Ask your Elder."

I turned and walked closer to Dane. I took his hands into mine."I want to be with you. Please, don't leave me." Dane hugged me close to him. He felt so right.

Dane whispered in my ear. "I don't understand, but I want to. I want to understand Nora."

Lonnie looked at me and asked."What is a boyfriend? Do they taste yummy? Well, do they?"

Link pulled Lonnie's ear. I laughed. Some things never change with them.

Dane was watching the scene with amazement. A green head poked from around Lonnie's back.

Lonnie turned around and got excited. "Nora! Nora! My sister Lana!"

Lana stepped out from behind Lonnie. Her eyes were lowered, and her hands were together as the flowing white dress bellowed around her. She resembled her brothers, but she was very regal-looking and very feminine.

Lana lifted her eyes to reveal purple, unlike her bother's green eyes. Lana began to speak, "On behalf of our Queen and King. Her Majesty sends her gratitude to thank you, Mistress Nora, for breaking our people's curse." She looked sideways at Lonnie, who had started eating another seed and frowned at him.

Dane looked at me and whispered loudly. "You broke a curse?"

I nodded. Dane just rolled his eyes. I whispered to Dane, "I'll explain later."

Link walked towards his sister. "What are YOU doing here? You are supposed to be with Queen Luna."

Lana replied, "And you, dear brother, should he be at court." she smiled with satisfaction.

Lonnie jumped into the conversation, saying, "And I am supposed to be personally overseeing preparations for the festivities of the new season. I think I will serve boyfriend as the main course!" Both Lana and Link looked at Lonnie and rolled their eyes.

Lana turned to speak to Nora, "Mistress Nora, after today's events," casting a look at Link."I believe magic has its guardian. This is why we were able to break through to you. Beware of sharing our existence. Boyfriend Dane, you are decreed a special honorary dispensation. Now that our curse has been broken, our magical powers are slowly returning. The stars are aligning, and once they are one, our powers will be fully returned, and evil forces will seek to take them away once more. We need to protect against that happening."

Lana took Nora's finger from the bench and held it in her hand, closing her eyes. "I grant you the keys to our people with the blessings of Queen Luna, who is a direct descendant of Her Majesty Ancient Queen Liv." A slight tingle raced up Nora's ring finger and encircled her wrist. The tiny heart on the bracelet glowed a bright white.

Lana looked up at Nora and smiled. "It is done."

Link, Lonnie, and Lana all bowed to Nora. Only then did Lana turn to Dane. "You were specially chosen by the Ancients themselves. Betraying this honor will ruin our people, and you will be cursed for the rest of your days."

Dane nodded. "You have my word of honor." Putting his hand over his heart.

Lana looked deep into Dane's eyes. "I accept and bond your words with the Elders."

Glancing at Nora, Lana smiled. "Mistress Nora, it is my honor to have met you."

Link hugged Nora's finger in farewell. "Nora, we will see you soon." Link bowed to her, and Link and Lana faded away.

"Link, you didn't apologize to Dane," I yelled out to Link. He turned around and smiled. I wanted to flatten him.

Lonnie waved to Nora. "I love you, Nora." I rubbed his fuzzy hair as he also faded away.

After Lana, Link, and Lonnie returned to their dimension, Dane and I stayed outside to discuss today's appearances. Dane quietly listened and asked a question here or there. He seemed satisfied with my explanations.

By the time I finished my story, several hours passed.

After I finished talking, there were five minutes of silence, and I finally blurted out, "Talk to me!"

The feeling of nervousness was getting to me. Dane took my hand, raised my palm, and kissed my wrist. His lips were so soft against my skin.

Dane, with a crooked grin, said. "I didn't want Link to attack me again." Looking up at the sunset and back at me. "It's getting late; I forgot to ask you earlier if you would like to come to a backyard party my parents are giving. Allison and Jewels are also invited. You don't have to if you don't want to."

The words flew out of my mouth. "As long as Allison and Jewels are with me, I will go."

Dane smiled. "Thank you. I hate to leave, but....I'll text you the info."

I nodded in agreement and hugged him goodbye. As he left smiling dreamily, I glided back into the house. I felt giddy. I still felt his kiss. I found Mom still in her studio painting.

Coming back to reality, my stomach turned as I thought about seeing Dane's parents again. I should have said no to Dane. I wanted to talk to Mom about the backyard party. I didn't want to go. I wondered if I could back out. Would he be mad at me? As I peeked around the doorway, I watched Mom humming while she painted. She was so totally focused that I didn't want to bother her.

Sighing, I went upstairs to my room. Maybe it will be different this time with friends to back me up. Maybe…

He texted me when he got home

Dane: Hey Me: Miss you already. Dane: Me too.

Me: Are you too freaked out from today?

Dane: No, well, sort of. It will be okay. Promise a Happy face.

HURT HEARTS

As the lively backyard party at Dane's house kicked off, I was in a different world, still on my bed, engrossed in my phone. Allison and Jewels were amid a heated debate over their outfit choices, their lively banter filling the air with energy.

Allison expressed her displeasure at Jewels' choice of bright yellow romper: "She will look like a banana!"

Jewels' bright yellow romper caught Allison's disapproving eye like sunshine. She swiftly plucked it from Jewels' hands and returned it to the closet.

"Surely, you have something else?" Allison asked, rummaging through my closet.

"I'm gonna burn this sundress; it has bad vibes attached." Jewels rolled her eyes as she threw the blue polka-dotted dress into a corner. "Leave it to me to save the day." Jewels grabbed her bag and pulled out a black romper with a skirt.

Jewels held it up, displaying it for us. "My Aunt sent this for Christmas. I will never wear it; it has flowers as if I would ever wear flowers. She tries to get me to wear' girlie stuff.' It's not going to happen," she declared with a dramatic flair, eliciting a chuckle from the group.

Allison took the dress. "Nice vampiric choice," she said, teasing Jewels about her usual black attire with a mischievous glint in her eye.

"Not all of us are pink princesses," Jewels teased, not one to back down. She rolled her eyes in response, their banter adding a touch of humor and camaraderie to the party.

<u>DANE</u>:

I stood in the doorway of my mother's room and watched her as she put on her jewelry. "I will not let you snub Nora again, Mom."

She looked at me in the mirror. Frowning, she glared at me. "The little urchin is not fit for you! Screw her and get it over with! You will marry into society, nothing else! Do you understand...son."

"Here is a news flash...Mother. I will marry who I want. It is not for you to decide. It's my life. Not yours."

Mom turned to face me. "You don't know who she is, do you? She looks so much like her father. The same eyes."

"I don't care who her father is. I want and will marry her. You will not stop me." I stood my ground.

Mom laughed. "You have such a wonderful imagination, son."

I had enough of her and walked out. I am so sick of her pettiness.

THE PARTY

When we arrived at his house, Dane was the first to greet us. He was dressed in a short-sleeved polo shirt and khaki pants—good. He was not dressed in a tie.

Jewels and Allison walked in first.

"What took so long?" he asked. Then he saw me. You look...incredible." Taking my arm, he led me into the backyard. "Did you bring your swimsuit?" he asked.

Allison punched Dane on the shoulder. "Do you know how long it took us to make her beautiful for you, and you want her to go swimming? Are you fucking insane? "

Dane flinched. "I guess not." He glanced over at Jewels, who was giving him a nasty look.   "Okay, truce. You win, no swimming." He held his hands up in defeat.

Jewels muttered something to Allison. "I think he wanted to see her in a swimsuit."

Both girls giggled. "Can't he just be happy with seeing her great legs?"

My stomach turned when I saw the servers and lots of well-dressed people. Is that the Governor? I thought. I'm going to be sick! Dane's mom lifted her head as if I were some sort of alien intruder. Dane guided me to the food table. We approached it, and my stomach twisted again. Jewels put her hand on my shoulder in reassurance as Allison talked to Dane's mom.

Cordelia turned her attention to Jewels. "Cordelia Alexander, so delighted to meet you. What an interesting outfit you are wearing." The tilt of her nose said otherwise, more like another bug to squash.   She looked down at Jewel's very short black leather skirt. Her shirt is just tight enough to reveal her ample boobs, and the bottom of the shirt ends just above her pierced belly button.

Jewels responded, "Thanks. I put it together myself today. Do you like it?" A defiant tilt of her head said she was anything but pleased.

Cordelia looked at Jewel's in blatant disgust. She turned her attention to me."Nice to see you again."

Allison jumped to distract Cordelia from any further conversation with me."Oh, Mrs. Alexander, your decorations and lighting for your party were fantastic." Taking Cordelia's arm and guiding her away while carrying on a nonstop conversation, pointing here and there, Cordelia pretended to listen to Allison attentively.

Dane twirled me away into the kitchen, where the caterers were busy making food and stuff. He backed me up against the wall and placed a light kiss on the corner of my mouth.

"You are stunning. Do you want to see my room?" he whispered as he trailed kisses down my neck. As we entered the house's main living area, I thought about how gorgeous it was. Sunbeams danced off all the chandeliers, which reeked of money.

Every piece of furniture was meant to show off wealth.

"Dane! Nora!" Cordelia's stern voice echoed."Where are you off to?"

I looked outside at Allison and Jewels standing on the other side of the glass French doors, both mouthing sorry. My terrorizing fear hit me square in the stomach.

"I expect an answer," Cordelia demanded. Her arms were folded. Her manicured red nails reminded me of daggers that had just dug into an unknowing dying victim.

Dane squeezed my hand in reassurance. "Nora needed to use the restroom." The lie seemed flawless to me.

Cordelia smiled. "There is one in the cabana. You know that, dear." She turned to look at me.   "May I see you for a moment…is it Nora?"

"You promised!" Dane growled as he tried to pull me behind him.

"I did no such thing." Cordelia's flash of perfect white teeth with her blood-red lipstick reminded me of a lion promising not to devour an antelope."Nora?"

My stomach felt like a lead balloon. My shoulders went back; I took a deep breath when I unhooked my hands from Dane's. I gave him a look of reassurance even though I felt like I was being led to the gallows to be hung for a crime I committed.

THE INQUISITION

I walked with my head held high and my shoulders back; I wasn't going to let this woman beat me again. Cordelia stood by the door and shut the heavy wooden door behind me.

"Now it's time for a little girl talk." Cordelia folded her hands together as she started with. "Dane is my only child. He mustn't get distracted by someone like you. It was fun while he was in school, but now it ends. You do not have the pedigree. So there are no misunderstandings; you are a plaything. Dane will marry a debutante in … society, well-bred and with lots of money. I will not allow him to lower himself with someone like you."

A tear fell. "He…can see anyone he wants." I almost choked on the words. This could not be happening. This is the twentieth century, right? I didn't time warp into some barbaric time where parents forced their children into marriages.

Cordelia laughed. "You are so much like your mother. My son doesn't love you. Your father never really loved your mother; it was a fleeting obsession. You are a plaything to Dane. That is all. I do not want you anywhere near my son again. Is that understood? Take your friends and go."

I stood a little taller at the mention of my father. "I know my father loved my mother, no matter what you say or think." Stepping up to her, I pointed my finger at her. "I'm going, but don't ever say my parents didn't love each other! Is that understood?"

My manners fled the scene. I lost who I was. I could feel magic creeping up, and I had to control it. Never use magic in anger, but I am so tempted. There was a thickness in the air.

I stormed past her, opened the door, and ran to where Dane stood with Allison. Allison was hanging up her cell phone, and Jewels was holding her arms out for a hug.

Tears were pouring from my eyes as I looked at Dane."It's over. Don't call me or come and see me anymore. Here is your bracelet." I was so upset I couldn't unlatch the hook.

Dane looked at me and then at his Mom. "Nora, no, please don't go. Please," he said, trying not to take the bracelet. Looking at his Mom, he yelled, "What did you do?"

Cordelia stood in the hall, arms folded, and smiled. This was precisely what she wanted—tapping those blood-red nails as if they were begging to do their damage.

Allison pushed Dane out of the way. "Let's go, Nora; your mom is on her way. I called her already." Allison and Jewels each put their arms around me as they ushered me out the front door. I couldn't stop shaking.

Mom was in the circular driveway waiting for us. We piled into the backseat.

Mom exited the car and stuck her head in the window, "I'll be right back." With that, she stormed into Dane's house without knocking.

Cordelia turned toward the door as it slammed closed. "I don't remember you being invited," she sneered. You have to leave. We have essential guests here."

Grace charged Cordelia until her back was against the wall. "You can't let things go, can you? You have to take it out on MY daughter. Grow up, Cordelia. Scott always thought you were trash! You may look classy, but underneath, you are pure evil."

Stepping closer to Cordelia, she said, "If you ever make my daughter cry again, I will do what I intended to years ago." She abruptly turned towards Dane and said, "You are welcome at my house at any time." With that, she left the house, slamming the door behind her.

MAD AND CONFUSED

After dropping Allison and Jewels off, she sat in a chair next to the kitchen island, rubbing her forehead momentarily. Mom looked at me and asked. "What happened? What did she say to you?"

I felt like a lost child again, being reprimanded for something I couldn't understand. I couldn't meet Mom's gaze, my eyes fixed on the floor. I mumbled,

"I don't know what I did. She said I was a plaything for Dane…" My heart was a storm of confusion and pain, and I, a whirlwind, was just a toy engulfed in a w of emotions.

Folding her arms, she prodded. "Cordelia Alexander just doesn't say one or two things. Spit it out, Nora. You have nothing to be ashamed about."

I couldn't say it—I just couldn't. When I looked up, I saw the determination in her eyes. Taking a deep breath, I blurted out,

"She said Dad never loved you. I said that it wasn't true. I told her never to say that again." My heart hurt, and my stomach hurt, and I couldn't control the tears that were gushing out. I was a mess of the hurt and confusion. emotions, and inability.

Mom's lips thinned into a straight line. "That woman is a viper. She will destroy anything to get what she wants. I had the misfortune once to stand in her way. Be very careful. Don't let her confront you again alone. Do you understand? "

"Why does she hate us? Is it the same reason Dad's parents do?"

She was holding out her hand as an indication to stop. "Don't go there! I can't do this today!"

My filter that keeps me from saying stupid stuff broke. This is what came out:

"You always say that! When you are older, I'll tell you. I can't today. When Mom? I want to know where I came from. I want to know my family history! I want to know why I am being torn from Dane!" My voice trembled with the intensity of my longing for answers.

Once again, the door slammed, and the clock on the wall rattled. If she won't tell me, I will find out alone. I thought. Running upstairs, I slammed my door shut, my mind already set on uncovering the truth. I was resolute in my quest for answers, no matter the obstacles.

I lay across my bed, my body wracked with sobs, my heart heavy with the weight of my emotional turmoil.

My dad, also known as The Elder, stood beside my bed. "Nora Rose?"

Looking up at him, "What do you want? You going to disappear again?" It was harsh, but I was in no mood to be excellent. "Why did you lie to me?"

"I did not lie; I am your Elder. It is against our laws to reveal who I truly was. The Ancients did not understand the love between a parent and a child. Right now, I am concerned about you." He sat next to me and put his hand on my back.

"I don't understand any of this," I said, trying to choke back tears. "What did I do? Am I the scum she thinks I am?"

Dad stopped for a minute as if reliving the memory. "Cordelia was so vile she went so far as to turn my parents against Grace. She spread lies and false rumors about your mom. She tried it with my Grandmother, but she failed. Grandma Rose loved Grace. You represent everything Cordelia hates. Didn't your mom tell you all of this?" Dad asked.

"No, Mom never talks about you or the past. Dane's mom tore my heart out. She...said I was trash, a plaything for Dane." I said, my voice trembling with emotional vulnerability as a whole new batch of tears started falling.

"Do you know Dane's mom, Cordelia? She said horrible things about you and Mom. Why would she do that? Why do that to me?" A fresh batch of tears began to fall.

"I know Dane's parents very well. Roger, Dane's father, was my very best friend. We went to school together since we were very young. In college, I dated Cordelia once or twice. I knew she was bad news. She tried everything to date me again; she was just a gold and status digger. She hit the roof when I fell head over heels in love with your mother. Cordelia targeted Roger to get to me. I tried to warn him, but he wouldn't listen. She thought he came from money when it was all mine."

I sat up and put my head against his chest as he wrapped his arms around me to comfort me. He felt solid as I held onto him, as I cried until I couldn't cry anymore. After several minutes, he let me out of his embrace.

"You are an extraordinary young lady. I know it hurts, but things will get better in time," he said as he placed his hand on mine.

"I can't stand Dane's mom! She is viscous, mean..." I couldn't say what I wanted to say. "Why do you like Dane? What makes him so different from Cordelia?" I couldn't help but ask.

"Dane is meant to do good things. Save peoples's lives...guard yours." Dad said. I felt like he was not telling me everything.

"What are you hiding? I have gotten good at knowing when someone is not telling me the whole story." I said suspiciously.

"The ancients are older than time. Feelings are foreign to them. They are the ultimate guardians of the universe; some would call them gods. They needed a human Elder to connect to this world." He drifted off in thought.

"Why? Why pick me? Why couldn't they choose someone else's Dad?" My voice almost sounded like a whine, filled with confusion and a hint of desperation.

"We were meant to save magic. A powerful queen foretold it." Dad got quiet as he looked off in the distance. "We need to change the subject, Nora Rose."

"What do I call you? Dad? Elder? What?" The question ignited my irritation again.

"I'm your father, Nora Rose. Call me Dad. This has to stay between us for now." My dad said, sighing. His finger brushed my cheek as he wiped away a tear.

"Do not stop fighting for what is right. Trust Dane; he is not the enemy. I must go. Be Strong and Be Well, Nora Rose." Kissing the top of my head, he disappeared.

THE RABBIT HOLE

Five days have passed since the party. I've refused to come out of my room. I needed time to think and time to stop hurting. Mom gave in and started leaving TV dinners and pizza by the door. Gigi finally stopped whining, and Dane came by every day after work.

The first day, he knocked on my door but made himself comfortable in the chair Mom had left. Dane continued a conversation through the door for a couple of hours. I refused to talk back; it hurt too much. While he spoke, I sat on the window ledge and turned up the music's volume with my earbuds on.

Allison and Jewels came by also. I still refused to open the door while they were there. All I could do was cry until I ran out of tears. I hadn't realized how hard I fell for Dane. I feel miserable and hurt. How could I let that happen? I need Link and Lonnie. I need my dad. I watched Dane walk down the street; the sight of him made it hurt more.

I heard a knock at the door.

"Nora, it's Allison." I sighed in relief. "I know you're hurting. Jewels will be here, but she has to see her brother tonight. She invited us to come over for a sleepover. We have your favorite junk food. You can't stay in there forever, you know. You have to be missing my wonderful personality by now."

I chuckled as she said that. "Nor? Please come out."

I opened the door. I did miss Allison. I reached for her and hugged her. "I do miss you guys," I said, wiping away a tear that escaped.

"Oh, geez, you look awful," Allison commented. "Already cleared it with your mom, so let's pack a bag." She marched into my room, started putting clothes in her bag, and made me watch her. "I'm almost done, hurry! Let's tell your mom bye."

I looked at her in stunned disbelief. "I never said I was going, Al. Put all of that back."

Mom came up behind me. "You are going if I must get Bennett to carry you there. Go have fun." Allison was smiling as she stood watching the scene.

"You are such a traitor, Mom," I said as she kissed me.

Allison took my arm and guided me out of the door. Mom kissed me one more time with a hug and waved goodbye. We walked arm and arm to Jewel's house. As Allison was about to ring the doorbell, Jewels' little brother Finch opened the door.

"Hey Finch, do you remember me? I'm a friend of your sister, child shook his head. "What do you have there?" Pointing at the stuffed animal, Finch held his stuff Opossum tighter while standing in the doorway.

"Finch, where are you?" Jewels yelled from the back of the house. "Finch! Don't make me call you by your given name!" Jewels rounded the corner. Jewels saw Finch had opened the door, and Allison and I stood in the doorway. Jewel's face changed from worry to a grin at seeing her friends. Ignoring her little brother, she walked past him and welcomed us in.

SLEEPOVER AT JEWELS

"Okay, I want the dirty details on Dane." Jewels lounged on the side of the plush sofa.

"I don't know; I haven't talked to him," I said as I spooned a mouthful of chocolate ice cream covered in chocolate syrup and whipped cream.

Allison grabbed a handful of popcorn and said, "He has been texting me, begging me to get through to her. He isn't staying at home; His dad is letting him stay with JoJo's for a while."

"Great, I'm glad he got away from the bitch." I muttered

"She is worse than a bitch. What would she think if she knew he kissed you?" Jewels said.

"Hey!" Allison squealed. "I'm supposed to know everything first!" Allison pouted.

I wanted to die right about now. "It was just a peck."

Jewels laughed. "Not from where I was sitting."

"Nora!" Allison squealed again.

I got up from the sofa. "It was just a freakin kiss!"

"Come back and tell us about it!" Both girls said at once.

DANE AT JOJO'S HOUSE

"So when is she going to talk to you again? You look like a lost puppy. I can't stand this anymore!" JoJo said as he waited for his turn at the video game.

My phone beeps with a text:
      Allison: The rabbit has left her nest
      Me: Really?
      Allison: Yep, we are having a sleepover at Jewel's place. Try once more tomorrow. She should be ready. Nice move with the kiss.
      Me: Thanks

"Dude, you kissed Nora?" JoJo asked.

"Yes," I said, not wanting to talk about it.

"Are you planning to get in her pants?" JoJo asked. "Dude, you have to!"

I turned on JoJo in a heartbeat, grabbed him by the collar of his shirt, and yanked. JoJo towards me. "Don't ever say that again! She is not that type of girl."

As I let go of JoJo, he said. "Dude, I'm sorry…I didn't mean it. I just…"

"You love her, bro. That's cool and sad at the same time." JoJo said as he straightened his shirt. "You better tell her soon. She has a fine ass. I heard some dudes talking about her. Better stake your claim."

"Anyone touching her, they are dead," I muttered.

"I will spread the word, dude. Let's play." JoJo said, yanking the remote out of Dane's hand.

NORA:

The clock ticked somewhere in the darkness. Jewels and Allison did their best to make the sleepover as fun as possible for me. We all played hide and seek with Finch. Once he went to sleep, we talked, laughed, and ate lots of junk food for most of the night.

After we settled down, I tossed and turned and finally sat up in a panic on the sofa, thinking I needed to return to my room—my haven.

I gently moved Jewels' leg off mine, tiptoed around Allison's hair, and slipped on my sandals, quietly leaving the back door. I sighed in relief.

Looking over to the metal sculpture in my backyard glistening in the moonlight. Something made me glance down at the heart on my bracelet; it was also glistening. 'A trick of the light, I thought.

With each step, I walked towards my house, and my bracelet became warmer and brighter. *"You have the keys to our people,"* fluttered through my thoughts.

I stood there momentarily and decided to walk over to the sculpture. I almost laughed out loud. 'There are no locks on the sculpture. What did Lana mean?" Curiosity got the better of me.

I reached out to touch the intersecting points of the pyramid. The next thing I knew, I was falling into a dark tunnel.

When I landed, my shoes fell off. I expected the fall to hurt, but it didn't. I landed on what I thought was grass or something that resembled grass.

Lana caught my attention."I did not expect you to arrive this fast, Mistress Nora; I forgot to tell you it's a bit confusing when you cross dimensions." She gave a slight bow. "Please forgive me."

It took me a minute to understand what Lana was saying.

"I'm in your world?" I asked, looking all around me.

I saw, in wonderment, tiny acorn houses on the city's outer rings. A sparkling pale lake, the color of cotton candy, surrounded the two inner circles. Rocks—I think they are rocks—glow various neon colors where the water meets the bluegrass. It was a sight to behold, a world unlike any I had ever seen.

The outer circle had mushroom houses closest to the lake. In the middle stood a silver tree. The silver reflected the lights of the mushroom houses, glinting on the pink lake. The tree rose above the houses, its branches curled to hold large silver balls.

Lana helped me up. *"Was I her size?"*I thought.

"Yes, you are our size. Come with me; the queen has requested your presence."

Pausing, I looked down at what I was wearing. "I'm in my pajamas. I'm not properly dressed to see the queen."

Lana's purple eyes sparkled with amusement."We do not judge by what is on the outside. What one wears is insignificant. That is one of human's greatest flaws."

Lana took my hand and guided me to the city. "We all do a job to provide for our Queen, King, and people. We have our emotions back now, and the ancient ways have been intact for centuries. Our Ancient Elder Mother, Queen Liana, was a very fair ruler, so there was no hate or wanting of others' things."

Curiously, I asked. "None?"

Smiling, Lana said quietly. "There was the evil I spoke about before. I can't say more."

The houses on the outer ring looked like giant acorns with windows. Lana turned to me to say, "These are our merchant's houses. Most are Carpenters, Farmers, and such."

As we walked down the path, residents were in their doorways, bowing to us as we passed. Some were holding brooms, others pails, or little ones hanging off their Mother's apron. The merchants followed us over the bridge, along with an orange-colored mother duck with blue stripes leading her ducklings.

Walking over the bridge, purple and green fish jumped out of the water to greet us. I stopped in amazement and saw a rainbow-colored fish jump out and wave with its fin before splashing back into pink water. Purple jellyfish glowed at the surface. Silver glittered rocks sparkling from the jellyfish's reflection glowing. The ducks waddled into the water and circled the jellyfish.

"Will the jellyfish hurt the fish and the ducks?" I asked.

Lana chuckled. "No, the jellyfish are not harmful here."

Lana and I walked along a cobblestone path that cut through the mushroom houses.

"The inner circle is where our Royal Council and Advisors live." Lana turned me around to face a massive group of curious faces. All were silent.

Lana said to the crowd, "This is Mistress Nora, the one who has broken our curse!" The whole village cheered when they heard who I was.

An older version of Link, with graying hair, stepped forward. "Mistress Nora, My name is Leroy, the father of Link, Lonnie, Lana, you know, Lann and Leo are away now." Taking his wife's hand. "This is my wife, Lulu; it is my profound and humble honor to be in your presence."

He stood like a proud soldier and bowed his head. Please let me welcome you to our village. I had the honor of escorting the young Elder..." He coughed. "excuse me, your father to the Ancient Elders."

I felt so honored and accepted here. "Thank you," I replied, feeling humbled.

Lulu stepped up with her head bowed, holding my shoes. "Mistress, your shoes." It felt weird when she put them on my feet. Lulu's hands glistened like glitter as she stood up.

After introductions, Lana took my hand. "We must see Her Royal Highness." I bowed in return as the village people bowed once more.

We walked through the door, and I saw Lonnie still eating seeds at the table with his Royal Hat on. He truly loves that hat. Looking around, I saw Link, where he was standing next to King Lukas.

He smiled and waved when he saw me. The Queen gestured for us to come forward, where Lana bowed, then stated, "Your Majesty Queen Luna, my, I present Mistress Nora of the Human World, daughter of an Elder."

I fell into a deep curtsy with my head bowed, hoping I did it correctly. I felt ridiculous in pajamas with unicorns on it. In my defense, it was a gift from Allison.

"It is so nice to meet you finally, Your Majesty ." I felt humbled to be in her presence.

A hand lifted my chin. "Please rise, Mistress Nora."

I did what I was asked to do.

The first thing I noticed was the queen's sparkling yellow-green eyes. Her translucent skin was stunning, and her blue hair fell to one side.

The Queen smiled."You are so very pretty. The Elders are so pleased that the curse has been broken. Link and Lonnie were on their best behavior, I trust…" She ran her fingers over the bracelet. Pausing with a smile, "Ahh, young love."

My heart twisted. "I mean no disrespect, Your Majesty, but I'm not talking to him."

The queen's only response was a chuckle. "Not all is as it seems. I have an informant who says boyfriend Dane talks to you quite often and is hurting just as much," Queen Luna said as she glanced at Link.

I also turned to look at him, and he looked guilty.

Lana stepped in. "Pardon, Your Majesty; the time has come for Mistress Nora to return to her world."

Queen Luna smiled."Very well. Remember the words of your Elder, Mistress Nora. Be well until we meet again."

The heart on my bracelet started to glow white when the Queen removed her hand from mine.

"It was an honor to meet you," Queen Luna said, smiling and placing her hand over her heart.

I hugged Link and Lonnie. Goodbye.

Lonnie asked, "Would you like some seed for the trip?"

With a frown from his sister, Lonnie quickly put the seed behind his back. It made it harder to leave.

Lana guided me to a small room. She put one hand over my eyes to say something in a language I didn't understand. I felt the wind brush against my legs.

Suddenly, I sat up and looked around. I was still at Jewels' house. Was I dreaming the whole thing?

***

Finch stood inches from me, just staring at me. "Did you see them, too?" He was still holding the stuffed animal."Did you? Spock saw them."

I looked down at Allison and Jewels, who were still sleeping.

Whispering, I asked. "Who? Who is Spock?"

He looked at me weirdly, holding up the opossum. "Spock," Finch said, turning to look at his sister. "The little green people. I saw them this morning. Did you see them, too?" Finch said louder. Frustrated, he shrugged his shoulders and walked over to his sister. With an evil gleam in his eye, he grabbed a handful of his sister's hair and pulled.

Jewels shrieked and jumped up, and Finch's self-preservation instincts kicked in fast and ran.

"Finch! Jewels screamed."Just wait until Dad gets home! You are in so much trouble!!"

PATCHWORK

I'm not sure I could blame Dane for wanting to make out. But the temptation to take it further was too great right now. Dane and I talked for a while about different things. The one thing we both agreed upon is we have to trust each other no matter what happens.

The conversation kept coming back to how our mothers knew each other.

Dane asked, "Who is Scott?"

"Scott is my dad," I said very quietly. "I look like him, Mom says; I have his eyes." My voice had gotten progressively lower. "My dad said he likes you." With a half-smile, I looked up at him. His questioning look made me realize what I had just said. "When I hit my head, he came down to watch over me. It sounds dumb; I know I just…"

Dane put his finger over my lips as if to say Shh. "I believe you. I don't think you are crazy or nuts. As for your eyes, they are lovely. You are so wonderful, Nora Rose." He said in a low, husky voice

I must have turned a hundred shades of red. No one has called me beautiful before, well, except for Mom. I like the way it sounded on his lips.

Dane rubbed the back of his neck. This was never a good sign. It meant that there was an uncomfortable subject on the horizon. "I don't mean to ruin a moment. I talked to my Dad, trying to get information from him. About the 'history' you know. I felt like he wanted to say something, but he locked down. Later, when packing some clothes, I overheard my parents arguing." I could tell he was nervous.

Dane continued, "The one thing that has been bugging me the whole time." Rubbing his neck again, he said, "I wonder if your mom knew who I was when…"

"I did. I knew who you were when I met you." Mom was standing in the doorway. We both jumped at her voice. "I came up to see how things were going. I'm glad the both of you patched things up. I have some pizzas downstairs in the kitchen. That shirt is a little small. Is it Allison's?" she said as she stood in the doorway.

"Yes, she let me borrow it." I tugged at the short midriff as it bounced back up. It was a baby blue shirt with embroidered cherries on the bottom stopped neckline. They're about an inch above my belly button.

"I love pizza!" Dane jumped up and grabbed my hand to pull me up.

I groaned in response. I feel like I am going to turn into a pizza. "Okay," I said reluctantly.

We followed Mom down the steps into the kitchen. Dane immediately started to put three slices on a paper plate. As I sat at the bar, I could only stare at Dane inhaling the pizza slices. Mom poured us each a glass of soda. As Mom was walking out, she stopped at the door frame.

Turning to look at us, she said. "I'll be in the studio if you need me. Dane, don't forget you promised to let me draw you."

Dane rolled his eyes when Mom turned her back to him.

The dog, however, was a different story. Gigi sat and stared at us the entire time while we ate.

Dane ate three more pieces of pizza while I nibbled on one slice. There were too many thoughts in my head—too many feelings to deal with, too many unknowns.

I felt the tug to see Lana. I finally pushed the plate away with the half-eaten pizza. I sighed, "I swear, I will turn into a pizza."

Dane smiled. "I'll still think you are beautiful." I rolled my eyes and laughed. He lifted another slice, and then it was gone.

Disgusted. "Finished? Or do you want another pizza?"

Dane smiled. "I'm still growing Nor."

"Pig!" I said, playing and throwing a napkin at him.

Looking at him finish off the last slice of pizza, I wondered if he ever ate pizza at home.

I still couldn't help thinking about why his mom would say those hateful things to me. His dad seemed nice. What was the big secret? I had to find out. I had to know.

A smile appeared on my face. Link would say, 'A secret mission.'

"Whatever you are thinking, I don't think I am going to like it," Dane said as he wiped his mouth and reached for a breadstick.

An evil smile crossed my lips. "Nope"

QUEEN LUNA

"Don't stay out too late, Nora Rose. Tell the girls I said hello." Mom relayed all this information, never looking up from her painting. Gigi gave her approval with an agreeable "woof."

We walked outside, never breaking our finger connection. The sculpture gleamed in the setting sun. Dane started to head for the bench, but I ushered him toward the sculpture instead.

Dane's pinky finger curled around mine. Shivers raced up my hand, encircling my wrist. The bracelet once again began stirring to life. Standing before the sculptures, I put our joined hands out straight.

Dane pulled me into his strong arms, "When we stand here…next to the pyramid, I want to melt into you. You are all I can think about, Nora."

His hands were on my waist, and I could feel him wanting more. He wants to touch me much, much more. I can hear his thoughts, and they are driving me insane.

"I want to feel all of her…" His thoughts were cut off from me.

Backing away from Dane, I looked up at him.

"I think Queen Luna is calling. Do you trust me to take you to see her?"

Dane looked at me for a moment and smiled. "Yes." "Okay, let's go," I said.

****

The next second, Dane and I were falling through the air. Landing on the same grassy substance as before, I knew we had made it, but looking around, I saw that it didn't look the same.

There weren't any houses; as far as I could see, it was just a bluegrass field. I turned around once or twice to ensure I wasn't missing anything.

My attention turned to Dane, who was struggling to understand what had just happened. I took his hand for reassurance.

Wide-eyed, mouth hanging open. "Where are we, Nora? Are we in the right place?"

I smiled. "It's okay. We are in Link and Lonnie's dimension, their world. We're their size now… I came here once before, but I didn't see their village this time."

Looking around in wonderment, he saw clouds flowing in the sky, their different colors reflecting different prisms.

The wind blew gently. "This is awesomely cool!" Dane smiled.

The blue-green grass blades swayed back and forth. It looked like the grass was playing a game no one knew about.

A daisy popped out from the blades of grass. It stretched its petals towards the sky as if it was just waking up for the day. The petals are neon purple with a pink center. The daisy was rotating around back and forth and side to side. It almost looked like it was a periscope. It felt like someone was spying on us from underneath the grass through the daisy. When the daisy spied us, her petals stiffened and ducked back into the grass. I giggled.

"Nora?" Dane said, trying to get my attention. I turned around and saw the stream.

"Don't touch the water. It looks dangerous." I ignored him and walked over the stream.

Dane followed and commented. "The water looks like pink-glittered slime."

"I like this color. It smells and looks like bubble gum or cotton candy. I can't decide which." I said to him

Laying on my stomach, I hurried to put my finger into the water. The rainbow fish swam around my finger. It lay on its side and flipped its fin back and forth as if he were saying hello.

I giggled. The fish stuck his head out of the water, and I petted him between his eyes. This is awesome, I thought. The fish looked over at Dane, wanting to play, but when he didn't, he turned to flick water in his face with its back fin. I couldn't help but laugh.

"There is a purple turtle…is it dangerous?" Dane eyed the strange fish swimming around in circles alongside the turtle.

Several more fish came to see what all the commotion was about. There was a red fish with black dots, a fish with black and white blocks, and a family of orange ducks with blue stripes. They were all gathered around us, wanting to play. I petted all the fish and ducks that came by to say hello.

"This is not normal, Nora. Are you sure we are in the right place? Are those glittered rocks?" Dane asked warily, pointing to the rocks under the pink water.

"Nothing here is dangerous. Relax. Why didn't you play with the fish, Dane?" he said, playfully pushing his arm.

I looked over at him. He is so close to me, I thought wistfully. My heart started to thud. He has perfect hair and straight teeth, a smile on my face, and handsome. I sighed.

A fuzzy yellow ball of fur hopped in between us. I turned my head to see what it was. A rabbit?

Dane and I sat up to look at this banana-yellow bunny. I reached out to pet it. The rabbit was delighted; he bent its long ears. The rabbit stepped closer to me as I stroked the yellow fur of his ears. I felt the muscles in his ears tense as he pulled them up.

"What do you hear?" I asked in a soft voice. For a second, the yellow bunny looked at me, then bolted.

"That was so cool. Where is Link and Lonnie?" Dane asked.

"Queen Luna and Lana brought us here. They will be here soon." I said softly, playing with a blade of grass.

Taking Dane's hand, I scooted closer to him. Discarding the blade, my fingers moved to trace Dane's hand. I traced the outline of his hand moving softly. His skin was browned from hours in the sun but still so soft.

Curious little white flowers started peeking out from the blue-green blades of grass. My heart felt like it was trying to pound its way out of my chest.

I started concentrating on his wrist. I didn't want to look in those eyes or his lips. If I do, I will turn to mush. His other hand lifted my chin to meet his gaze. My brain went on automatic shutdown. His knuckles skimmed over my cheek and then over to my ear. His fingers cradled my head as he tilted it upwards. He leaned down, where his soft lips met mine. It felt like thousands of fireworks were exploding throughout my body at once. It was pure magic.

Opening my eyes again, he was still so close to me. Looking down at me, his lips were turning up in a grin. The tip of his finger traced my lips.

"You are so beautiful." He whispered. His finger continued down my chin, my neck. I am going to die!

His fingers started at my waist, then moved over my belly button. His hand flattened over my stomach. The magic was so strong here that it surrounded us in what felt like a private bubble. My body was fully alive with the need for his touch…demanding it. Dane's eyes darkened with desire, his hand inching under my short cutoff shirt. I remained silent as Dane touched his lips to mine, and his hand brushed the underside of my breasts.

He ended the kiss, trying desperately to catch his breath. Leaning his forehead to meet mine, he says,

"Nora, please…"

The pull was so strong here. I needed him to touch me. "Yes…"

The invitation barely left my mouth before Dane lifted my shirt and looked at me once more…Dane lifted his head to look at something. "Uh, Nora?"

"Hmm?" I answered, still in my dreamlike trance. I was reaching up to run my fingers down his cheek.

"Nor…" Dane said a little louder, pointing.

I reluctantly looked up and followed his gaze. Tall flowers were everywhere, swaying in the light breeze. The flowers had turned to face Lana, Link, and Lonnie, standing under the sunflower that materialized at that moment.

Lana stepped out from the sunflower. She bowed, her cheeks pink. "Mistress Nora, Dane, Welcome Back." Keeping her head lowered to conceal her grin.

Dane and I both stood up. He whispered, "You're right. We are their size."

Lonnie smiled and jogged over to hug me. "I am so thrilled to see you, Nora.

Lana said she would make you a hat if you still want one. Do you?"

Link was scowling. He looked at me, shaking his head. I leaned over to hug him. I whispered, "I will always love you more." He smiled then and returned my hug. Link returned his focus to Dane.

Link went to stand toe to toe with Dane. "Don't let my Nora get hurt again. It is my job to protect her! Do we understand each other?"

Dane looked at Link with a smile on his face and softly chuckled. "You have no worries. Nora is everything to me. She is my world... my universe." He turned to look at me and smiled.

Lana interrupted by saying. "Gentlemen, the Queen is waiting if you are finished playing barbarians. Now play nice, boys." Lana gestured toward the sunflower, where Queen Luna sat upon the throne made up of daisies.

The Queen smiled as we approached the throne. The Queen's dress was illuminated with magic. It gathered on one side of her shoulder, where dozens of flowers cascaded along the length of her body. Tiny lights shimmered as if she had dozens of fireflies. Sparkling twinkles were within the texture of her gown. Every time the Queen moved, or the wind blew the material, the dress glowed in response.

Once everyone assembled under the large canopy, like sunflowers, the Queen greeted us as we walked up.

"I am pleased to know, Princess, that you are his universe. It does my spirit good to know this. Now...who do we have here, Mistress Nora?" Queen Luna asked, as her gaze was squarely on Dane.

I curtsied, "Your Majesty, I want to present Dane Alexander." Taking his hand in mine, "Majesty, Queen Luna."

Dane bowed to the Queen. "It is an Honor to meet you, Your Majesty," he said.

Queen Luna then motioned for Dane and me to be seated. A single rose blossom materialized; one of the petals formed a seat for us to sit upon. The fragrance coming from the flower was delightful.

Queen Luna took a few moments to look at Dane. She sighed, addressing me. "Mistress Nora, this young man is more than just a boyfriend."

Dane looked at me and then nervously back at the Queen. His hand found mine; the magic was still there, still lingering between us.

Queen Luna chuckled. "I do like you, young Dane. Do not worry; to be chosen as a Guardian is a great honor, especially when you were chosen by the Ancients themselves." She stood up and walked towards us.

Dane looked confused. "I'm sorry, but what are the Ancients? And why did they choose me?" he asked.

Queen Luna frowned, then sighed. "The Ancients are from a time before time. They are the final word on everything. Only a few are still with us. Elders are the enforcers of the Ancient's will. We never question the Ancients because they created this world and dimensions we live in." Queen Luna said as she looked closely at Dane. "I am a descendant of an ancient race. A descendant of a powerful Ancient. "

"I am sorry, Your Highness, I should have known," Dane muttered.

"Nonsense, how could you have known? May I?" Her hand tilted Dane's chin up as she analyzed his aura. She was placing her hands on his forehead. "A premium breed you are, Dane. There are not many left in this world like you." She sighed. "I find myself in a very odd position. You see, Ancient magic is potent. This magic must be guarded with equal power. Long ago, the first Queen could balance it with her King. Then, she placed the powers with the sisters, hoping to unite them. When jealousy tore them apart, magic became vulnerable. Evil influenced one of them to curse our people. True love is the only thing that will hold and balance our magic."

Queen Luna stopped for a moment."We do not fully understand our new emotions, and until that is possible, I must protect our magic and our new way of life. I am required to ask your permission, Dane. We will respect your choice, whatever your decision."

"What makes me special? I am just a normal guy?" Dane asked.

"You are a true protector. You will put yourself in harm's way to save another life. Your children will be protectors, and this trait will live on through the generations. When you love, you love with all your heart and soul. Your heart is pure." Queen Luna smiled.

The Queen looked back at Lana, who nodded in response. Her attention settled back on Dane. "If you accept this responsibility, it should not be taken lightly. You will be bound to Mistress Nora for all time. There is no turning back. You can't be separated, and you will share one soul."

The Queen turned, and the wind caught her dress. As green material lifted into the air, dozens of sparkles passed. Queen Luna once again settled onto her throne.

Lana stood up. "Dane, I understand Link's visits stressed you, and we apologize. It was very hard for Link, or any of us, to see Nora so sad. We can't interfere in the human world by our laws, although we may have bent some of the rules." Lana looked guilty.

Dane stood up. "Your Majesty, Lana. I accept the position; I accept being Nora's Guardian. I love her."

Queen Luna smiled. "As you wish."

The Queen looked at me. "Mistress Nora, you have not only broken our curse but have also safe-guarded our magic. I can make no promises outside of my dimension, but I will do everything I can to see that you are well rewarded for your service to us."

Pausing momentarily, "The second part was to allow us to regain the balance of our magic, which required you to allow your heart to be held by another. Mistress Nora, the love in your heart has grown beyond our dreams; we will be forever grateful for that. For the journeys ahead will require an extreme amount of bravery and courage."

"Journey?" I asked. "What kind of journey, You're Majesty?"

Queen Luna smiled."Your heart was closed to the world. No one could get in. Link and Lonnie made a crack to open you up to the beautiful possibilities of your world, friendship, and young love. Therefore, breaking an ancient act of vengeance upon us. This was the first part of your journey."

Lana bowed her head, taking a moment to pause. "Your journey will go beyond time and space. You will defeat the Evil one that is breaking free as we speak. As you broke our curse, you also released the evil that caused it. It is time for you and Dane to return to your world. Be well, Mistress, Nora."

DANE:

After I left Nora's house and walked into my house, the sun was setting. I wanted to stay at JoJo's, but my dad texted me to come home.

He met me at the door with his usual glass of amber liquid in his hand.

"Where have you been? I texted you hours ago." Dad asked.

"Out," I replied. How do you explain that you went to another dimension?

"You look different. Are you on drugs?" Dad asked.

"Really? I wouldn't tell you the truth if I was." I had a big mouth. I hated being here. One more year until I turn eighteen. One more freakin' year, I have to deal with this.

"You are pissing me off, Dane." He stepped before me to ensure I didn't pass him up.

"And I hate being here!" I yelled back.

"What are you going to do? Live with Nora? Yeah, I know exactly who she is. It took some time to figure out who she was. When Grace came here after the party, I knew." Dad set the glass down and folded his arms. "Have you fucked her yet?"

"No! It's none of your damn business. Leave Nora out of it!" I wanted to hit my dad.

Dad smiled. "But you want to. I see the way you look at her."

"Again, none of your damn business, Alcoholic! Go find an AA meeting." I was furious.

"Well, if you do, use protection," Dad said.

"She'll trap you." I turned to walk back out the front door.

"Where are you going?" Dad asked.

"Out and not coming back," I replied.

THE BALANCING ACT

The next couple of days, we were passed in a blur. The weekend arrived for our annual block party, the day when all the neighborhood descended on our cul-de-sac to argue about politics and eat BBQ, hamburgers, hot dogs, and whatever else goes on the pit.

Tables are set out with watermelon snacks and other variety for the kids running around. Mothers are in constant motion. The older members just sit under a large canopy with fans and complain about the heat.

Around the perimeter of all the lawns, mainly Mr. Cranky's lawn, there were big signs indicating not to walk or throw trash on his lawn. To do so would be violating a strict neighborhood code.

Since we didn't have grass, I figured we didn't need to put the signs up. So when I went out this morning with Gigi, Mr. Cranky insisted on knowing where our lawn signs were.

I plastered a smile on my face. I replied, " If we don't have grass to walk on, why must we put the signs up?"

Mr. Cranky set down his watering pot. "When will your mom start growing something besides weeds in her yard?"

I rolled my eyes. "I'm not sure. But I'll ask. I've got to go." As I walked away, he grumbled something under his breath.

I waited until he was gone and returned to sit on the porch. While relaxing, I watched everyone having fun.

Allison showed up with a broad white brimmed hat, oversized sunglasses, and a massive sequin tote bag for 'just in case stuff.'

On the other hand, Jewels wore a black sun hat, glasses, tank top, and shorts. The girls have apologized to Dane since we announced we got back together. He forgave them but warned Allison there would be payback if she used glitter around him.

I glanced over to see Dane talking to Mr. Cranky. This can't be good, I thought.

The thunderous roar of a truck announced Baby Blue Eyes' arrival. Here, he comes carrying an ice cooler and several cases of soda. He caught the eye of all the females out in this insane heat. Bennett wore only cargo pants and a pair of sunglasses. He was shirtless, as usual. I could hear every female's heart beat faster, causing them to swoon.

He walked past Jewels and Allison, who were reclining in chairs, trying to catch some sun. Their mouths fell open. He dropped off the cooler, clapped his hands, and headed straight for Mr. Cranky, standing at the grill. Oh, this is going to be fun.

Bennett offered to 'man' the grill, which sent Mr. Cranky into the stratosphere. Mr. Cranky started waving the spatula in Bennetts's direction. An argument erupted between the two as to who was qualified enough to BBQ.

Bennett just wanted to help Mr. Cranky grill so he could enjoy the party. Dane walked over to settle some of the tension between the two men. It must have worked. Both Bennett and Mr. Cranky had sour looks as they worked together, grilling hamburgers and hot dogs.

After settling the grilling debate, Dane saw me sitting on the porch.

He approached me and asked, "What are you doing here? Hiding?"

"It's been a whirlwind of a summer. I needed a minute to take it all in." I answered wearily, "No, I am not hiding. I'm just watching everyone having fun. Nice work, big guy, for smoothing things at the grill."

"It feels nice to be a superhero," Dane said proudly, standing tall, his hands on his hips, and looking at the sky.

"You're not a superhero. You're a Guardian. Which reminds me, does it still hurt?" I asked as I took his wrist in my hand. I turned it over to see what it looked like. Now, it was very close to a henna shade. Several smaller symbols were woven into a larger one, with a spell written within all the symbols.

"Lana said it would fade soon. I'm not worried about it. Do the girls know about the kiss yet?" Dane asked.

"How long have we known Allison? Of course, they know." I started to blush. "I told Mom, too. She started crying and saying things like her baby was growing up. Then she started talking. It was one of the first times Dad missed." I sighed.

Dane reached for my hand as he sat down next to me. I looked over at Allison and Jewels. "I think Allison needs to find a boyfriend."

As if I was calling her name. Allison turned around in her chair. "Hello, love birds! Come join us ." Waving her arm back and forth to make sure she was seen.

We looked at each other and smiled. Hand in hand, we walked over to the curb to join them.

Allison said, turning towards us. "Hey, guys. Oh, Nor, guess what? I found out some cool information about kissing." She didn't stop long enough for us to answer. "Did you know the brain shuts down because it tries to process so much information simultaneously? It takes in information, like whether the person is chemically compatible. Who knew the biology of kissing was so complicated? "

"I wonder if that lady with the curlers is an alien disguised as a human," Jewels wondered, altogether avoiding the whole subject. "I mean, you never really know who's real anymore. Aliens breeding with humans? She could be an alien in disguise." Pausing to think. "Nor have you seen Finch around?"

Looking around, I answered, "No. I haven't." Turning to Dane, I said, "Have you seen him?"

"Nope, but I'll go look for him." Dane got up and went to look for the young boy.

Jewel's head popped up. "Now that he is gone tell us all the gory details and leave nothing out! All the details! I am dying to know!"

Allison turned to face me. "Spit it out! I want to know everything!"

Turning a bright shade of red. I blurted out, "It was one of the most magical moments of my life." I couldn't keep from smiling.

. Jewels smacked her lips as she applied chapstick to her lips. Dreamily, she said. "I bet he is a great kisser. Too bad he's taken. However, I like dark, mysterious guys that have issues. Makes it interesting. What kind of guy would you like, Al?"

Allison paused for a moment. "He would have to be a Prince Charming, love glitter, and have glittering green eyes."

I wondered if that particular Prince Charming exists. "Anyway, It was so romantic. I melted like goo. He has soft lips." At the mention of his lip, I started turning red again.

Jewels smiled. "Look at Nor; she's grinning like a Cheshire cat."

"Hello? Earth is calling Nora." Allison's sarcastic tone did not escape my notice. Allison clapped her hands together. "So what happened next?"

"Not to change the subject, and I know I'm new here, but...." Jewels lifted her sunglasses while sitting up. "Did anyone notice that weird guy talking to Mrs. Erma, the one with black hair? It looks like a horrible wig."

I glanced over to see the guy. He seemed like he didn't belong. "When did he get here? I don't remember the Clover's moving out," I thought. I got this weird feeling while looking at him.

Allison sighed. "Okay, this is not a conspiracy show. This is real life, not a television or YouTube. Maybe it is a TikTok ploy. Do you see cameras? Maybe he is house-sitting. Why don't you ask Mr. Cranky, he knows everything."

I started getting chills even though it was boiling outside. I decided not to let it bother me, but it still nagged at a part of my brain.

"Jewels!" Finch ran towards his sister. Nora has a dog. She is lovely, but she tries to eat Spock. I told Gigi she was a bad dog."

Dane sat down next to me. "You look tense. What is up?" He took my hand and turned my palm up. He started drawing little circles in the middle of my palm. The tingles it left in my hand made me feel so much better. "There, that should help."

I whispered. "You are my superhero." I leaned over to hug him.

"Excuse us," Allison complained. "Save that stuff when we are not here. Eww." Allison dug in her sequined bag.

"It's cute," Jewels commented, smiling. She glanced over at the strange guy pretending to talk to Mrs. Erma. He was caught looking towards the girls and quickly looked away. "That man is bad news no matter what you say," Jewels muttered.

Finch started to whine. "I'm hungry, Jewels."

Jewels rolled her eyes. "Then go get something to eat, squirt."

Dane got up once more. "Come on, man. Let's go get a hot dog." Dane took Finch's hand to walk him over to the table.

Jewels turned to Nora. "If you want to get rid of Dane, let me know. I will take him in a heartbeat," Smiling Jewels added. "I'm only kidding," she said as she saw the look on my face.

For the first year since we moved here, I had a lot of fun at the neighborhood party and thought of all the fun stuff we did today. We threw watermelon slices at each other. Jewels took out the hose when we got bored with the watermelon fight. We played in the water.

We ended up accidentally spraying Mr. Cranky while we were playing around. He wasn't happy. It's nice having good friends.

***

The strange man gave up trying to blend in. He retreated into the house. He would have to do this the hard way.

He removed his wig, threw it on the table, and settled into the recliner chair. Being in this circus of a neighborhood was coming to an end.

He wouldn't be here if he weren't getting paid so much.

ACT II

It was one of those mornings when I didn't feel like getting out of bed. Yesterday, I ran into Dane's mom at the mall, and all those feelings returned. I burrowed deeper into my comforter.

"Nora Rose, you up yet? It's almost noon!" Mom said, knocking on my door at the same time. "Nora?"

I responded. "I need a mental health day. Not getting out of bed." FYI, it's not a good thing to say to a mother.

My mom sat on my bed. "I'm not going away. Talk to me." She pulled my comforter down.

I tried pulling it back, but she wouldn't allow it. Instead, I put my head on her lap, closing my eyes. Mom started gently playing with my hair.

"What is it, Nora?" Mom asked softly.

"I strongly dislike Dane's mom. We saw her at the mall yesterday." I was quiet for a minute. "I miss Dad, Mom."

Taking a deep breath, Mom replied. "So do I. How can I make it better, Nora?" I hugged her tighter.

"Wait a minute. Nora let me up for a minute. I will be right back." Mom walked out of my room and down the steps.

A few minutes later, she was back in the room. "Sit up." I did what she asked.

Mom held out a man's school ring and a picture of my dad. "It was Scott's...your dad's college ring. I want you to have it. Put the ring somewhere safe. I want you to have them so when you miss him, you'll have a keepsake," She paused for a while. "You look so much like your dad. I'm sorry for keeping this from you for so long. I guess I wasn't ready to face losing him. I feel so responsible for his…'

I hugged Mom. "You know it's not your fault."

"I sent him for ice cream." A tear fell from the corner of her eyes. We were watching a movie, and I craved ice cream. You had started kicking me. Your dad insisted on playing with you. Every time you kicked, he would try to touch your feet and make you kick me harder. He would never leave for work until he kissed you and me goodbye."

Her smile faded away. "That night," she paused, "Before he left, he gave you a kiss on my stomach and said, 'I will always love you, Nora Rose.' Then he kissed me goodbye and said he would be right back with my ice cream and that he loved me, and he left. I should have gotten some at the grocery the day before, but I forgot. If I had only remembered the damn ice cream!"

Wiping the tears from my eyes, "Dad told me it was his time. To give yourself a break, it wasn't your fault. He is always close by."

There were several minutes of silence between us. Looking down at Dad's picture, knowing he was alive was weird. When I see him now, I know he isn't.

Looking at my mom, holding both the ring and picture, I said, "Thank you so much for this. You have no idea what this means to me." I gave Mom a big hug.

"Your mental health day has officially ended. Let's get the day started." Mom said, wiping her tears away. "How about a girl's day?"

"That sounds good to me," I said, going to bed and jumping out of the ring and picture on my dresser. I can't wait to get started on having a great day with Mom.

As Mom left my room, I looked at his photo and thought how lucky I was to meet him, even briefly.

My phone buzzed with a text:

Dane: What r you up to today?

Me: girl's day

Dane: We need to talk.

DANE:

Scott looked at the young man sitting on the edge of the tub. He was torn between being an Elder and a father, and like any father, this was a very uncomfortable situation. "Dane…your Dad needs you. Things will get worse before they get better," the elder said.

"No disrespect, but how do you know my dad? What do I call you? How can I see you?" Dane asked.

Scott smiled. "Queen Luna has given you magic so that you can see me now. You can call me Scott. That is my human name. I know Roger very well; we were lifetime friends. He will need you. Your job as a Guardian will not be easy. You will know things you must keep from Nora for her protection and hear things you don't want to hear. You will have to endure the rituals of spells into your body to keep my daughter safe. Don't confuse magic with lust. It needs to be her decision on how far things go between the two of you."

I hoped I wasn't blushing. This is her Dad, and he knew.

Scott continued, "This is a lifetime commitment. You are Nora Rose's protector. She has made mighty enemies emerge from its prison. Luna neglected to tell you this when you agreed. Nora's magic is getting stronger. This is not a video game to be played. The more powerful she gets, the stronger you need to be, and you can't falter. Do you understand? You can not fail her in any way."

I felt a surge of responsibility to protect Nora. I knew that she was mine, and I had to defend her. "I won't fail her…ever."

Scott chuckled. "So you say. Being a Guardian is not easy. It is the hardest thing you will ever have to do. Nora Rose's life always comes before yours. Your children will face the same things you will. Cherish this time you have together, free of magic, for once the stars meet, a huge burden will be bestowed upon you." And he was gone.

***

I climbed onto Nora's roof and tapped on her window. I smiled when she jumped and looked at me as if I lost my mind.

"What are you doing? Did you climb up here?" She asked as she opened her window. I was pretty pleased with myself.

"Yes," as I crawled inside her room. Taking her into my arms, I kissed her.

She pushed back. "Dane?"

"What?" I continued to kiss her neck. I loved that she went to mush when I did that. I could feel her giving in as I approached the sensitive spot behind her ear.

"Dane….I… thought you needed to talk." Nora tried hard to be unaffected. I sighed as I gently bit her earlobe.

I whispered, "Yes, in a bit." Muttering before claiming her lips. My hand slipped under her shirt. Shit, she had a sports bra on. But I still felt her body's response to me. Her nipples were hard, and all I wanted to do was to wrap my lips around them.

"Dane, we can't," I barely heard her say. I inhaled and reigned myself in, but my body protested loudly.

Looking into her eyes, I knew it was hard for her, too. "You are so irresistibly beautiful." Her mouth formed a smile.

"What did you have to talk to me about? How did you get up here?" She asked.

"I climbed the lattice on the side of the house. I need to know how you feel about... us," I asked, nervous about her response.

My cell phone buzzed with a text. "*Get home now! From my dad*".

When I looked up, Nora had unshed tears. My heart fell.

A tear ran down, and I caught it with my finger as it fell.

When she finally spoke, my phone buzzed again. I ignored it. "I don't know what I feel, I know... I want you desperately, but I can't handle your mother. She hurt me too much, Dane."

That statement hurt my heart. "What if she wasn't in the picture? I love you, Nora. Luna requires me to do guardian lessons; I want to do this for you. I am volunteering at the fire station as soon as it gets approved."

"Since when?" Nora asked.

"I have been staying with JoJo since I started. He has a friend who is a volunteer firefighter. He introduced me to the guys. I needed you to know. I love you, Nora."

I could see her hesitation and worry; no, I felt it.

She smiled. "I will support you."

ROAD TRIP

Dane spent all his free time with Queen Luna. I, however, spent that time pouting. I could have hung out with Jewels or Allison, but they were busy doing something else. So, I am in my room, lying across my bed, holding my teddy bear, sulking.

"Why are you sulking? That is not like you, Mistress Nora." Startled, I looked over to see Lana standing next to my soda.

"Don't you have Guardian lessons?" That wasn't very nice. "I'm sorry, Lana." Turning my head to look at my bed to face Lana while still looking at her, I shifted.

"Mistress Nora, I know this has been hard for you. The path you have taken is not an easy one."

Lana came closer to sit on a book I had been reading earlier. "How can I help?"

"I don't know. As for a path, I don't have one." I said, becoming more prickly.

"Mistress Nora, I realize you are upset. You are to embark on travels that will be one of the most distressing for you, but just for a time. Dane, Allison, and Jewels will be alongside you to help you find the things you need to know."

Lana put both her hands on my hand. "I do not know what you must learn, but it is essential. It was requested that I speak to you right away. I have a feeling that there will be a time element to it. Oh, Is that Scott in the human form?" Lana said as she looked at the picture I had on my dresser.

"Mom gave me the picture and my dad's college ring the other day," I answered.

"I must hurry, Mistress Nora. Remember these words. Tears of old never lie, so don't pass her by. It's been so long since this long-lost Love sang her song. Forgive. Forgive, because she doesn't have too long." Lana faded away.

I was so confused.

Just then, my cell phone started ringing. The caller ID said it was Allison.

"Hello," I answered in a toneless voice.

"I AM Freaking out, Nora! Guess What!" squealing Allison."I'm so excited, Jewels, Let's tell her together!" Together, they squealed, "ROAD TRIP!"

ALL ABOUT THE BOUGIE

Conversation amongst the friends had ceased several hours ago once the excitement wore off. Allison was playing a game on her phone on my opposite side, slightly humming a song. Jewels sat in the very backseat, sleeping. I was leaning against the window, watching the trees go by in an endless blur, thinking about the last couple of days.

Allison's dad won a competition at his job. The prize was three days, four nights, in an all-inclusive five-star wilderness lodge resort. There were no strings attached. Invite all your friends; lucky for us, Allison's parents don't have friends. The Spencers keep to themselves for the most part.

Mrs. Spencer and Mom are complete opposites, but they get along well. Mom even painted a very neutral painting to bridge the gap between their personalities. The gift worked. The two moms started having coffee every other morning. I'm glad Mom has a female friend to talk to; I can be a handful. I'm assuming Mrs. Spencer vents about her handful, too.

The Spencers are excessively conservative, so they met with Jewels' Dad and my Mom to ensure all the parents were on board. Mom, Jewels' Dad, and Finch were invited because they could ask as many people as they wanted.

The entire trip was completely paid for. Jewels' Dad had another business trip planned so that he couldn't go; he hired a nanny to watch Finch during the day while Jewels was gone. Mom was thankful for the invitation, but she made some excuse of having a commission painting to finish for a client and offered to help babysit Finch at night.

"Here we are, guys!" Jack Spencer announced. "Wow! Look at that!" As we rounded a corner, a beautiful lake came into view. "Wow, look at that lake! Good fishing girls!"People were standing on the pier fishing on the lake.

"I don't fish, Mr. Spencer."Jewels said."Besides, I refuse to touch a worm."

"Jewels?" Allison asked. "It's how they did it in old times. Don't listen to her Dad. Oh Wow! How awesome is that view of the lodge?"

The lodge sat on top of a hill in a rustic, elegant style. The bottom floor had large windows and glass doors. White ducks waddled down the hill towards the lake. Trees dot the landscape. We're all craning our necks, looking at everything, taking in the lodge's views.

"Where is the pool? The brochure specifically said there is a pool here." Allison whined.

"I'm sure it is on the side we can't see yet, Al," I said.

Flowers lined the driveway as we drove and stopped at the front entrance. Valets dressed in a full tux with a top hat and white gloves walked up as we pulled under the awning. The valet opened the car door for us and welcomed us to the lodge. We piled out of the car, stretching our legs from the long ride.   Mr. Spencer went around to the trunk to take the luggage out. The valet put his hand out and told Mr. Spencer that a luggage carrier was coming.

I tried to grab my bag, but the valet stopped me."I got that, Miss." He turned his attention to the parents,

"Your luggage will be brought to your rooms, Sir. The check-in desk is through the doors." The valet informed us. Mrs. Spencer thanked the young man and ushered us into the lobby.

The lodge's exterior may have looked wealthy. Massive chandeliers hung in the lobby, and the carpet was burgundy. The check-in desk was dark wood, and everything had gold accents. There was not a speck of dust anywhere rustic, but its interior screamed.

The clerks behind the desk wore black skirt suits with pearl necklaces. Their hair was perfect, and their makeup was flawless.

We were given two separate suites that were connected. Computer-chipped bracelets that were given to all of us, which room keys we had to wear at all times while we were at the lodge.

Even the elevator reeked of money. It had a burgundy carpet with a gold h in the center of the elevator. Even the elevator doors were brass.

As they opened onto our floor, a sitting area with a couch, two tall lamps on either side, chairs, and a table welcomed us. The hallway was lined with beige wallpaper to compliment the same burgundy carpet with fleur-de-lis going down the middle.

To say our room was upscale would have been an understatement. We saw a sofa, a glass table with different little figures, and two armchairs when we first entered. On the other side, a desk sat, with a leather chair tucked neatly into its place.

Allison was already looking for a plug for her phone.

***

The bedroom was massive. A mammoth king-size bed dominated the room, with two side tables topped with marble and dark wood underneath. Crystal lamps stood like silent sentinels on either side of the bed. The comforter looked soft, and the sheets were cream satin.

The first thing Allison did after plugging in her phone was belly-flop on the bed. "I call this side!" she shelled around on her back. Oh, it's so comfortable!"

Jewels and I looked at her as she sat up; she had her place up. "A room could go for about two thousand a night. I feel sorry for the person who has to pay this bill." she continued, "You know I looked it up," Allison said as she fell back on the feather pillows.

Jewels walked into the bathroom and ran her fingers along the marble vanity. "I wouldn't doubt it. I can't wait to see what is served for dinner."

I opened the window curtains. "Come see this view." It was stunning. I opened the balcony doors and walked out to see the view. You could see a waterfall in the distance if you stood just right. Both girls exited the balcony and gasped at the beautiful view before them.

A knock on the door brought us back to reality. Allison piped up, "I got it. It's probably our luggage, and I desperately need to unpack." She took several steps, turned back to us, and said. "You know I read this place is haunted too. Isn't that cool?" Allison opened the door.

The porter quietly rolled the luggage into the room. "Where would you like the luggage, Miss?" he asked Allison, waiting for her answer.

Allison answered. "Please put it in the bedroom. Thank you."

The porter nodded in response. Allison dug into her purse to tip the man when everything was unloaded.

He shook his head no. "It has already been taken care of. Thank you."

The porter looked at me, and his mouth fell open but quickly closed. He nervously nodded and hurried out of the room.

Allison asked, "What was that all about?" Opening her suitcase, she thought, "What are you wearing for dinner, Jewels?"

Jewels walked back into the room. "This is what I am wearing to dinner."

"Travel clothes? Didn't you bring a dress for dinner?" Allison asked. "Nor what are you wearing to dinner?"

"Is that why you have three suitcases?" I asked, looking over at the pink fuzzy luggage with a big silver sequin "A" on each piece, plus a large makeup bag.

"There are only two suitcases for clothes. You know I have to have matching shoes for each outfit, and this is my makeup luggage." Allison put her hands on her hips.

Jewels rolled her eyes. "Really?" She walked out of the room, shaking her head in disbelief, and went to sit on the sofa in the adjoining room.

Allison is the most organized person I know. She had a full schedule of everything, including times for dinner on her phone. It took Allison almost an hour to shower, get dressed, put make-up on, and brush her hair approximately forty times on each side. As soon as her lip gloss was applied, her phone beeped to announce it was time to go down to dinner. A minute or two later, her parents knocked on our adjoining door, saying, "Let's go to dinner."

The hostess asked us to wait momentarily at our table as we arrived downstairs. Jewels walked over to the wall where a large ornate oil painting of a couple hung on the wall.

"Hey Nora, come see." I walked over to where Jewels was. "Look at the plaque under the picture. It says, 'Abner and Rose Beckett.' Are they related to you? Rose sort of looks like you. She has your eyes, and oh, look at her mouth." She pointed.

I looked up at the photo. "I was named after my grandmother Rose. But there is no way this is her." The queasy feeling started in the pit of my stomach, asking what if?

Dinner was beyond delicious. I barely had room for dessert. This time, the four sets of forks didn't intimidate me. I even helped Jewels figure the forks out. We all talked and laughed at Allison's dad's jokes during dinner. Mrs. Spencer rolled her eyes a lot. I like Allison's family; it makes me feel normal. Looking around the large, elegant dining room, I thought I had caught a glance at the weird guy from the neighborhood. I was just seeing things, maybe.

Allison announced plans, which jarred me out of my thoughts. "I made nine reservations for massages for the girls tomorrow. Spa day, girls! Dad, you can do whatever you want; what about golf? Or fishing?" Allison announced to the table as she was keying something in her phone.

"I'm trying to schedule a ride to the waterfall or the zip line for the day after tomorrow. For some strange reason, I can't change the reservation for dinner. I spoke to the concierge, but she wouldn't budge."

I whispered to Allison, "I'm going to the pier to call Dane." I stood up and thanked Mr. and Mrs. Spencer. I made an excuse about going to the powder room. Putting my napkin on the table, I got up, walked out into the hall, and went through the glass doors onto the pier facing the lake.

Walking down to the pier, I'm captivated by the sun's setting; it's so beautiful here, peaceful, breathing in the fresh air. Making my way down to the pier, the water was calm like glass. I closed my eyes, taking in the peaceful scene.

My bracelet started to tingle again. I looked around; there was nothing that looked out of place. The only other people were an older couple walking hand in hand towards the pier.

The bracelet again started to tingle. It usually indicates magic was close by, but there is none here. It began to get me a bit nervous. The older couple were about to pass me up and were about 10 feet away looking at the lake. The lady, however, kept glancing at me more often than I was comfortable with.

"Are you Enjoying yourself?" Dad said, appearing next to me and scaring me half to death. I jumped and was about to speak when he motioned for me to keep quiet and to walk over to a set of chairs a few feet away.

I followed him, and once we were far enough from the older couple, I took out my cell phone to pretend I was talking on the phone.

"I will get you a bell to wear around your neck! And to answer your question, no. I miss Mom and Dane. Why is my bracelet tingling? There is no magic here."

"Nora Rose, you need to know something important." Dad sat in the opposite chair quietly, my hand.

It was the older couple walking from the pier. They were standing a short distance before me, just looking at me. I looked over to my Dad and back to them. They looked old enough to be grandparents while still looking incredibly young.

The lady wore a coral shirt with white shorts and a wide-brimmed hat that matched her outfit, as she had just walked off a cruise ship. The man wore a blue golf shirt, pants, and sunglasses.

The lady came over to me and spoke first. "I'm sorry. I thought I left my cell phone by your chair." Her voice was very shaky. She stood there just staring at me.

The man spoke next, "Come on, Abigail." He touched the lady's shoulders and gave her a slight tug. "Let the young lady finish her phone call." He gave her another tug.

I could tell she wasn't telling the truth, but I was confused. "Sorry to bother you, Miss."

They walked away in the direction of the lodge. I gave them a half-hearted smile.

I turned to Dad. "I think they sat by us at dinner. What did you want to say?" He didn't move. He was looking in the direction that the couple took.

Dad hesitated for a minute. "I..." He looked around nervously.

"Nor where are you?" Allison called out.

I stood up. "Hurry, tell me." I looked at Dad, pleading with him to answer. Still, he didn't.

Dad disappeared as Allison approached me ."What are you doing out here? It's getting dark. Besides, Mom wants us to stay in the lodge; you know how weird she is. We have an early breakfast." She stood there waiting for me to do something.

"Are you okay? I told Jewels she had to sleep in the middle since she was the skinniest." I barely registered what Allison was talking about.

I couldn't speak. I didn't know what to think. Whatever had just happened was downright weird.

"Yeah, I'm okay." I tried to shake the bizarre scene off.

Allison glanced at me sideways and shrugged as we walked together to the lodge. We returned to our room, where Jewels were waiting for us.

"It's about time you showed up. What were you up to?" Jewels looked at me like she could see straight through me. You look like you just saw a ghost."

Wow, what a choice of words, I thought.

SECRETS AND SHOPPING

As promised, the spa day was incredible. We had an hour before dinner. Jewels said we needed to check out the shops downstairs before dinner. Allison's mom was napping, so we left her a note. We headed downstairs to the gift shop.

We stepped off the elevator on the main floor. The hallway was busy with people coming down for dinner and going back and forth with shopping in various shops.

There were coffee shops, bagels, or whatever snack you may want, and this gift shop was enclosed by glass. Three tables of shirts with logos sat at the entrance, and on either side of the entrance, tables of different types of coffee cups were lined up.

Jewels and Allison hurried into the gift shop. I slowly walked to look at the shirts. I wondered what I should get as a souvenir for Mom and Dane.

I was lost in thought when I glanced up to see the older couple from yesterday. They were sitting at a table drinking coffee. The older woman looked at me and smiled again. I smiled, not knowing what else to do.

My bracelet started tingling. I rubbed my wrist to ease the prickly feeling. I saw Allison going straight to the jewelry section. I decided against the shirts outside the shopping. I stepped in. I wandered around, hoping something would jump at me to bring home. I stopped to look at the key rings.

"Excuse me, I wanted to apologize for bothering you yesterday." It was that lady again. Send to me in greeting. "My name is Abigail. You can call me Abby, and this is my husband, Jasper."

It still bothered me that I knew them from somewhere. Jasper kind of extended her and looked like my dad...odd.

"I'm Nora ." I held out my hand to return the greeting.

She looked at my hand for a moment, hesitating to touch it. Then, gently cupping my hands in between hers, she touched my hand. My bracelet warmed around my wrist when she felt it. A tear fell from her eye.

"Oh, my, I am so sorry. I don't know what has come over me." She looked at me again nervously. "You are such a pretty young lady. Jasper, isn't she beautiful?"

More tears started to fall. Now I'm getting nervous. What is up with this woman? Why is she acting like this? Am I on some sort of hidden camera show?

"Nor where are you?" Jewels called out.

The woman snatched her hand away from mine. I almost fell forward.

"I'm coming, Jewels," I called out, looking back at the older couple. Feeling awkward, I started to leave, but turning around, I began to tell them bye, but Jasper spoke instead.

"Nice to meet you. We don't mean you any harm, my wife..." He grasped his wife's hands. "We lost a grandchild long ago, and you look very much like her. I apologize if we scared you." Jasper said diplomatically. "Abby, it's time to go."

Abigail looked up at Jasper and smiled. Another tear escaped the corner of her eye, and she smiled.

"It's so nice to have met you, Nora Rose." She glanced at me once more. Turning away, they walked arm in arm toward the elevators. As they waited, Abby rested her head on Jasper's shoulder.

I stood there stunned. My bracelet continued to tingle. I felt I should know them, even though I knew I didn't. Did I tell her my middle name? That was so eerie.

Jewels and Allison came with baskets full of things to bring home."You haven't started yet?"   Allison asked. "Wait here while I get you a basket." Jewels lifted my arm as she walked off, which I wore on my bracelet.

Looking into my eyes, I said, "The bracelet is trying to tell you something." I tried to pretend I didn't know what she was talking about, but her intense stare dared me not to argue.

Jewels stayed close as I walked through the shop, looking at different things on each counter. I picked up a super cute purse shaped like an ice cream cone. The bottom "cone" part was gold holographic, and the ice cream part was white glitter with a red holographic cherry on top.

I smiled at Jewel's. "It reminds me of Dane."

"Well, get it." Jewels said.

I flipped the purse over and looked at the price tag; it said a hundred and fifty dollars. My mouth fell open, and I put it back.

Jewels pouted. "Why aren't you getting the purse? It's all paid for."

Allison came up to see what we were looking at. She was sipping on a straw. "Oh, that is pretty. Get it, Nora. Sorry, I got sidetracked," Allison advised as she sipped her frozen coffee. "Mom never lets me have these. She says it makes me too hyper."

Hyper, I thought. I could already see her mind bouncing. "The purse is too much. I'm just going to bring Mom and Dane something small." I put it back on its hook, as I said. "I don't need it."

"So, Nor, who were those people you talked to earlier?" Allison took another sip of her drink.

I shrugged my shoulders."I don't know." I didn't, so it was not exactly a lie. We checked out and headed back to our room.

After another delicious dinner, Jewels, Allison, and I wandered around the lodge. True to Allison's word, she was extremely hyper and talked nonstop, more than usual.

When we got back to our room, a box with my name on it was at our door around nine o'clock. It was wrapped in cream wrapping paper with a white ribbon.

"Don't touch it! It could be a trap." Allison exclaimed as she observed the package. "Is it from Dane?" Jumping up and down, clapping her hands.

Jewels grabbed Allison by the shoulders and pinned her to the wall. "Al, you are not allowed EVER to drink coffee again! Do you understand?"

Jewels tried to be patient with Allison all night, but this was the last straw. She bent down, picked up the present, and handed it to me. She turned around and opened the door. After we walked in, I set the present on the bed.

"Aren't you going to open it?" Allison asked. "Are you? Are you?"

"Be Quiet! You are the one who said it was a trap." Jewels stated as she picked up her pajamas.

I looked at the present, untying the bow carefully. "Okay, so far, so good," I thought. Ripping through the paper, I opened the box, and my heart stopped momentarily. It was the ice cream purse I had been looking at in the gift shop.

"Well, who is it from, Nor?" Allison and Jewels asked.

"I don't know. Let me open the card." I said.

The card simply read: From Abby and Jasper.

I replaced the top of the box and put the package on the side of my luggage. I was throwing the wrapping paper in the garbage, so I changed into my pajamas.

Allison and Jewels finally went to sleep after a long conversation explaining who Abby and Jaspermet were and how I was. I was still wide awake. I ensured Allison and Jewels were sleeping before I quietly got out of bed, tip-toed to the balcony door, opened the glass door, walked out, and closed the door behind me. I leaned against the balcony.

"I want to apologize," Dad said as he appeared beside me.

I jumped. "I'm not talking to you. Go away!" I hissed as I continued to look at the lake. "And wear a bell while you're at it."

"Whether you do or not, you still need to hear what I say. Remember when I said that Cordelia spread rumors about your mother?" He waited. "Look at me, Nora Rose."

I turned to face him. "You left. You left me! Who are those people? What if they hurt me? You left!" I was hurt and close to tears.

"They are my parents...you're grandparents." His words echoed in my brain.

I could barely breathe for a moment, and my heart stopped.

"How...is that possible? They disowned us?" Time seemed to stop. "I don't understand. You're lying!" I didn't want to believe him.

"I never got along with my parents, even when I was little. They tried to force me to be something I wasn't; that is why I spent so much of my time at Grandma Rose's. I left that life behind because I loved your mother. I hoped to mend fences with them when your mom became pregnant with you. They didn't budge...and then it was too late. It was easy for them to blame your mom when I passed away. Your mom had so much to deal with: a new baby, grief, plus everything else...too much."

I sat down on the chair as he sat beside me. He took my hand in his. "It has been so long since I've seen them. I remember how much I love my parents."

"What do they want? They have been following me around. It's creepy. They sent me a purse," I said, pointing to the room. Jasper said they lost their grandchild. Why now? Are they trying to buy my love?"

"I can't answer any of those questions for them. I am asking you to forgive them, please." Dad's voice was low and sincere.

"Don't do that again," I said, my irritation slightly subsiding.

"I can't promise that. There are lessons you will need to learn; it is part of your journey that you must take." Dad took my hand. "I hope you understand. Things will get harder before they get better, but I will be by your side to guide you."

"You have to promise never to leave me like that again. I forgive you for now." I muttered. We both stood up, and he gave me a big hug.

"I love you," Dad said near my ear.

"I love you too. I'll forgive you for now." I muttered. We both stood up, and he gave Give me a big hug.

We spent a full day at the waterfalls the next day and went zip-lining over them. We had a lot of fun and topped it off with another delicious dinner. However, there was no sign of my Grandparents during dinner.

My friends and I walked up to our room; we were exhausted. Another gift wrapped the same way was waiting by our door. I picked the package up and carried it into our room.

Allison and Jewels gathered. I opened it right away. It was a key ring that matched the ice cream purse. Abby and Jasper also gave it to me.

On our last day, Allison's Dad was checking out. The desk clerk handed him a card envelope with instructions to hold on to it until Jewels and Allison fell asleep. Jewels slept on the furry pillow she got from the gift shop, and Allison slept on her unicorn.

I quietly opened the envelope. Allison's dad looked at me through the rearview mirror. I guess he was curious; Dad looked at me, too.

The cover said, '*To my Granddaughter.*' As I broke open the seal, I pulled out the handwritten note, which read:

Dear Nora Rose,

Please know our intention was never to frighten you. Only to get to know our only grandchild. I could not find the words to tell you in person that we are your Grandparents. I know a few gifts do not make up for the years we missed in your life, but I would like to be a part of your future.

I have terminal cancer and can't bear the thought of never knowing my only beautiful granddaughter. Please call us so Jasper and I can cherish the time I have left with you.
Sincerely,
Abigail and Jasper Beckett

I closed the card and put it back in my bag. Mixed feelings swirled in my head. I closed my eyes and fell asleep. When I woke up, we were back home.

***

Mom was outside waiting for me when we drove up. As I got out of the car, she was there with open arms, waiting to give me a big hug.

"I missed you." Mom said as she squeezed me tight. The dog barked in the window, leaving spit on the glass.

"I missed you too, Mom." My stomach hurt knowing I had met my grandparents, and I couldn't tell Mom. "Is Dane on his way?" I asked.

Mom smiled. "Of course, I texted him when Allison's Dad called. He has a surprise for you."

Allison turned to her Dad. "I want to stay to find out what the surprise is." Her dad looked up as he was getting the suitcases out from the back of the car; he was shaking his head no.

"But... I want to see Dad. Mom?" Allison whined.

"Allison, we are tired from traveling," her mom said. Get back in the car so we can go home."

"But I never get to see Nora's surprises," Allison complained, adding a foot stomp for good measure.

"Allison, please get in the car!" Her mom yelled. I could tell they were exhausted from driving.

Jewels and I hugged Allison goodbye, whispering in her ear that I'd call her to let her know my surprise. I thanked her parents for including us. Allison reluctantly got back in the car. We waved as they drove off.

"Lala! Lala! I missed you!" Finch was running towards his sister with Spock in his hands. Jewels welcomed his hug, dropping her luggage and shopping bags to return his hug.

"Missed you, brat." She said as she hugged him back.

As Allison's parents were turning the corner. A silver SUV turned onto our street. It looked like Dane's Dad's car, and that's when I saw him.

Dane was driving his dad's SUV!

BREAKING BONDS

"When did you get your driver's license?" I asked as I hugged him.

"Yesterday," Dane said, picking me up and spinning me around. "I missed you."

"D!" Finch ran to Dane to give him a high five. "Can we play cars today?"

"No can do, little dude," Dane said. "We'll play later. I see Spock came to meet your sister."

Jewels put her hands on her hip. "Since when have you been playing cars with my brother?"

Mom came to the rescue with an answer. "Your Dad's babysitter's car broke down yesterday, so Dane and I took over." To Finch, she said. "We had fun, right?"

Finch turned and smiled at my Mom and back to Jewels. "I had the most fun playing with D, Jewels. So did Spock."

There was an emotion that crossed Jewels' face that I couldn't quite understand.

"Is everything okay, Jewels?" I asked.

Jewels blinked." Yeah, come on, Finch, let's go home." She hugged me and bent to pick up her suitcase, but Dane offered to carry it to her house.

As all three walked next door, Mom turned to me and said."What's going on?"

"Nothing," I lied. Hoping she wouldn't notice.

"Regarding Dane driving, should we talk about being alone in a car with a boy?" The uncomfortable undertones in her voice made me squirm, like when she wanted to have the 'Your body is changing talk.'

"Mom, eww? You have to bring this up now?" I watched as Dane walked out of Jewels' house.

"Nora," she looked over. "We will talk about this later." Mom walked back into the house.

As Dane was walking towards me. "What was that all about?" His phone started ringing. He looked, then sighed. "It's my Mom."

***

When she was mentioned, I stepped back, and my heart beat faster. I didn't mean to overhear his conversation, but she spoke loudly.

"I need you to pick up my dry cleaning after work. Are you at work?" his mom asked.

"They didn't need me the pool, and Nora just returned from her trip. I wanted to welcome her back." He said as he held my hand. "How did you know where I was anyway?" He was on the verge of yelling.

"Don't question me! Did you tell her yet?" She sounded too pleased with the statement, and my stomach twisted.

His eyes flew to meet mine. "No! Bye!" Dane hung up on her and turned off his ringer.

My heart dropped.

Whatever Dane was about to say, I didn't want to hear it. I pulled my hand from him, starting to back up. I can't handle this. I can't do this now. I thought to myself.

I put my hand up in defense. "Whatever it is, don't say a thing. I can't do this now." My voice was shaky, and my stomach felt hollow.

I backed up to the porch steps, but my legs couldn't hold me. I sat on the bottom step and put my head down, starting to cry.

"Go away, Dane. I...I can't take any more." I said between sobs. I put my hands over my head as if I could keep anything else from hitting me.

Dane squatted in front of me, feeling helpless."You promised to trust me through anything." He kneeled to my eye level. "Mom has transferred me to a new school, Nora; you know I had nothing to do with it. Look at me, please."

He lifted my hands off my head. I gently lifted my head so I could look him in the eye.

Darn, those hazel eyes.

A stray tear fell from my eye; he caught it with his finger. "I can't do this anymore. I don't want to break up with you, but we can't be together anymore."

"No!" Dane grunted in pain. He fell back on the sidewalk, holding his stomach.

"What's wrong?" I jumped up to help him up. "Are you okay?"

Dane winced and curled up on his side. "I'm fine." He said between gritting his teeth, cringing in pain. As the pain settled, he looked up at me. The agony on his face caused me to forget all the negativity between us.

I knelt beside him. "Dane, talk to me...please."

It took Dane a few minutes to answer. "Magic" was all he could say, and he closed his eyes again.

I helped Dane to sit up. "I'm not breaking up with you; we'll talk. I can't fight your mom right now. She will tear us to pieces; she already is. What is wrong with magic?"

A foreign voice came out of Dane's mouth. "Your distrust allowed evil to break free. Magic is vulnerable; therefore, you are too."

"Who are you?" I asked.

Dane replied. "An Elder"

SEWING LESSONS

Dane's knock on the door usually sent me running for the window ledge to hide. Instead, I leaned my head against the door.

"Nora, if you don't want me to come by anymore, I won't return, but please open the door."

I opened the door. When I looked at his hazel eyes. I started to close the door again. Dane held his hand out to stop the door from closing.

"Don't shut the door." It hurt to look at him. "Don't lock me out again. Trust me. Please."

Everyone is telling me to trust him. What does everyone know that I don't?

"You don't understand what it feels like to be told you aren't 'good enough'! Now I know why my grandparents want no part of me. It hurts Dane!" I threw my hands up in defeat and returned to my room.

I bent down to pick up a pink teddy bear, which Dane had given me as a gift. I smiled as I hugged the bear close to me. I sat down on my bean bag. I decided that I would trust him, for now, to hear what he had to say; I owed him that much.

Dane paced back and forth for a little while. I watched in silence as he tried to get his thoughts together.

"Jewels is… is…freaking making voodoo dolls of me by the truckloads. She keeps giving me the evil eye and muttering under her breath whenever she goes to the pool with her brother. I'm scared that I will start losing teeth or hair or something! Allison! Allison! There is a pound of glitter in all of my swim stuff. You can't get that stuff off!"

I had to admit Allison is ruthless with glitter. I tried hard not to laugh, putting the teddy bear in front of my face.

Dane taking a deep breath to calm down. "I'm so mad at my mom that I am crashing at JoJo's while his folks are on vacation. Nora, you must understand this is our Mom's fight, not ours. Dad said it's a good idea to stay away from mom for a little bit."

"I have no idea what you are talking about," I replied

"Your mom didn't tell you?" I shook my head, no, so Dane continued. "Something about an old threat and your dad thinking my mom was trashy. Your mom almost took my Mom's head off the night at the party."

I could tell he was trying to gather more details. "I can't remember all of it; something happened long ago." Dane rubbed the back of his head with his hand and grimaced. I sure don't want your mom mad at me. She has sharper fangs than a lioness."

Bits of Dad's words echoed in my ear. He tried to warn me. *Trust Dane.* Tears collected in my eyes. I didn't listen to my dad; he only wanted to help me.

"Allison, really put glitter in your stuff?" I said so I wouldn't entirely fall to pieces.

Dane bent down and took off both of his tennis shoes. True to his word, the soles of his boots were very sparkly. Yikes!

Dane sat down next to me. "I would never hurt you or anyone you love, even Link, little annoying green pest," he made a weird face.

"What does Link have to do with this?" I remember Queen Luna telling me about her "informant." Of course, she would send a Link, I thought, rolling my eyes.

"Link would show up in the middle of the night, wake me up! He started talking about stuff that made no sense! He said I must learn to sew, bind, blend, glue something. I know nothing about sewing! It was the middle of the freakin night! I asked him about it, and he always said, talk to you! Every night!" Those hazel eyes were looking at me, almost pleading while trying to catch his breath.

I stopped and rested my head on my teddy bear. The pieces of the puzzle were falling into place. Link for all of his complaining; he always wanted to protect me. I had been so miserable I completely missed the fact that I had people who cared about me.

Link tried to get Dane to help me.

"Link meant sewing lessons. You need sewing lessons." I put my hand on his chest. "To mend a broken heart. He wanted you to fix my broken heart." I said softly.

Dane ran his fingers along my cheekbone. I scooted closer to him. "Nora, please forgive me, please." He said as he leaned closer to me.

At this point, I would forgive him anything. Leaning into his arms, he pulled me close to him. His lips touched mine gently. Electricity crackled between us. Gentleness gave way to a deeper kiss. Pulling my body closer to him until our bodies touched, a flood of warm sensations tingled all over. Dane gently bit my lower lip, opening my mouth to him, and his tongue slipped inside. Oh my god, what do I do now? I shyly responded with mine.

My hands slipped under his shirt, feeling the soft skin along his back. Dane pulled back, ending the kiss. We looked at each other, almost like we were stuck in a trance. His finger outlined my lips as a small smile crossed his beautiful lips.

"So, does that mean I'm forgiven?" Dane smiled as he kissed the spot behind my ear. Shivers raced down straight to all my girl places.

"Yes," I whispered as his mouth glided down my neck. I breathed in as his teeth nipped the hallow of my neck…

"Nora, are you up there?" Mom called from the stairwell. "Yes," I yelled back.

HELLO EVIL

Tossing and turning for several hours, I finally gave up trying to sleep. The day I had been very emotional. I rolled out of bed and slipped on my shoes. I was quietly tiptoeing down the steps and out the back door.

When I touched the sculpture and felt the familiar fall, I knew I must learn how to land. My next thought was, *Why aren't my feet hitting the ground?*

Falling further through the darkness, I landed in a pile of twigs. I looked around and tried to stand up. It was some kind of forest. It was dark; the only light was an eerie glow from the neon branches. Or were they trees? There were neon greens, purples, pinks, blues, and yellows. I took a step into the darkness. The crunch of the twigs below my feet didn't feel right. They felt alive.

"Hello?" I called out.

The sway of the branches was the only answer I received. Another step caused the branches to pull back to either side to form a path straight down. I think this is an eerie version of the Yellow Brick Road.

I took several steps down the path. I heard a rustle of leaves. A glowing yellow bunny hopped close to me. I bent down to pet it. He snarled and hissed, turned red, and ran away.

This is the first time I ever felt afraid. I needed to turn around and get out of here. As I was about to turn, a voice echoed in the darkness.

"There is no way out, sweetheart. Hello, nice to finally meet you." A sultry voice cooed.

"Who are you?" I tried to sound brave, but my voice wavered, and my teeth started chatting.

"I know who you are. You're a thief. You think you're smart by stealing magic from me." The voice sneered. "It will be mine once again, thanks to you. Follow the path so I can take back my magic and rule like I was supposed to from the beginning..." an evil laugh followed. "If you survive..." The words were more of a sinister purr.

"Dad? Dad, where are you?" I called. "Dane? Queen Luna? Lana? Somebody please help me, Please!" I pleaded, turning around and looking for some way to escape this nightmare. This can't possibly be happening.

"I have you, my Princess." another female voice assured.

"Oh, you are not playing fair. Well, come to think of it, my sister did not either. I won't allow Elders of the light in this realm, but I made a small exception for you, sweet child. You see, I need your magic. The Ancients are... well, can we say becoming obsolete? They tried to revitalize themselves by adding a human Elder. What a joke." Her voice was temptingly and seductive.

"Come out where I can see you," I commanded. "Are you afraid of me?"

"Do not antagonize her." the voice whispered.

"What form would you like me to take? Give me some of your magic, and I will take any form you choose." She paused for a moment. "I know; how about the cute young fellow you are so fond of?" She fell into a fit of fiendish giggles.

A branch off to the right cracked and started to move independently. "Oops, too late, they chose for you." She laughed again. "You're just too fun for words. I haven't had this much fun in a long time. Since cursing my sister." More cracks and bending of the branches followed.

"She is angry you broke our curse. I have you. I am Queen Liv, this horrified creature's half-sister." she whispered.

"Did the human Elder not teach you anything about your magic?"

I didn't answer.

"That is such a shame," the voice purred. "Hand your magic to me, and I will let you go. Cross my heart." the evil voice cackled once more.

The branches were shifting and moving closer to me. Instinctively, I started backing up. Branches encircled me; some grabbed my feet and legs, trying to wrap themselves around my ankles.

I kicked and swung at them as they tried to hold my arms. I was trying not to panic as a branch pulled my feet out from underneath me; I fell and hit the ground. The sound of laughter was so loud it drowned out the crackling of the branches as they entwined themselves around my legs.

From somewhere, I heard, *"Trust me."* The words calmed me.

I screamed; the branches now had the lower half of my body, and they were quickly wrapping themselves completely bound around my chest and mouth. Then everything went black. I was standing in nothingness. Wisps of fog are floating past me as if I were standing in the clouds.

The voice was very close to me; I couldn't see anything. "You see, I have been stripped of a name... yours is such a pretty one. How about I take yours?"

Something pointy grazed the back of my neck, sending full chills down my spine. "If you hope to get rescued, you can get that thought out of your little head. No one can rescue you here." Something slithered across my foot. The voice laughed. "Humans. They are so fragile. Don't fear. My pet will not hurt you. Now let's get back to you giving me a name." The silky voice seemed a little further.

"Why did it get taken away?" I asked.

"Did my sister not tell you WHO I am?" The voice sneered.

"I don't know your sister. I don't know you either." I was beginning to get to her.

I wanted to play dumb and throw her off her game. I was playing a game of psychological warfare. But I wasn't very good at it, although Cordelia was helping.

"I would have believed you, but you hold the key to my sister's dimension; not even the Elders have a key." She was so close now I could feel her breath on my neck.

A hand slid down my arm. I had my bracelet on; I tried to pull my arm away, her hand curled around the bracelet, and razor-sharp nails sank into my skin.

Squeezing, my eyes shut against the pain as tears stung in my eyes.

"Don't let her hear you cry. She enjoys the pain. Here he comes." Queen Liv said softly.

I saw pure white; it radiated from a pinpoint and enveloped everything. Embracing the whiteness, my fingers started to tingle. I wasn't sure if it was because of the blood that was pouring out of my wrist, excruciating pain, or it was familiar magic. A pair of hands were reaching out for me, but with my wrist bound, I couldn't move.

I struggled mentally to reach the hands.

"Help me!" I screamed in my mind. I was getting weak. I imagined Dane reaching for me—my protector, my everything.

It gave me a renewed strength to fight more. I gritted my teeth, reached deep down, and with everything, I pulled out every ounce of strength I had to fight back. An explosion of pure white knocked me back as I screamed. Was it someone else screaming? I wasn't sure. I felt the energy explode from me, and then there was nothing.

I felt like I was falling back into space. Someone caught me. I was so weak I couldn't lift my head to find out who it was. I felt safe in his arms, who I don't know.

DANE:

I was in my room, listening to my earbuds and playing a computer game, when I felt the abrupt shift in magic. A sharp pain in my arm got my attention. I looked down to see Link holding his sword and Lonnie frowning.

I took out his earbuds and looked down at the little green man, "Was that necessary, Link?" I asked, rubbing my arm.

Link raised the sword once more."Some Guardian you are! Nora was stolen! She is hurt, and you need to come with us now! She may be dying!"

Crying, Lonnie said, "Dane, she is hurt. Bad. We need you. Please!" Lonnie lifted the end of Dane's T-shirt to blow his nose.

Taking a second to look at the spot, Lonnie blew his nose on.

Jumping off the bed. "Did Lana create a portal for us to get back?"

"Why did the Queen make this moron the Guardian?" Link grumbled to Lonnie. All Lonnie could do was shrug his shoulders.

***

The Royal Guards were on high alert for any evil that may have escaped during my rescue. I lay motionless on the blades of the blue-green grass of Queen Luna's Kingdom.

The villagers came to hold vigil but could not get too close. Queen Luna was trying to tend to my wounds with water from the lake. She then started wrapping them with material the villagers had given from their homes. Lana joined Queen Luna and Lulu as they tried to help me.

"Lana, I'm unsure if I am doing this correctly?" Lulu asked how to care for me…to care for a human.

Lana just nodded. "You are doing fine."

"You're Majesty," Leroy bowed as he approached Queen Luna. "Link and Lonnie have gone for the Guardian. All the Ancient Elders and Nora's Dad are petitioning for entrance to our dimension."

The Queen's head popped up. "All of them? " Her eyes widened. Lulu's head also popped up. She quickly returned her attention to me.

Leroy turned back to the Queen. "Yes, Your Majesty. The portal will close once the Elders are present for their safety and ours. The Guardian is on his way. What shall we do? " Lana asked.

"Please ask the Elders to be patient with us." Queen Luna placed a hand on my forehead. "Nora would never forgive us if we don't bring her Guardian to her." Queen Luna took a deep breath.

It was unheard of to make an Elder wait, much less than all of them.

"Yes, You're Majesty." Leroy bowed and went off to relay the message to the Elders.

"Your Majesty the Guardian is here," Lann said, trying to catch his breath, motioning with his hand "right behind me."

The Queen looked beyond Leroy to see Dane and Link running, with Lonnie trying to keep up.

Dane was running so fast that he almost ran past me. When he saw me, he dropped to his knees. He looked down at me, seeing how pale I was.

"What happened?" he asked, breathing deeply.

The Queen was first to speak. "Guardian, you must not get upset. The Elders are on their way. The younger stole her and attempted to steal her magic. She was badly hurt. You must go with Leroy's family now. Only the Seer and I are allowed to confer with the Elders."

"No! I'm staying! I'm her Guardian!" Dane protested. "I saw her Dad already."

"This has been done by evil, Guardian; I am commanding you to go with Leroy and the boys so the Elders can help her." Queen Luna nodded at Leroy.

Dane hesitated to follow Leroy. Link bowed to the Queen. Lonnie's eyes filled once again with tears as he gently laid his hand on my forehead, and he, too, followed. Lulu curtsied, gently taking Dane's arm as she guided him to follow her family.

Once Queen Luna was alone with me, The Ancient Elders circled my limp body along with the Queen. Queen Luna curtsied as my Dad walked towards her.

"Thank you for allowing us to be here, you're Highness." His eyes are looking at me, resting on the ground. Dad was torn between being an Elder or a loving father. Right now, he had to be an Elder, he decided.

"My deepest gratitude for caring for my child in her time of need. She will be healed soon. Someone stopped the venom from entering her bloodstream, but Nora had lost an extreme amount of blood. She will need to rest; you will continue watching Nora Rose until she is well. I will explain things to her if I have your permission to return."

"Of course, you are welcome. What shall be done about the wounds on her arm? We don't know how to treat her," Queen Luna said.

The Elders responded. "We will tend to her wounds and her injuries. Have Lana consult with the Elders to set up training for Nora Rose. We did not realize how strong her magic had grown until..."

"May I ask what happened?" Queen Luna asked.

The Elders conferred in silence for a moment. "She destroyed the entire dimension of the younger."

Queen Luna's mouth fell open, and her eyes widened in surprise. "It will be done as you ask."

The Queen bowed once more to the Elders as they walked from the circle toward her village.

QUEEN LUNA'S DIMENSION

The Elders had assured the Queen that by the time I was well enough to return to my world, only a few hours would have passed on Earth.

After the Ancient Elders tended to my injuries, the Elders brought me to Leroy and Lulu's home. Dane kept watching me but was told to return once I woke up. He held my good hand as I slept.

Since it was Link and Lonnie's family home, they were a constant presence at my bedside. Villagers dropped off offerings of cakes, bread, and flowers, and the little ones even made crafts for when I woke up. Lonnie was caught once or twice eating some of the cakes.

Lana entered my room."Guardian, I must give her a potion before she wakes; this will not be pleasant for her." Dane stepped out of Lana's way.

"What is that?" Dane asked cautiously.

"An elder requested that I give her this. It is safe; I give you my word." Lana lifted my head to pour the liquid into my mouth.

My hands instinctively went straight to block my mouth; as the potion slid down my throat, my hands fell to my side as I subsided once again into a deep sleep.

It was the first time Dane saw my wrist. The bracelet was gone, and the scars were still visible but healing fast.

"There was severe damage done. She will be good as new soon." Lana smiled. "She will be waking soon. An Elder has requested to speak with her."

Lana sat down next to Dane."Do not worry. Nora's magic is powerful, and they will find a way to defeat those who come between them. I know you are hurt and concerned; have faith, Guardian. I can't give you a key, but I can give you a connection to us. Lana pulled a braided twine bracelet from her pocket.

"Wear it always. We'll communicate this way if there is an emergency in the future." With that, Dane returned to his room.

***

Lana was rubbing oils on my scars, as prescribed by the Elders, when my dad appeared. "How is she, Lana?" He asked.

Lana curtsied."She is doing well."

Scott leaned over me to place his hand on my head. A moment later, I jumped up and gasped. Looking around in a panic, it took me a minute to focus.

"You are safe, Nora Rose." I looked at my dad. I threw my hands around his neck and hugged him. "Thank you for saving me."

"There is much you need to know. I have to get you back to your time." Dad said as I hugged him once more.

Dad and Lana told me what happened and what they witnessed.

In the human world, I was sent back to my room with a stern warning to take it easy.

I closed my eyes once I settled into my room. I was jarred awake by my cell phone ringing. I fumbled to answer the call. I barely got "Hello" out when I heard...

"You didn't call me to tell me the surprise!" Allison pouted. "Well, what was it?"

"Allison?" I asked, still half asleep.

"Who else would it be? Do you have a new best friend I'm unaware of?" Allison waited.

She could hear Nora breathing, so she roared, "Wake up! Why am I always the last one to find things out?"

A WISH GRANTED

Several hours later, I sat at the pool under the awning with Jewels and Allison. Finch was Dane's constant shadow. When the lifeguards rotated, Finch followed along behind Dane.

Jewels lifted her head and tilted her sunglasses down. She was looking at my wrist. "Allison, come here now!"

"Wait, there is a cute guy on the other side of the pool." Allison adjusted her sunglasses to get a better view of him. "When exactly are we going to get into the water?"

"Now Allison! Here!" Jewels insisted. I tried to pull my wrist back, but it was still sore.

"Stop it, that hurts," I whined. I quickly pulled my arm back.

"Nor where is your bracelet? What happened? You haven't talked to your man all afternoon. He has been watching you every chance he gets." Jewels is now highly concerned.

Allison took off her sunglasses and faced Nora. "Spit it out. Do I have to glitter him again? Again, why am I always the last to know?"

"No! It's my fault; I called a break. His mom is monumentally evil. She is tracking him! That is so uncool."

My stomach twisted as I looked at him for the billionth time today. When the lifeguards blew their whistles, the kids had to leave the pool while taking a break.

"Look who is coming to talk to you," Allison said, practically singing it.

"I have eyes, Al," I said, getting nervous.

As Dane walked closer to the girls, he said to Jewels. "You may want to check on Finch; he is getting red."

"Come with me, Allison." Jewels said, dragging Allison away from Dane and me.

Once the coast was clear. Dane put his hand on my bad wrist. "You okay?"

I looked up at him. "They brought you in? Why?"

Dane looked away for a moment and looked back at me. "I'm not supposed to talk to you about it, but Lana knew I would anyway. I don't know if you know the whole story, but you were hurt badly. Link and Lonnie came to get me. I stayed with you... held your hand while you slept. Everyone in the village came out to check on you. I'll give you your break, but I must know you are okay. Can we at least talk?"

"I would like that," I said quietly. Dane picked up my wrist gently and pressed his lips against my wrist.

"You look gorgeous in that swimsuit. It's hard to concentrate," Dane said, looking at me like he wanted to eat me.

"You look sexy too, Mr. Lifeguard," I said.

Later that afternoon, Allison, Jewels, Finch, and I ended up in my room. Finch passed out on one of my bean bags from playing all day. Allison took up her usual spot at the foot of the bed, reading a magazine. Jewels, lying across the bed as I sat at the head of the bed.

"So Nora, what happened between you and Dane? How did you lose your bracelet?" Jewels asked.

"It broke. I told you before we are on a break because of his mom." I said, It was sort of the truth.

"Jewels, you know you have been acting super weird lately. We are all worried," Allison commented.

"I appreciate your concern. This summer has been hard. So many changes have been happening." I tried to explain.

"What changes?" Jewels asked.

"Jewels, why is your dad gone all the time? Isn't he ever home?" Allison asked.

Jewels sat up. "We are not talking about ME. We are talking about Nora right now. Got it?" An intense stare followed the question.

Allison pouted. "Got it. What changes Nor?" Jewels laid back down.

"I met my grandparents—the ones who disowned me. I ran into them at the lodge. The older couple that I was talking to at the gift shop. Mom doesn't know yet. I don't know how to tell her either," I admitted.

"Wow, what are they like?" Allison asked.

"I don't know. It's not like I sat down and had an actual conversation," I tried to explain.

"Well," Jewels started, "When Mom died, Dad checked out. So I take care of Finch...or try to." Jewels glanced over at her young brother sleeping. "I don't like talking about it. So the subject is officially closed."

With that, things seemed to quiet down between us.

***

Later that afternoon, after the girls left, instead of a phone call, the doorbell changed everything.

"Nora Rose, get down here right now!" Mom screamed from the doorway.

I had been enjoying my pity party when Mom screamed my name. That tone of voice sent icy-cold chills down my spine that no teenager wants to hear.

"What happened now?" I thought glumly. I ran down the steps to find Mom holding a box.

"Do you care to explain this?" Mom asked as she held up the box.

I stopped at the last step. "I don't know what it is. I didn't order anything." I said as I looked at the box.

"It's addressed to you from your grandparents. It's from your father's parents, Nora." Mom's tone hadn't softened any. "Explain this!"

My heart dropped to my stomach. "How do they know where I live?" I thought.

"I'm waiting for an explanation." Mom had that stare that could drill holes through a lead.

"The lodge, they uh, ran into me. I didn't know at first, I swear." I stuttered every single word.

"You met them!" A shriek tinged her voice. Mom gets scared when she hits this pitch.

"I...I didn't know who they were, Mom! You have to believe me. I didn't know. Just wait... I have something to show you."

I ran up the steps and grabbed the card from my bag. When I got back down the steps, I handed her the card; as she read the card, her persona softened around the edges.

"Why didn't you tell me?" Mom asked as she handed the card back to me.

"Because I figured you would yell," I said honestly.

She looked at me for a minute as if trying to figure something out in her brain. "What did they say to you? What gifts?"Mom finally asked.

"They didn't say much. The first gift was an ice cream purse and a matching keychain. What's the big deal?"I asked.

Mom walked into the kitchen, set the box on the kitchen island, and continued to the cabinet to grab a wine glass with one hand and a wine bottle with the other. She took what looked like a sip. As she set the glass down, she said, "It is a big deal, Nora."

"I seem to be the only one who doesn't know what is happening," I said. "You never talk to me. How was I supposed to know who they were? Things are happening all around me, and I'm clueless about what they are. It's not fair, and you know it. I'm not a baby anymore."

With another two big sips of wine, Mom looked like she was fighting a major battle in her head. She then looked up at me.

"You win." Another sip of wine and a deep breath.

She took my hand as she began the tale."She hit below the belt when Cordelia realized she could never weasel into your dad's heart. I had to attend my last art class, which I had to model for that night. Cordelia took the opportunity to spike Scott's drink with something at a club. She claimed he assaulted her in the bathroom of the club. No one listened to her because his friends had seen another guy all night, Cordelia dancin', and Roger said he drove Scott back to their apartment shortly after he started passing out. It only served to infuriate her more."

Mom continued."Cordelia's plan B was to go to his parents and tell them Scott got her pregnant in hopes Abigail and Jasper would force Scott to marry her. She knew Scott and his father never got along. They believed her lies, and a major falling out was between father and son. Jasper and Abigail tried to force Scott to marry her. The more your dad denied, the angrier Jasper got. His dad eventually took your dad out of his will, which didn't go well for Cordelia. She admitted she lied, but it was too late. Cordelia is greedy, self-centered, and only thinks of herself and no one else."

After finishing the story, Mom was starting to have a hard time. "The real damage was to Grandma Rose. All this fighting in the family so hurt her. Grandma Rose cut Jasper out of his inheritance. When Scott announced he was still marrying me, his parents thought I was also a gold digger since I didn't come from money."

I could tell this was painful for Mom, but she continued."Grandma Rose adored your dad. She let us marry in her rose garden and left her whole estate to him...us. He didn't need it; by that time, he had a thriving business. She got to hold you once before she passed away. Your dad's death was too much for her fragile heart."

She paused. "When we found out I was pregnant, your dad tried to make amends with his parents. He brought the sonogram pictures to show them, and it broke his heart when they turned their backs on him. He grieved over the loss. It was the only time I saw him cry."

"Can I open the box?" I asked quietly. Mom turned around and retrieved the scissors from the drawer, opened the box, and slid it over for me to open. I peeked inside.

A pink box sat within the cardboard box. I wiggled the pink box out and set it in front of me. A card was taped to it.

It said: Better late than never. Abigail and Jasper B

I handed the card to Mom. I took the lid off of the box and set it aside. I removed the tissue to reveal a fragile porcelain doll resembling me in a green dress.

Another note sat on top of the doll's dress.

"This belonged to your great-great-grandmother. I hope you love her as much as she did."

"She is so beautiful, Mom," I said as I ran my hand over her brittle, delicate dress. A worn brown tag was tied to her arm. "My name is Kat." I read the tag out loud.

Mom closed her eyes. "Kat with a K, I remember, It's Katherine." Mom looked like someone stabbed her in the stomach. She closed her eyes in pain. Tears fell. She was reticent for a few moments until she regained her composure.

Mom and I talked for a while after the box opening. However, much to my extreme discomfort, we had the "driving alone with a boy talk." It was worse than having the "your body is changing talk."

"Mom, I know you're worried; I'm not gonna do anything stupid," I said.

Mom walked over to me and hugged me. "I love you."

"I love you too, Mom," I said as the phone rang.

Mom answered the phone. By the look on her face, she was not happy. "I understand," she replied while looking at me. I don't know, but I'll ask." Mom pushed the mute button on the phone.

"It's Jasper; Abigail has had a relapse. She is at the hospital in town. Do you want to go see her?"

"Is it okay with you?" I asked.

Mom nodded yes.

Unmuting the phone, she said, "We'll be there shortly. What room? Okay." She hung up the phone and sat down next to me. "

Are you feeling okay? You look a little pale." Mom rubbed my forehead to see if I had a fever." Why don't you return to bed, and I'll call them back?"

"Mom, I want to go see her." It came out almost like a whine.

"Well, then go put something nicer on." Mom said.

I went upstairs to change when I heard a little voice calling out.

"Nora! It's me, Lonnie."

I looked around. "Where are you, Lonnie?"

"Right here!" Lonnie emerged from under my bed, dragging my teddy bear with him. Link stuck his head out and waved.

"What are you doing with the teddy bear Lonnie? And why aren't you helping him, Link?" I sat down on the ground.

"I want a fuzzy, soft thing too, Nora," Lonnie said, breathing deeply.

"The little human here earlier had a soft thing; now Lonnie wants one. Is this my punishment?" Link asked.

"Do you mean Finch's opossum? It's a stuffed animal. Lonnie, wait. I will get you one in your size, okay?" I said. Link, be nicer to your brother."

Link folded his arms."We have been under the bed all day. Lana wanted to know how you are feeling."

"I'm okay," I said.

"We're here to deliver a message from Lana, 'If there is an emergency, Dane has a communication device."

"But..." I tried to speak.

Link raised his hand to stop me, "We know you are not talking to him. Dummy never left your side, not even for a moment."

"Nora!" Mom called. "Let's go."

"Tell everyone I am doing fine." I kissed both Link and Lonnie on the head."I have to go." I ruffled Link's fuzzy lime hair.

"I am thrilled you are doing better. I love you, Nora." Lonnie said as he gave my finger an extra hug.

"I love you too, Lonnie. I love you, Link; both of you are my heroes." A portal appeared, and they walked through it, waving goodbye to me.

I changed as fast as I could. The ride to the hospital was tranquil and awkward. I didn't talk during the ride because I didn't know

**

Mom sat still with her hands on the steering wheel when we arrived at the hospital and parked. "What are you thinking about, Mom?" I asked hesitantly.

"I haven't seen them since the funeral. They wouldn't hold or look at you during the services. I couldn't bury my husband without them blaming me for everything, and now here I am ."

Mom took a deep breath, looked at me, and smiled ."I know deep in my heart this is what your father would want me to do. So let's go before I change my mind."

We walked up to Abby's room. I peeked inside. Jasper was sitting next to the hospital bed, holding Abigail's hand.

He looked up when he saw me standing in front of the door. I looked at Mom and motioned for her to come in with me.

I saw my Mom's face look fearful. I smiled at her, took her hand, and the fear disappeared. Mom and I walked a little way into the room.

Jasper's face registered shock for a few minutes. He collected himself for a moment and held his hand out in greeting.

"Thank you for coming, Grace." He looked down at Abby, looking back at Mom, and said, "I've lived by one stringent rule my whole life. I never apologized to anyone. I will change that rule immediately, starting with you, Grace, and Nora. I apologize for everything we put you through. I can't imagine the pain we caused you. I hope you can find it in your heart to forgive us."

Mom smiled."Would you like some coffee, Jasper? Give Nora some time with Abigail". Jasper nodded in agreement, kissed me on the head, and walked down to the cafeteria to get coffee.

I walked over to the bed and touched Abby's arm. It wasn't that long ago I was just as weak as she was. Abby looked completely different since I last saw her. She looked frail, older.

I sat in the chair next to the bed, closest to the window. The monitors had a steady beat. I wondered if she would wake up now that I was here, almost willing her to.

"Don't leave now, Abby. I just got here." I whispered.

A bright white light appeared on the other side. "Dad?" I asked. The center was a bright white concentrated center, with rays of different colors radiating.

"I am the first of my kind, the Eldest of all of what many call me Ancient Elder." That being said. "Would you like me to take a human form so it will be comfortable for you? Do not worry about formality; it is not needed here."

"How did you know what I was thinking? Why are you here?" I asked. I stood up and faced the beam of light. "How do I know you are here to help?"

"You are learning." The bright light transformed into an older man with grey hair, a plaid shirt, brown pants, and a sweater vest. He had a standard pair of reading glasses tucked at the point. He dug into his pocket and pulled out the bracelet Dane had given me.

"It's good for you to be untrusting," he said.

I put my arm out as he clasped the bracelet on my arm. The gold shimmered as it fell into place on my wrist.

"I wanted to meet you personally. I admire your courage to face evil and your passion for the ones you love, strengthening our magic." The Ancient Elder sat in the chair. Your Guardian was the one who saved your life.

Your father was not allowed to interfere. Dane knew you were in trouble, so he called for you, reached for you, caught you, and brought you safely to Queen Luna's Kingdom. I wiped his memory of what happened. I have my reasons. Your fight has just begun. This will not be the last you have heard from her."

I looked over at Abby sleeping, then at the Elder. "I have no doubt; I felt her vengeance and her hate. She wants my death, and one day, she may have it, but not today. I wish for more time…for my…Grandmother…please." I didn't want to beg, but I was prepared to do so.

The Eldest smiled. "Such brave words for someone so…young… so inexperienced. You know nothing of us. How can you make those claims?"

"Because she is my daughter." My father appeared beside the Eldest. "You forget she holds the last of our magic."

"Humans, Why are human feelings so important?" The Eldest asked, nodding to the hospital bed.

My dad answered carefully. "This woman is my mother. She has things to teach, lessons for Nora Rose to learn."

I stood watching the two Elders. It seemed like they were communicating without speaking.

My dad finally spoke. "I understand my job." Dad looked at me and smiled, then disappeared.

"What did he say?" I asked the Eldest.

"You will find out soon enough. Humans are so complicated; I will never understand your kind," the Eldest said as he stood up. He looked at Abby, who was lying in the hospital bed. The Eldest walked next to her and laid his hand on her head. A bright glow radiated around her head. He chuckled. "Humans with their outdated medicine. She will not be cured of her illness, but this is your gift so that you may spend more time with her. Learn your lessons well."

He extended his hand to me, and I took it. "Be well, Nora Rose." And then he was gone.

Looking at my grandmother, she opened her eyes. "Nora Rose?"

"It's me, Abby." I sat next to her on the bed."How do you feel?" I asked.

"Better. Where is Jasper?" Her throat was dry. I leaned over to get her cup of water. She sipped a little bit. "You look just like your father. The first time I saw you, the pain of losing Scott started all over again." She took my hand. "I am so very sorry, Nora Rose."

"How do you know my middle name?" I asked.

She chuckled weakly, "Scott always said if he had a girl, he would name her Rose. It seemed your mom got to choose the first name."

"I did," Mom said as she and Jasper stood in the doorway, holding coffee cups. Abagail, how are you?"

"Grace, your daughter is everything a young lady should be," Abigail said as she patted my hand.

We didn't stay long, but I promised I would come by to visit tomorrow. On the way home, I texted Dane. "The bracelet was returned." I put a heart emoji next to it.

"How?" Dane texted back.

"Magic" with a smiley face. I texted

"What are you doing tomorrow?" I asked.

"Got a day off. Prob nuthin." He answered.

"Can you ditch your stalker? I want you to meet someone." I asked.

"Let me see what I can do," Dane answered.

Walking into the house, Mom wanted to know how I enjoyed my visit. I told her the basics and escaped to my room.

"Dad?" I silently whispered, but no response

"Talk," Dad said. I jumped again."Yes, I know I need a bell." He sat down on my bed.

"I thought I would hate them when I finally met them. It's the opposite. Then, the Eldest gave Abby more time. I don't understand any of this, Dad. I don't understand why that thing happened to me. Why come after me?"

"There are no easy answers, Nora Rose," Dad said.

"Fine. Don't tell me. Have you joined Mom's Don't Tell Nora Anything club?" I turned away from him.

Dad did not answer. Just smiled."You were lucky today; you spoke to the Eldest with disrespect. It is not done."

Dad held my hand as he said. "I have to speak to you as your Elder now, not as your father. You were taken because true love needs to be bound to what we call a Soul Covenant. The stars will soon collide, and you must have a Guardian when it does. We learned our lesson from the Ancient Queens. We will not allow magic to fall into evil hands again." He paused. "I have persuaded the Ancient Elders to allow you to choose. A Soul Covenant would mean you would be bound together in a magic marriage, as Dane is already bound to you as your Guardian by magic, but this... is soul bonding forever."

"Why is this such a big deal?" I asked.

He replied, "The human world is like a chess board; good and evil are the players. Evil has dominated the Earth for millennia. You have tipped the balance. This is why magic is extremely vulnerable right now. You broke your bond with Dane, so you were taken to stop magic from being locked into the light. Others will do the same. There are plenty of evil predators, and they are all after you."

"Excuse me, Elder," Lana said from the doorway. "I have a message that the Eldest has assigned guards to protect Nora," Lana said quietly. "For Mistress Nora's protection, she is to stay in the human world until the Eldest decrees all is safe. I will come to you, Mistress. Also, in an emergency, the Guardian can contact me."

Looking at both Lana and Dad, I said. "I feel like I'm being punished. Why does it have to be me? Why do I have magic?" I complained.

"I can't lose you again. You need to be very careful; You are in real danger. Consider the Soul Covenant carefully."And then he was gone.

GUARDIANS

I sat on the island, eating a bowl of cereal. A heavy cloud of guilt overshadowed the anticipation of seeing Dane today. I couldn't shake the feeling that I was constantly pushing him to take risks for me. The desire to discuss what had happened was there, but it was futile. Dane's memory had been wiped clean, leaving me with unanswered questions and a mountain of unanswered guilt.

Now, I have friends, a Dad, and even grandparents—everything I had ever wished for since I was old enough to walk. But now that I have it all, I find myself even more miserable than before.

Gigi started barking at the back door. I threw cereal pieces on the floor to keep her quiet. Barking turned to growling, so I got up and pulled out one of her biscuits.

"What is wrong with you?" Gigi wagged her tail and circled a couple of times, waiting for another treat. Her ears perked up, tied with a growl, to keep her quiet and lip baring her front teeth.

"Fine, now I must deal with a demented dog like you." Gigi as she started a whole new barking fit. Suddenly, there was a knock on the back door.

"Hey," I said, opening the back door and returning to finish my cereal.

"Where is your mom?" Dane asked, looking around. Looking down at Gigi, he yelled, "SHUT UP!" Gigi went quiet but continued to bare her teeth at Dane.

"What the hell is wrong with you? You never yell at the dog." I asked. Dane continued to glare at the dog. "Dane, look at me!" Dane put his hands around my wrist. My bracelet started to sting and burn.

"What are you doing?" I yanked back my arm, but Dane grabbed my other arm and started to sneer at me. Drool oozed out the side of his mouth, and his pupils dilated so that no color was left in his iris. "Let me have it!" Dane said as his whole eyes started turning completely black.

"No!" I said, trying to pull my arm away. He wasn't letting go. Gigi was barking loudly in the background.

"GIVE ME TH...." Whatever it was stopped in its tracks as he looked behind me.

I looked behind me to see two substantial translucent, nine-foot stone lions; they wore collars of solid gold with a football-sized emerald at the center, with large eyes of stone glinted with pure menace. Sharp fangs of stone demonstrated fierce anger, paws the size of a car, lifted, sealing the fatal fate of the imposter. Roaring, growling, the masquerader shifted into a solid black figure.

The honest Dane came in through the back door and scooped me out of the way as one of the stone lions picked up the entity with his fangs, tore off his head, and ate it. The other lion gobbled up what was left and swallowed him. Once he was gone, both lions sniffed the air; one leaned back on his hind legs, roared, and disappeared.

Dane and I huddled in a corner. His arms and body protected mine. Tears flowed down my face. When he was sure everything was safe, Dane let me sit on his cheek and up. I put my ha light surrounding Dane.

"Thank you," I said.

He bent down and kissed me. Tingles raced up from the bracelet. I wrapped my arms around his neck and pulled him closer to me to deepen the kiss.

"Never, Never let you go." Fluttered through my mind.

Suddenly, Dane pulled back. Breathing deeply, Dane helped me up into a standing position. He ushered me to sit at the bar. "What were those things?" He asked.

"The Eldest assigned guards for me," I said softly.

Dane didn't say much for a while. "Lana is alerting the Queen." He said as he held my hand.

"I thought it was you until the bracelet began to burn. Its eyes turned black and..". tears started to fall.

He wanted to get my mind off that creature, so he changed the subject. "I had coffee with Jasper. He wanted to know if I was working now, going to college, or if I had a career picked out. When I told him I wanted to be a firefighter, I thought he was going to have a stroke. 'A nice-looking young man like you should go into business.' Then I choked. I told him my dad is in business and that I have no desire to be cooped up in an office all day. Then he wanted to know what kind of business dad was in."

Gigi came back, trotting into the kitchen, wagging her tail. "Hello?" Jewels said, "I found Gigi wandering around, walking in circles outside. Thought I would return her to you."

"D!" Finch went over to hug Dane.

"Thank you, Jewels, for bringing Gigi back and closing my back door, which I left open for some reason." Jewels said as she observed the tension between us.

"What's going on? Why are you on the floor?" Jewels asked. Dane helped me up to a standing position. Jewels looked at the bruise forming on my arm. We must have looked guilty because Jewels asked. "Are you okay?"

I smiled. "Yes," We both said together.

"D, I'm going to a new school soon. Spock can't go. I have to be a big boy and go by myself." Finch said, looking at his sister.

"You are a big boy," Dane said, ruffling Finch's head. I must go home, but I promise I will take you to the park before you start your first day at school. Okay?"

"Okay, D. Can Spock come too?" Finch asked.

"Yes, he can," Dane said, smiling down at Jewel's little brother.

"Will your 'Warden' let you out to play?" Jewels sneered.

Ignoring jewels, Dane turned and kissed me on the head goodbye.

Turning to Finch, I tried to distract him from Dane leaving. "Guess what I got? An ancient doll."

"Really? Can I see Nora?" Finch asked.

"Sure, I'll go get it." I looked at Jewel's. "Thank you for bringing the dog back." I hugged her.

"We'll have to talk about what happened, Nor. I felt bad vibes, bad magic," Jewels whispered.

"I know. I can't tell you everything, but you were right when you said I had magic. I just can't explain it right now; it is too complicated." I was trying to find the right words.

"I understand. Go get the doll; I'm curious, too." Jewels said with a smirk.

I stopped in the middle of the staircase; I put my hand on my stomach. I feel like I have been punched as the tears started falling.

I had overwhelming thoughts going through my head, I muttered to myself. I feel like I have a target on my back. I can't win—the pressure to secure magic with a Soul Covenant. If I secure magic between Dane and me, Cordelia will be a thorn in my side forever.

If I don't enter the Soul Covenant and leave my magic unsealed, I will be a walking target for every evil maniac who wants my magic. I don't know what to do. I just don't know!

As I continued up the steps, I wiped my tears away. Picking up the pink box, I turned around and turned back down the steps. Rounding the stairs, I set the doll's box on the kitchen island.

"Oh, a pink box; Allison would love it." Jewels remarked sarcastically.

"Open it! Open it!" Finch jumped up and down.

"You have to be very careful with the doll. It's ancient." I said. Taking off the lid, I flipped the tissue to the side and tilted the box.

"She is beautiful, Nor." Jewels said. "I'm not much of a doll person, but wow."

"I want to see!" Finch whined.

I took a breath and gently picked up the fragile doll. As I lifted her, a folded sheet of paper dropped back into the box.

"She is pretty, Nora," Finch said.

A sheet of paper peeked out from under the tissue in the box. I grabbed the paper and put it on the side while I put the doll back in its box.

Jewels handed the paper to me. Her phone rang, and she answered with a few clicks. Looking back up at me, she said, "Dad is back. "

"Yippee, Dad is home!" Finch squealed while jumping up and down.

Jewels gave me a quick hug. I thanked her again for returning the dog with a promise to let her know what the letter said.

"Come on, Lala, I wanna see Daddy," Finch said, pulling jewels out the door.

As I refolded the tissue, I put the letter inside the box and put the top back. Mom walked in with Baby Blue Eyes, and they were laughing. They both stopped when they saw me.

"Where did you go?" I asked.

"Bennett asked me to breakfast with him." Mom said.

"And all you left me was a Post-it? 'I'll be back,'" I asked.

"Nora Rose, you are going too far," Mom said sternly.

"Here is my Post It, 'I'm going to my room.' I gave Baby Blue Eyes a nasty look as I walked around him with the pink box.

I heard Mom say something to him, but I didn't care.

 I got almost halfway up before Mom at the bottom of the steps said, "Stop right there; what is wrong with you?"

"Nothing!" I turned to continue up the steps to my room. Slamming the door closed.

After locking my door, I retrieved the letter from the box. Opening it, I saw that the handwriting was beautifully written. I leaned back against the door and slid down to read the letter.

My Dearest Great Granddaughter Nora Rose,

I hope this letter finds its way to you one day. I held you for the first time today and instantly fell in love with you. For you see, Your father was the love of my life. I brought him up from a little boy. Scott and his father did not get along very well. Jasper's life revolved around running a business and money. I always told Scott to follow his heart and do whatever he wanted to do in life. This infuriated Jasper regularly.

I must admit that I did not do such an excellent job raising Jasper. I was at home caring for or raising a baby. His father drilled business into him from the moment he started to walk. Jasper had little to no childhood. Looking back on my life, I realize that one of my greatest regrets is that I didn't protect his childhood. I tried to correct that with Scott.

You will inherit the bulk of my estate once you come of age. A board of my trustees has instructions on all that business nonsense. But, you must beware of those who want you only for your money. Greed is an ugly thing.

Your father was genuinely lovestruck when he met your mother. She was all he ever talked about. Scott was over the moon when he found her again. I remember that night he called me so excitedly. When I first met Grace, I knew she was the one for him. Cordelia had other plans. She tried to convince me that she carried Scott's child. I marched her to the doctor's office, but it was false. I demanded an apology, one I never got. I knew her Grandmother; we grew up together. Our two families have been rivals since my mother married into the Mayer family. Here is another long story—a tale for a later time, my Rose.

I wish only the best in life. I feel my life slipping away. My husband is close by, waiting for me. Think of Me Whenever You Smell a Rose

Love you, my namesake Nora Rose.

--Rose Beckett

TRAINING

I folded the paper and set it down on the box. I closed my eyes and leaned my head against the door.

"Hello, Princess." A male voice said.

I jumped, stood up, looked up, and saw a young man sitting on my bed. He had dark hair with modern hair, dark skin, and brown eyes. He wore a dark grey T-shirt, jeans, and white hi-tops. This guy had a cocky grin like he knew more than I did.

"Who are you?" I asked quietly.

"I'm crushed. Didn't Daddy tell you I was coming? Oh, I forgot the Eldest punished you in this world." He laughed. "My name is Hunter. I'm your trainer. I'm an Elder, too," he said, smiling.

"Get off my bed," I said, honestly irritated.

"Make me," Hunter said. "If you are worried about your Guardian, He knows." Hunter looked at the expression on my face. "Classic! He didn't tell you either. Oh, Wow, this is going to be fun after all." Hunter swung his feet and set them on the floor. "Damn, you are pretty."

"I thought Elders were celibate." I sneered.

Hunter laughed and laughed. "Oh shit, that's a good one! I have had more women throughout the centuries, and you…" Hunter stood up and started backing me up against my door, putting one arm on either side of me, trapping me.

"Do you know who I am? Of course, you don't." He laughed. "I have trained every great warrior, in every dimension, from the beginning of time! What I am is a bit more complicated. There are not enough human years for you to understand. Humans are too feeble to understand complicated stuff."

"I don't care who or what you are, so let me go!" I was getting furious. Swirls of light formed around my fingers, making their way up my arms. I could feel the heat around my shoulders.

"Good. Remember the feeling you have right now," Hunter said. He lifted his hand; the magic that had encircled my arms was now drifting across the room.

Hunter gently caressed my face and traced the curve of my face. "Very pretty," leaning closer, I closed my eyes. I could feel his lips close to mine. "Sweet princess, how about I take what I deserve from you?" His fingers ran down my body. "It is very nice." His lips were gliding down my neck. I just wanted to die. It's not like Dane's kisses.

"Elder's Magic," he whispered in my ear. "Coming from a human, what will they think of next? It's almost comical." He bounced the power ball of light back to me. As I caught the ball, the light disappeared.

"I didn't ask for it," I said quietly.

His eyes glowed to an amber color. "This is not a game. That thing that attacked you at your house was not a game; it was a skinwalker, evil's minions. Just one kiss, Nora?"

I felt his lips. I squeezed and leaned in, so I closed my eyes, trying not to make contact. He was making my skin crawl.

"Pity," Hunter said as he backed up and grabbed my elbow. His hand began to glow.\

I kneed him in the groin. He bent in pain.

"You Bitch!" He growled.

"Stay the fuck away from me! You are not allowed to touch me again!" I felt my mind scrambling for Dane's.

"Lesson one, Princess." Hunter leaned in close to my ear, "Do not piss me off, then he disappeared.

I fell to the floor, and tears began to fall. Then my cellphone rang. It was Dane. I answered the phone.

"Why didn't you help me?" I asked.

"I can't, Nora. You need to learn to defend yourself. It is not easy for me." Dane replied.

WHO ARE YOU?

With the departure of that arrogant trainer, I was very frustrated; I headed downstairs to hear Mom and Brainless laughing at something. Trying to avoid them, I headed out the back door.

Mom called me, "Did you come down to apologize, Nora?"

"No!" I said as I walked out the back door, slamming it shut.

I am so frustrated and confused. I want to see Lana, Link, and Lonnie. I want out. I want to stay where the lakes were the color of cotton candy, and fish were the color of the rainbow, a place where things were carefree. Things aren't confusing there. I looked up at the sculpture, my bracelet starting to tingle. I looked around to see if anyone was looking—no one.

Or so I thought.

"Don't do it," Dad said. He stood behind me. "Look at me."

I kept my back to him. "No, you caused enough trouble. I'm getting my driver's license and will never return here. I don't want to have magic!" The breeze caught a tear falling from my cheek.

"It will follow you wherever you go, Nora," Dad said. "You can't outrun magic. You are half Elder; as such, every being knows who you are. You must decide on the Soul Covenant, Nora, or this will continue."

I turned around. "You have an answer for everything. I was just fine before all of 'this,'" Gesturing with my hands. "Hunter almost….He almost molested me! Do you even care?"

Dad's facial features softened. I felt his sadness. "I did 'this' to you. I am sorry for your pain. I am not sorry for being able to spend time with you, even if it is this way. You need to decide soon."

"I don't want to be stuck with Cordelia, and oh, by the way, I want another trainer!" Stomping my foot as loud as I could on the ground.

"I did not choose Hunter; he is the best. You do not question the Eldest's authority. I would happily escort you if you want to visit Link and Lonnie." Dad waited for my response.

I could feel the light wanting to come out again. "I am not a child! I can't win either way! What do you want of me?"

"You don't have much time with your grandmother. Your grandparents have rented a house close by. My mother is out of the hospital. Call them," Dad said as he watched me storm past him, and I returned to the house.

This time, Mom didn't say anything to me as I passed. Up the steps and back in my room.

Dad appeared sitting on the bed. "You can't get rid of me that fast. You have no choice. You can't beg for the Eldest's help and turn your back. You have much to learn and battles to fight. You are the hope of every being in this universe. Do you understand Nora Rose? You have to get your priorities together!"

My anger flared. "So easy for you to say! Popping in and out like a fairy! 'You must save the universe.' No, that is your thing, your fight! This fight is not mine! I want to be a normal teenager! I just want to have a family, have a boring life, and grow old!"

Dad frowned and stood up. "I was hoping you were different." He stood up. "You are no better than my parents and the generations of Becketts before them. Selfish, conceded, and…"

The words stung, venom straight to the heart, tears falling uncontrollably. "All right!" I screamed.

"Who are you, Nora Rose?" Dad asked.

"I am just…me! Just a plain girl…a girl no one saw! No one cared about it! A girl who
lost her father and spent her birthdays wishing he was here with her! Watching her mother cry herself to sleep and feeling guilty for being alive when you were gone! Then you show up immediately and tell me I must save the universe!" Tears were choking me. "I can't fight that psychotic woman! I can't fight something I didn't do! I didn't do this! I want to have a family with Dane." I couldn't bear it anymore. It hurt too bad.

Dad scooped me up in his arms and let me cry. "You will have a family, Nora. It will be different, but you will have your own family."

"

CORDELIA:

"So let me get this right." Cordelia walked around the sofa behind Roger. "You allowed my son to see that little bitch?"

"Cordelia," Roger said calmly.

"No! Do not go there! We agreed!... No, you agreed, jackass!" Cordelia screamed, grabbing a bottle of wine and pouring herself a full glass.

"Agreed on what Cordelia? You, you started this shit at the BBQ. You went after Grace's daughter when you damn well knew better!" Roger turned to face her. "You have been a fucking thorn in Grace's side for years! Why? Jealousy? She was better than you?"

"Bullshit! She was a money-grubbing slut who took off her clothes for money!" Cordelia spat, drink the rest of the wine.

"She was an artist. She was paying her way through college, not sleeping through it. Fucking every professor you had for grades." Roger said. "Well, the men, at least. What did you do to your female professors... fuck I don't want to know. "

"Shut up! Shut up! Shut up! I did what I had to do!" Cordelia screamed. "I didn't have a cash cow like you did!"

Roger stood up. "You have a bad memory. I think your boy toys are screwing up your head. I worked my way through college. I worked long fucking hours interning with Scott. We were going to be partners. You are nothing but a whore, and will always be a whore. I want out. I want a divorce,"

"I will take you for everything you got!" Cordelia yelled as she threw the glass across the room.

"I don't have shit. You took it all. Have our accountant that you are fucking, check into it!" Losing his tie, Roger took the wine bottle and entered the pool house.

Cordelia gritted her teeth in anger.

GETTING AWAY TO ALLISON'S

I asked Mom to bring me to Allison's for a sleepover and get me in a bet. One of my favorite places in her room is an oversized stuffed chair. I was flipping through a magazine but wasn't looking at the pictures.

"You have been looking at the same picture for twenty minutes. What is going on with you?" Allison asked.

"I think Mom is getting serious about Baby Blue." Trying not to cry. "I don't want him anywhere near my Mom."

"Oh, Nor," Allison leaned over to hug me. Her hair smelled fruity. "I don't know what to say," she said as she sat back, a look of concern on her face.

Sniffling, "There isn't anything you can do, Al." I brought my knees up to my chest, wrapping my arms around my knees.

Allison's face brightened. "I can spike his stuff with glitter! Would that help?"

I couldn't help it. I started laughing. "It took Dane weeks to get rid of most of the glitter you cursed him with." We both laughed at the thought.

My cell phone rang; reaching over to get my phone, I saw that it was Abigail. "Hello, Abby"

"Hello, Nora. I was wondering if you, your Mom, and your friends are available this Saturday night for Dinner?"

"I don't know, I could ask. I have been meaning to call you. Is it okay if I can come by tomorrow?" Not early, only because I'm having a sleepover by Allison's house. I'll ask her tonight if she wants to go on Saturday.

"Jasper and I have rented a house near you. I'll text you the address.." Abigail stated.

"Good, I'll see you tomorrow," I questioned

"Sounds good. Talk to you then, Nora Rose." Abigail said.

"Goodbye, I'll see you tomorrow," I said.

Allison and I spent the night discussing Great-Grandma Rose, Abigail, Dane, and Mom. We laughed and cried and ate chips, popcorn, and Pop-Tarts. The Spencers don't like to keep junk food in the house, so I packed a bag of goodies for us to eat. This is one of the reasons we always sleep by my house.

ALLISON'S BRIGHT IDEA

The next day, I called Mom to make sure it was okay if I went over to Abigail's house for a while.

My grandparents sent a driver to pick me up. Allison was impressed and immediately demanded I call her with all the details. The driver pulled into this long drive; my mouth dropped open to see this vast mansion.

It was more opulent than Dane's parent's house. The driver looked in his rearview mirror and said we have arrived, and please wait so he can open the door for me. I have to tell Allison about this. I knew they had money, but wow! As I approached the door, an older man opened it for me.

"Welcome, Miss. I will show you to Mrs. Beckett." I followed him through a vast hallway until he stopped, and I almost ran into him. I heard him announce that I was here. I could hear Abby say to send me in.

I looked around the corner. Abby looked better than she did when she was in the hospital. Her silver hair was pulled back into a neat braid that rested on her shoulder. Abby had very little makeup on. She was in a chair with a blanket placed over her lap.

"Nora Rose, it is so good to see you. Did you have fun at your sleepover?" Abigail asked. "Sit," she indicated, looking at a chair beside her. Do you want something to drink or eat? Jasper is playing golf so that he won't be here this morning. He said he would see you tonight."

I smiled in response."No, Thank you, Abby. How are you feeling?"

"Better. The doctor couldn't figure it out. 'First time this ever happened,' he said." Abigail said. "I'm glad I have a little more time to get to know you. Rose, Jasper's mother, before she passed, told me she got to hold you. She said it was like holding a piece of heaven."

"I found a letter from her behind the doll you sent me," I said nervously.

"What did it say?" Abby asked, surprise showing on her face.

"She felt guilty about how she raised Jasper and how she tried to do things differently with Dad." I stopped because I didn't know how far to go.

"I know about your inheritance, dear. I'm sure she told you. I'm curious to know if she said anything about Cordelia. My question would be, how do you know Cordelia," Abigail asked.

I hesitated. I spent several minutes figuring out how to get out of this.

"Nora Rose? I asked you a question." Abigail said sternly.

I wondered if I looked as guilty as I felt for lying to Abby. "Cordelia is Dane's mother. She hates me. She says I'm not the debutante she wants her son to marry." Saying the words after all this time still hurts.

Abigail laughed. "She said what? That you aren't the debutante SHE wants for her son?" She continued to laugh.

"I don't understand why you are laughing. It's not funny." I could feel the tears starting to form in my eyes.

"Oh, my, Nora honey, you are worth more money than anyone can spend in ten lifetimes." Abby patted my knee for reassurance. "She was rotten then; she hasn't changed much in all these years. My only regret is that I believed her and not my son..." Abigail became thoughtful, taking a deep breath of resignation... "There are many things I regret. Things I can't leave this world without correcting. I hope one day Scott forgives me."

"Tell her I do," Dad said telepathically. "I will love her always."

"I know he forgives you. He loves you; you're his mother." I smiled.

"You are a sweet child. Would you like to stay and visit until everyone comes over for dinner?" Abby sat back for a moment. "Is Dane coming for dinner?"

"I'm sorry he can't unless he can sneak away. But I doubt it." I said.

Abigail picked up her cell phone and started texting. After a while, she looked up and smiled.

"I would love to stay; the only change of clothes I have with me is pink unicorn pajamas," I said, smiling. I loved that smile I saw on her face.

"Call your mother and ask her to bring a dress for you. I understand we also have a young fellow attending," she said.

"How do you know?" I asked.

"I know a lot of things." Abigail commented, "The Becketts are a force to be reckoned with."

***

I was excited that Mom, Jewels, Finch, and Allison were invited to dinner. I just wished Dane could have eaten with us.

The dining room was just as luxurious as the sitting room. The light dusty blue walls held different types of platters from years past. A long mahogany table could easily seat sixteen people comfortably. The chairs were upholstered with a light gold fabric. There were ten place settings.

I smiled when I saw that there were only four fork place settings. Two crystal chandeliers hung above the table. Allison, her parents, Jewels, Finch, Mom, Jasper, Abigail, me, and an empty chair to my right sat around the table.

"Who's the chair for?" I asked no one in particular.

Abby smiled, "A surprise."

Small talk pretty much stopped as the first course came out. The plates of pears and camembert appetizers were placed in front of us.

The second course was Roasted Beet salads with goat cheese. The third course was cheese plates being handed out when Dane walked into the dining room wearing a blue suit and a light blue shirt. He smiled, and my heart did a flip-flop.

A plate of Brie, Blue Danish, and Apple Walnut Smoked cheese served with cranberries and olives, with jam and honey, was placed in front of me.

"Forgive my tardiness for dinner," Dane said as he walked in.

I was shocked. He was here. Dane leaned in and kissed me on the cheek before he sat beside me. I was wondering why there was an empty chair next to me. I just thought it may have been an extra chair. I'm not good with etiquette stuff.

"Welcome, young man. Please sit so we can proceed with dinner." Abigail's smile brightened. It looked like a thousand-watt bulb glowing.

I was already half full when the lemon and garlic roasted chicken was served; for dessert, angel food cake stuffed with whipped cream and berries.

When everyone was finished with dinner, we retired to the living area. Allison started everyone with a game of charades. Dane leaned over and asked if I wanted to take a walk. I looked over at Mom and Abby. They both nodded in approval.

"I want to walk with D too, Lala," Finch whined. Jewels whispered in his ear, and he quieted down.

Dane took my hand, and I followed him through the pool lights illuminated by the floating candles. Looking around, I saw the twinkling lights lining the gate's perimeter. The atmosphere was serene, with glass doors. It is so romantic. We sat on the outer bench closest to the pool.

"You look very pretty tonight," Dane said.

"Thank you. I miss you." I paused. "It is so frustrating that you keep things from me."

"I still can't tell you a lot of things. You have to trust me." Dane said, shifting. "It is part of the job, part of being a Guardian. We have to trust each other."

"I do." I reached for his hand.

He took my hand and pressed his lips against it. "I don't know how to do this; I don't want to mess it up." Dane looked so severe. Turning to face me, he took my right hand.

"What are you doing?" This was getting me very nervous.

Dane pulled out a small box. "It's not much, but I hope you like it." Fumbling, he opened it. Inside the box was a ring with an infinity symbol.

Shock showed on my face. A ring?

"Close your eyes." I did what he said. "Let your magic flow..."

A white fog passed in front of my eyes. A couple of butterflies passed through the mist.

"Describe what you see, Nora," Dane said softly.

"Butterflies. I feel like I'm flying through the clouds. Now I'm walking through a park. A family is playing ball. A toddler with black hair is pulling her hair and trying to eat it. A mom is turning around. Two smaller toddlers are holding their hands up, wanting to be held. I can't see her face, but she is pointing away from her."

I stopped talking as the vision continued. I looked in that direction—an older couple sitting on a picnic blanket. She waved to me. She turned her hand so I could see the infinity ring glowing on her finger. She leaned in to kiss the man she was with. Waving again, the scene closed.

As I opened my eyes, Dane smiled. "I wanted you to have it before you went back to school. I wanted to find the right time to give it to you."

I let him put it on my finger. It was significant but adjusted automatically to my size. It felt right. He pulled me closer and kissed me.

People started clapping in the background. We both turned in the direction of the noise. The dinner party was standing there, watching us, clapping.

"They knew?" I asked Dane.

"Do you expect Allison to keep a secret?" Dane said.

I shot Allison an evil look. She shrugged her shoulders as she smiled from ear to ear.

When Dane was getting ready to leave at the end of the night, he put on his jacket and asked me to walk him to his car. I followed.

He opened the driver's side door and turned to face me. "I need to ask you something. I only told you a half-truth; I did need Allison's help." He took my hand.

"Okay?" I said, "Wait, this isn't about the Soul Covenant thing?"

"Nora..."

"Dane, I'm not ready yet. Your mom..." I said softly.

"I am leaving the second I turn eighteen, Nora. I love you desperately, and I feel like you don't...." I cut in before he could say more.

"Your mom started this. I don't know what else to do." I felt like a total idiot. Why do I always let her ruin things? Take the happiness and run.

DANE'S HOUSE:

As Dane pulled into the driveway, he noticed the light was on in his father's office.

"This can't be good," he thought. As he walked through the door, his dad was waiting for him.

"Had a good time, son?" Roger stood in the foyer, leaning against the door with his arms folded and a drink in one hand.

Dane said, looking at his Dad, "Yes."

He proceeded to walk around his father.

Roger stuck his arm out, "You are treading on dangerous waters. Walk away, son. For Nora's safety, let her go."

Dane turned around, his voice tense."Don't."

Roger's hand landed on Dane's shoulder, his grip firm.

"You are skating on thin ice, son. You have no idea what you are dealing with. Walk away." His words hung in the air, heavy with warning, the gravity of the situation pressing down on them.

Dane pushed his father's arm away, his voice firm.

"It's not going to happen, Dad. I think you should take it easy."

With that, Dane continued to his bedroom, his steps echoing upstairs his determination to avoid his father's advice.

FIRST LESSON

I lay on my bed, my hand held high, looking at the ring Dane had given me. Sighing, I closed my eyes.

Once I settled down, the visions of hearing leaves rustle and walking through trees.

Butterflies fluttered past me, lifting a finger to let one of the butterflies land. "Run, Nora," they whispered.

Something shifted on the ground, and the butterfly flew away. I felt something on my shoulder. I turned to look; it was a branch. I tried to move away, but it wrapped around my neck.

"Where do you think you are going?" The words hissed into my ears. You see how badly I need your power, sweet child. Now be a good girl and hand it over."

"What makes you think I will hand it to you?" I sneered as I put my hand on the branch.

"Any good girl would have listened to her Daddy by now. You don't even have the mark of the Elders yet. Poor baby. But it will not stop me from getting what I want." The branch started tightening around my neck more.

I closed my eyes and raised my other hand on the branch, searching for the trigger. "Trust Me" rang through my mind.

The infinity symbol, I could see the white light starting to rise.

"That's it. Hand it over." Nails were starting to pierce my neck.

Dane! Focusing all my energy on the branch around my neck. I pushed all the energy into the branch, and whatever evil was connected to it exploded into a million pieces, followed by a scream.

I was startled awake as my phone announced a text message.

"Are you Okay?" Dane texted me.

"Yes," I replied.

I looked up to see Hunter sitting on the edge of the bed. "Nice moves, Princess. Have you learned your first lesson?" Hunter said with his ever-present cocky smile. "You didn't destroy 'her' in your little showdown; she will come after you again. This time, she won't be nice. You need to be prepared. Soul Covenant or no, she will have her vengeance."

I glared at him. "I thought the Covenant was supposed to cure all!"

"Lesson two: Ancients don't play by the rules, sweetheart," Hunter said.

"Why are they pressuring me?"

"Evil wants to retain the power of magic; you, my dear Princess, are tipping the scales in the other direction. Be prepared to work; you will never know when you will be tested."

"School is starting soon." I didn't want to do this.

"Trust me, Princess." Cocky smile. "Here is another fact: you're not getting rid of me so fast. So get used to it...Princess."

"Stop calling me Princess!" I yelled.

THE SLAPDOWN

The following day, Abigail Beckett rang the doorbell of the Alexander home.

Cordelia answered the door. A look of shock passed across her face as she recognized Abigail. "What do you want? I thought you were dead already."

Abigail ignored the sarcasm, smiled, and said, "Sorry to disappoint you about that. We need to talk."

"No, we don't." Cordelia sneered.

"I have a DNA test that says you will." Abigail smiled sweetly

Cordelia's eyes widened, and she stepped back to allow her in.

Abigail walked into the house, went straight to the dining room, pulled out one of the chairs, and gracefully sat on a white chair. She watched as Cordelia followed her and sat in the chair beside her.

"Tell me how you got this supposed evidence on me." Cordelia struggled to keep her composure.

"Although I may have been gullible enough to fall for your lies once, I won't make the same mistake twice. Is Dane here?" Abigail asked.

"Why do you care?" Cordelia asked.

"I don't want the sweet young man to know how horrid his mother is," Abigail stated.

"You don't know my son," Cordelia said.

Abigail smiled."You don't know your family very well, do you? Well, I guess not enough to know what's happening in your house. You see, I know more about what is happening than you do. I'm disappointed in you."

"I don't know what you know or think you do, but you must leave now," Cordelia shouted.

"I know who Dane's father is. He consented to a paternal test. Guess what, Cordelia… Roger was completely excluded from being a contributor to your son's DNA." Abigail calmly said. "Who would have guessed? Roger's DNA is not even on the radar. Hmm, wonder how that happened?"

That stopped Cordelia in her tracks. "How?" Cordelia's face flushed with fear. She held this secret for years without anyone knowing.

Abigail smiled again. "Leave Nora alone. Your son will date her and, one day, hopefully marry her. You will give your blessing to your son to do so. If I find out any different, I will pin you to a cross and burn you at the stake, just like the witch you are. Is that clear?"

Dane walked into the dining room."Hello Abby. I fully intend to marry Nora as soon as possible," Dane said as he picked up his car keys. I already know Dad isn't my biological father; I found out about three or four months ago."

Cordelia looked at Dane, horrified. "How?"

"In Biology, We had to do an assignment on blood types. I asked Dad because you were too busy. Dad's (Rh) factor is positive, meaning if he were my birth father, I would be positive as well. I wasn't sure it was right, so I asked Dad to redo it. I brought the results to my teacher, and the look on her face said it all." Dane said solemnly. "I didn't have the heart to say anything to him."

"Let me explain, Dane." Cordelia stuttered. "I..."

"I don't want to hear it," Dane said. I'm going out. Catch you later." Dane kissed Abigail on her cheek. See you later, Abby," he said as he walked out the door.

Abigail turned to face Cordelia."Intelligent young man, isn't he? I want your agreement. Ah, one more thing, put Dane back in school with Nora."

Cordelia hissed. "You spiteful old hag! I hate your entire family! I'm only sorry I couldn't kill your son myself!"

Abigail took out her phone and pushed a few buttons. A man in a dark suit with a briefcase came in. He handed Abigail a folder of papers.

"I had some documents drawn up by my attornies. It's everything we discussed." Abigail slid the papers for Cordelia to sign.

"You can't prove any of this," Cordelia spat. She picked up the papers and ripped them.

"Go ahead, I have copies. Now I know how you cheated your way through college. Cordelia, you should know me better than that. I can prove everything. A specific Executive Chair, a Professor at the university, is Dane's father...correct. Here is a pen."

Cordelia gritted her teeth as she signed her name to the document. Cordelia pushed it back to Abigail.

"Rot in hell!" Cordelia yelled as Abigail signed her name and handed the document to the attorney.

The attorney put the papers in his briefcase and turned to exit the house.

Abigail stood up, putting her purse on her shoulder. "I probably will, but I will feel better knowing my granddaughter will be free of you. Oh, I would be more discreet with the pool boy, your attorney, your accountant, that man on the boat, and the husband of your friend, the ditzy, mousey one, from now on. I'm sure your social club friends would love to see the pictures I have of you and them."

Abigail walked to the front door and let herself out. Cordelia sat in stunned silence in an empty dining room.

<u>DANE:</u>

Scott put his hand on Dane's shoulder, saying, "Let's talk elsewhere."

Scott took Dane to a field near the town of Queen Luna's Kingdom. Once there, they started walking together as they talked.

Scott started to explain."Roger was my best friend. I know he is not your father." Scott stopped to face Dane. "The reason why I am telling you this is that I can see your anger towards him. He needs your love right now."

"Why would he pretend all these years?" Dane asked.

"Roger had a complicated past. Things were never easy for him." Scott explained.

"His mother worked for my Grandmother, and because I lived with my Grandmother, we played together. His mother died a few years later, and Rose took him in. We were like brothers. He was always caught between two worlds."

"Are we gonna talk about my mom now?" Dane asked.

"No, she can talk for herself. Her sins are hers alone," Scott said. You have the choice to forgive her or not." Scott continued walking. "We need to talk about Nora. I want to emphasize that your souls will be connected. I want Nora to finish school. Be careful. I know how it is to be your age." Scott shot him a look as Dane blushed.

"Nora said that the...younger?... the younger is still after her. Is this true?" Dane asked.

"Yes, she will come after Nora Rose for vengeance. Hunter will train her well." He paused. "Thank you for saving my daughter..."

"She said Hunter tried to...kiss her and touch her." Dane said he was still furious that another man touched her.

"It will be dealt with," Scott said.

SEALING MAGIC

Mom was spending the day at an Art Fair in town. I still wasn't talking to her, so she left me alone at home. Lying on the sofa watching TV, the doorbell rang, and Gigi started barking. White sparks jumped from my fingers. As I walked through the hallway slowly, the sparks had become interlaced into one spark that slid through my fingers.

Looking through the curtains, I saw Dane leaning his head against the door. "I can feel you, Nora; please let me in."

"What was the name of our waitress on our first date?" I asked through the door.

"Georgia, I need to talk to you," Dane said.

I opened the door; Dane had tears in his eyes, and I hugged him as tightly as possible. After several minutes, I leaned back.

"What happened?" I asked as I wiped his tears away.

Dane walked into the foyer so I could close the door. Before I could turn around, he spun me around, backed me up to the wall, and looked deeply into my eyes.

"Nora, please..." His fingers curled around my finger, which held the infinity ring. He brought it up to his lips and kissed the infinity symbol.

"It's not foolproof. 'She' escaped; she wanted to kill me. I can't defeat her, Dane." I said, wanting him to kiss me.

"We can do it together. Sealing ancient magic to the side of goodwill..." He leaned his forehead against mine. He was so close that I could see the changes in his eyes. "Nora, you know we belong together." Dane said as he traced my lips. "I love you with all my heart. I would have never sacrificed my soul for anyone else but you."

"You did what?" I asked.

Dane's lips curled up into a smile. "Queen Luna looked into our future. She knew I would give anything to protect you."

"Magic has changed you. I never noticed the light in your eyes before." Dane backed up, turned around, and lifted his shirt. His back was covered in intricate designs.

"I thought it was only your wrist." I gasped.

Turning to face me, "Each Symbol has a complete spell within it; there are over a hundred. Only magic can see it, like the one on your arm soon." He lifted my arm to expose my forearm.

He traced it with his finger. "I'm going to ask you one last time. Nora Rose, please."

He said, placing my hand over his heart."agree to the Soul Covenant to save magic."

"Yes, I will," I whispered.

Dane kissed me until my back hit the wall. He lifted me, and I wrapped my legs around his waist. I felt him through his jersey shorts and my biker shorts. I was open to him.

His erection swelled as he kissed me deeply, rubbing into my softness. I felt utterly liquid the more he rubbed into me. My nipples hardened, and all I knew was that I needed him inside me.

"Dane….upstairs,…my room," I said in-between pants.

I didn't have to ask twice. I was on my feet, racing up the steps. My door was closed behind me. Dane took off his shirt. His chest was incredible. Dane sat on the bean bag, and I sat atop him, wanting his feel against me. I flipped up my shirt and took off my sports bra.

He looked at me as his hands caressed my breast. Then he took my hard nipple into his mouth and sucked. His teeth nibbled and sucked my hard nipple, shot jolts of sizzling electricity straight to my girl parts. I moaned, and he looked at me. Desire was intense in his eyes.

"I love you, Nora Rose." He said as he leaned in to kiss me. "I want to make love to you, claim you as mine."

A coughing noise came from behind Dane. I leaned around him to see my Dad.

"Dad?" I was irritated at the intrusion. I watched Dane close his eyes, wanting to melt through the floor. Dane straightened his shoulders back.

I grabbed my shirt and bra and put them on, and my dad gave me some privacy while I put my shirt on.

"Dad, what are you doing here?" I asked.

"I have a Soul Covenant to get you to," Scott said.

"Now?" I asked.

Dane quietly put his shirt on. He was embarrassed getting caught.

"Yes, now," My dad said. " I'm sending you to Luna's now."

"Why now?" I asked.

"Link and Lonnie missed you, and you need to change, Nora," Scott said.

The next thing I know, I am in Queen Luna's Dimension.

Lana smiled. "Hello, Nora. I'm here to help you dress. Where is Dane?"

SOUL COVENANT

A curtain of hanging vines opened on both sides of the cotton candy-colored lake. The lake was lit from within the water. The glittered rocks sparkled with every movement of the fish and turtles. I could see fuzzy purple stones.

The glass bridge was yellow, blue, and lined with mint green ribbons. In the middle of the bridge was a glass table with a vase and two cups on either side. A small box sat with the lid open, revealing the ceremonial ribbon.

Leroy, Lann, Leo, Link, and Lonnie wore Queen Luna's royal uniform and hats. I could tell Link was very unhappy wearing his royal hat. Lana was dressed in what looked like a Renaissance dress. Lulu wore a simple dress with flowers in her hair.

Queen Luna wore the dress she wore on the day of the Sunflower Court. The King wore the customary uniform, with a gold sash across his chest and a sword by his side.

The village witnessed the ceremony; the ancient Elders appeared on the glass bridge. They stood on both sides of the glass table. Hunter also attended; he stood apart from the other Elders but wore the robes of the Elders.

I looked down to see that I was wearing a simple dress. It reminded me of a prom dress. It was strapless, and stars covered the bodice, going down into the skirt.

I felt like a bride…well, I was. Flowers were braided in my hair. I felt pretty. I wish my mom could be here.

I walked to the bridge with Link on my right side and Lonnie on my left. The Queen walked behind me, and Lana followed behind.

Dane and Dad were waiting for me at the foot of the bridge. Dane wore white pants and a white shirt, a navy blue sash crossed his chest and tied at his hip. Link whispered that it was to identify him as Guardian, and Indigo was his color; the ceremony would seal the spells on his back.

Dad stepped in front of us; he looked back at me and smiled. He then took his place among the Elders. Link and Lonnie started walking, and as I walked with them, Dane followed a few steps behind.

Once we arrived in the middle of the bridge, the Eldest transformed into his human form. He nodded at me. He took my arm. "I will give you the magical brand identifying you as a Half Elder." The Eldest waved his hand over my arm, and symbols were imprinted on my forearm.

"All magic will know who you are." The Eldest said.

Then he motioned for Link and Lonnie to retrieve the two cups from the table. They walked to the cotton candy-colored water, scooped water into the cups, and returned to the Eldest.

"Thank you," the Eldest said to Link and Lonnie. Nora, Guardian, please take a cup." I took the cup from Lonnie, and Dane took a cup from Link.

The Eldest gestured for us to come to the table. "Each cup represents a separate self. We are here to seal and ensure our ancient magic cannot become vulnerable. Pour your glasses into this vase to represent one being."

We both poured our glasses into the vase. The Eldest continued. "Where you were two, now you are one. Pour the water back into the lake to signify the flow of life you will undertake together."

The Eldest walked towards Dane and placed his hand and mine on his back. He looked into the sky. Everyone's eyes followed upward in the distance, and a large explosion of light shattered in every direction. A beam of light is shown straight down into the Ancient Elder and through his hands into us.

"I seal these spells with the light of ancient magic. The foretold restoration of magic is now sealed within the chosen Princess who will bring peace to all dimensions." A golden glow traveled from the Elder's hand to follow the path of every symbol and spell on Dane's back, sealing the spells.

Queen Luna guided her hand over the ribbon which rose from the table. The ribbon floated with Queen Luna as she turned around to face us.

"Place your hands together," Queen Luna ordered. I placed my hand on Danes's, and the ribbon wrapped around our hands.

The Eldest placed his hand on top of ours, "Guardian, Nora Rose, Princess...

TO BIND, I TAKE YOUR HANDS
IN MINE AND WITH THIS RIBBON, I WILL ENTWINE YOUR POWERS I'LL FOREVER BIND FROM NOW
TILL THE END OF TIME. YOUR SOULS ARE BOUND
TO BALANCE AND RESTORE ANCIENT MAGIC
TO IT'S RIGHTFUL PLACE"

"May Ancient Queen Liv and Queen Liana smile upon us on this special day!" Lana said.

The infinity ring glowed bright as the ribbon was taken from our hands. Queen Luna smiled as she said. "They are well pleased."

Cheers from the villagers cheered. My dad came over to kiss me on the cheek. I hugged Link and Lonnie, who were both misty-eyed. Turning around, I hugged Lana, who had just joined us.

The day I seemed to pass in a blur. Luna's village celebrated all day with games, dancing, and eating, which Lonnie enjoyed tremendously. I enjoyed being with Link and Lonnie again. I miss them in my dimension.

Towards the end of the day, I just needed to be alone. I walked to the last mushroom house at the edge of the village. Knowing I would find a peaceful spot.

I sat down by the pink water. Bending over in a strapless dress wasn't the easiest thing to do. My finger was in the water, and my rainbow fish swam to greet me. I petted his forehead, and he laid on his side and flipped his fin.

I giggled. "You need a name," I said.

The fish wiggled in response.

"I'll call you Bo. Do you like that name?" I asked.

He did a flip in response. "Okay, Bo, it is." I smiled.

"Who are you talking to, Nora?" Lonnie asked. "I brought you a seed."

"Thank you so much. I saw you were having fun." I said as I patted the ground for him to sit by me.

"I didn't see you, and I missed you. Magic was shut down after....after..." Lonnie didn't want to say it.

"Thank you, Lonnie, for taking care of me." I gave him a quick side hug.

"Aw, it was nothing." Lonnie sighed. "Why are you here?"

"I just needed a break. I thought I would come to visit Bo." I said wistfully.

"Who is Bo?" Lonnie asked.

"A fish, this rainbow fish." I pointed to the fish, which brought me pebbles and threw them back in the water.

"Oh, hello, Bo," Lonnie replied.

Dane walked up to us. He changed into his t-shirt and pants. "Hey Lonnie, can I talk to

Nora for a minute?"

"Sure, I think they put out new muffins." Lonnie stood up, kissed my head, and hurried off to claim freshly baked muffins.

Dane sat down next to me. "You okay?"

Looking up at him, thoughts of our whatever that almost was filtered through my head. "I don't understand why I feel so sad," I said, looking into his hazel eyes, which changed to a deeper green.

"It's me. You're feeling what I'm feeling. There is so much I haven't told you. When I came over earlier, I found something out about my dad..." stammering,

"My dad isn't my biological dad. I don't know the details; I don't want to know. I love my dad... Roger....whatever, and I'll always love him."

"About... before...us," I paused. I was not sure I could look him in the eye after I bared my body to him. I feel...

"When we are both ready. I want you more than anything, but I want this to be right for you. Not lust, not magic, us." Dane looked at me with all the love I felt.

"Do we get a wedding night?" Stupid? Dangerous? Yes, it was. I looked at him, leaning in to kiss him.

"I wish. The desire you're feeling is mine. I want to taste you again." Dane's lips covered mine, and something flew straight in his face.

Somewhere close by, I heard Hunter's laughter behind us.

Not thinking, I threw my hand back towards the source of the laughter. A wave of distortion flew toward Hunter, knocking him off his feet. I could hear him hit the ground.

"Nice going, Princess!" Hunter said.

I looked at Dane, and we started laughing together.

SURPRISE!

It was the first day of school. I stood on the school's curb with Jewels and Allison, just staring at the building.

"I'm telling you there is something different about Nor." Jewels said. "Look at her."

"I am! She looks the same as yesterday, Jewels." Allison shook me. "Nor promise no gum in your locker this year. I bought you a trash can for your locker, so I don't have to wait an hour for you again."

"An hour? Nora?" Jewels exclaimed. "What do you think the chances of me finding my true love this year?"

I stood silently, not saying anything. Dane wasn't here. I'm not ready to do this without him, not seeing him in the halls, passing him notes, or walking to Scoops on Fridays.

"Nora, you okay? Are you in there?" Allison asked as she waved her hand in front of my face.

I continued to stare at the school, not blinking.

"I think something is wrong with her, Jewel," Allison said, grabbing Jewel's arm.

"Has all the glitter hairspray finally killed all the neurons in your brain? I just told you that!" Jewels told Allison.

Jewels hugged me. "I know you are upset, but you can do this; I know you can."

My eyes filled with tears. "No, No, I can't." I turned around to walk home. "I gonna talk Mom into homeschooling me," I said, backing away from them. "I can do that."

"Nora, you'll see Dane after school. Abigail is having dinner tonight, and Dane will be there," Jewels said. Come on, we'll walk together, all three of us."

Allison turned her attention to something in the parking lot, not hearing what Jewels said.

Jewels started walking Nora to the school; she realized Allison wasn't with them. "Allison! Focus! Let's go!"

Allison turned around once more and went back to Jewels. "Okay, I'm coming! I got distracted." Allison ran to catch up with Nora and Jewels.

***

Allison put the tiny garbage can in my locker with strict instructions to empty it every other day. I sat through the first two classes, doodling again in my notebook. The bell rang to go to the next class. Not looking where I was going, I ran into a solid mass.

I looked up and saw Hunter smiling down at me. "Hello, Princess."

"What are you doing here?" I hissed sarcastically. I dropped my books as I was bending down to pick them up.

"I thought you would be nicer. I'm a new student." Hunter said as he started following me to my next class.

"Go away. I don't need you here." I kept walking.

Jewels caught up with me. "Hi, I'm new too. I'm Jewels, and you are?"

"Hunter, my pleasure." He said, giving Jewels a slight bow.

I turned around, pointing my finger in his chest. "Leave my friends alone, do you understand."

"Someone is in a rotten mood," he said as he laughed. I grabbed Jewels' arm, pulling her toward our next class.

<u>DANE:</u>

Dane looked at the man he had called dad his whole life. He was supposed to go to school today, but this was his only chance to talk to him. Dane noticed last night that his dad was sleeping in the pool house. At the door of the guesthouse, Dane knocked on the door, and his dad opened the door looking hung over.

"Are you going to work today?" Dane asked.

"Took a sick day. What do you need, Dane?" Roger asked.

"Can we talk?" Dane asked.

"Don't you have school?" Roger asked.

"Mom is trying to transfer me back to my old school," Dane explained. Roger stepped aside to let Dane in. They sat across from one another, and Dane couldn't help but notice the empty liquor bottles.

"I'm listening," Roger said as he sat back, putting his feet on the table.

"I don't know where to start." Looking down, Dane said.

"You know that I'm not your biological father; your mother is having affairs? I know, son. I can see you want to know why. When you were born, the nurse told me your blood type; I knew then. I was going to divorce Cordelia until the nurse put you in my arms; I instantly fell in love with you and will always love you."

He was leaning back, rubbing his forehead, trying to clear the fog of the hangover. "Scott was there when you were born. As he held you, I told him about it. He gave me some excellent advice, 'Be his father Roger. You'll make a great dad.' Scott died not too long after that."

"You stayed for me? I always thought you hated me." Dane said.

"I could never and will never hate you. How about spending the day together?" Roger asked.

"Sure, that would be great. How about dinner at Abigail Beckett's house tonight?" Dane asked.

"She is still alive? No, she'll skin me alive." Roger said.

"I bet you ten bucks she won't." Dane smiled.

***

Dane and Roger arrived about an hour before dinner. Roger followed Dane into the sitting room where Abigail was resting.

Abigail looked up as the butler announced their presence. She put down the magazine she'd been reading.

"Welcome, Roger. Nice to see your time. Dane, come kiss me." Dane did as he was asked to do.

"Dinner will be casual tonight. After all this, I am not feeling well. The girls are in the pool. I had my car pick them up after school. I was surprised that you were not with them."

"Mom is getting everything straightened out. Don't tell Nora I want it to be a surprise." Dane asked.

"You are such a sweet young man, a welcome addition to our family. Don't you agree, Roger?" She asked.

Loud giggles prevented Roger from answering. Jewels, Nora, and Allison froze in the doorway when they saw Roger.

"I don't think we formally met. I'm Roger, Dane's dad." He seemed nervous.

"Jewels," waving her hand

Nora looked at Dane, and when he smiled, she shook Rogers's hand. "Nora"

"Allison, the first best friend. I'm armed with glitter so that you know." She looked at Roger intensely.

"Al, back off; Abby said it was okay for my dad to join us," Dane said

"Glitter?" Roger asked.

"It's lethal. Al is not afraid to use it, I know." Dane said.

"My mom is coming, Dane. How could you?" Nora whispers.

Grace walks in at that precise moment. Her mouth falls open when she sees Roger. Roger waved. "Grace"

Warily, she said. "Roger. Where is Cordelia?"

Abigail shouted, "That trollop is not welcome in my home! Let's eat. Tonight is casual, so there are no formalities. Dane, can you be a sweetheart and bring my wheelchair?"

Dane went to retrieve the wheelchair. Instead of the formal dining room, everyone entered the kitchen/den area, which had an oversized island with chairs to accommodate everyone.

"Abby, you sure you're ok?" Dane asked.

"Had a big day yesterday," Abigail said.

I lagged behind everyone, for I saw my dad from the corner of my eye. I asked him, "Why can't I heal her dad? Why can't the Eldest come back to help her?"

"You don't have that ability to heal yet. She was tired from her exertion yesterday, which affected her health. Elders do not decide who lives or dies. We do not decide the fate of beings. Go, or they will wonder where you are. I'm glad Dane took my advice."

I started to go but turned back to look at him again, but he was already gone.

After dinner, everyone but Grace and Roger left the kitchen to play charades. The game was becoming a tradition.

"What are you doing here, Roger?" Grace asked. "Go back to Cordelia."

"Dane invited me. Have you remarried?" Roger asked

"No," Grace answered.

"Why not?" He said. "You're stunning."

"I can't talk to you about this." Grace stood up to leave.

"Grace, wait," he said."I'm sorry I said it. We are going to have to get along. Dane will marry Nora one day. You and I both know it."

"I don't know anything anymore. Nora barely talks to me now." Grace replied.

"How about coffee sometime? We'll talk." Roger.

"I don't think so, Roger. Thank you for the offer." Grace walked out of the kitchen.

"I'm leaving Cordelia, Grace," Roger said. Taking out one of his business cards. "If you change your mind about coffee." He said as he handed a business card to Grace

"You better be careful she doesn't stab you in the back," Grace said as she walked out of the kitchen.

"That's what I'm afraid of." He muttered as he watched her walk out.

<u>NEXT DAY:</u>

I was getting ready to walk to school the next day, "Bye, Mom. See you later."

Waving goodbye, I picked up my school bag. As I opened the door, I saw a silver SUV with Dane sitting in the driver's seat.

I strolled up to the passenger side of the car. He rolled down the window. "What are you doing here?" I asked, the words flowing out in a relaxed tone.

"Picking you and Jewels up for school." Dane smiled.

"Your school is across town. You won't make it in time." I stated.

"Surprise, I'm back!" Dane said.

EPILOGUE

After school, Dane brought Jewels and me home. We entered the house to find Mom waiting in the kitchen. She was drinking a glass of wine, which made me very nervous.

"Sit down. I'd like to talk to both of you." Mom said. "How serious is this thing between you two?"

Dane and I looked at each other. "I intend to marry Nora after high school," Dane said.

"What does your mom say about that?" Mom asked.

"Abigail came to the house the other day to talk to mom. I overheard Abby threaten Mom with something, which I didn't hear. All I know is that my dad is not my biological father. I only found out about it several months ago myself. I talked to Dad yesterday; he and Nora's dad knew Mom's secret from the beginning."

"Scott knew?" Mom said.

"Dad said it was several days before..." Dane whispered the last words. "he died."

Mom put her hand on her stomach.

Dad appeared and stood by my side. "Tell her I didn't want to upset her."

"Maybe Dad didn't want to upset you," I said.

"I remember he went to the hospital for Roger. Scott was always loyal to your dad, Dane." Mom said. "I'm sure if he was alive today, he would still be loyal to him."

"Yes, I would," Dad said.

"I'm sure he would," I said.

Mom turned around to face me. "You sound so much like him, Nora Rose. I wish he could have seen you grow up. To walk you down the aisle, oh no!" She sat down, putting her head in her hands. "Oh God, this is happening so fast?"

"I'm not getting married now, Mom," I said, trying to understand what was happening. What are you worried about?"

"Nora?" Mom said, lifting her head to look at us. Please tell me I don't have to worry about 'things happening' between you two."

Dane and I looked at each other again. "Mom! We talked about this! Stop embarrassing me!" I said, again sending a nasty look to Dad. He had the nerve to smile.

"Both of you just go." Mom said.

"We were going by Abby's to swim while the weather was still hot," I said. I just needed to get my suit."

"Go. Don't come back too late. It is a school night." Mom said.

I hurried upstairs to pick up my swimsuit. When I came back down, Dad was by the front door. "Let me see what I can do."

"How are you going to talk to her?" I asked.

"I don't know it's impossible until I try. Go on, Nora. Dane is waiting for you," Dad said.

***

Walking into the kitchen, Grace was still cradling her wine glass on the kitchen island. She started muttering to herself. Even though Grace couldn't hear Scott, he still replied, hoping she could feel him nearby.

"Oh, Scott, what am I going to do? Nora is growing up so fast." Grace said

"Let her grow up, Grace," Scott replied.

"I wish you could have watched her grow up. She is so much like you." Grace said wispily.

"I have watched her grow. I have to disagree with you; she has your beauty and strength," Scott said.

"Dane wants to be a firefighter! I can't handle them marrying; I'll forbid it!" Grace said.

"You can't stop it, Grace; it is already done. He has protective spells to keep him safe. It's not like you to worry so much." Scott said.

Gigi rounded the corner and looked at Scott, lifting her ears and tilting her head to determine if Scott was a threat.

Scott bent down to pet the dog, which Gigi loved. He stood back up and looked at Grace.

"Call Roger, Grace." With that, he disappeared.

Grace grabbed her cell phone.

I texted Roger, "When do you want to meet for coffee?"

Made in the USA
Columbia, SC
27 July 2024

252ea65c-3c5c-4cc0-8316-d55c3e4a8bcdR01